More prais
A Gentleman's Guide to

D1110576

"Michael Dahlie was a cipher to me before I read his wonderful new novel, *A Gentleman's Guide to Graceful Living*, and a cipher he shall remain. It's funny, but not Carl Hiaasen–Christopher Buckley funny. Dahlie takes bigger risks, not pushing down so hard on the pedals, not pulling out the comic stops. He trusts the reader to be smart, relax and laugh. I did, a lot."

—Alex Beam, *International Herald Tribune*

"The endearingly understated story of a New York aristocrat who, under better circumstances, might have wound up in a Louis Auchincloss book. But he is undone by haplessness and self-doubt, rendered with dry acuity of observation. There is no old-money playground where Arthur Camden, congenitally maladroit, is safe from his own ability to bumble."

—CBS News (Summer Reading Pick)

"Dahlie's dark humor and light touch elevate this debut about a damaged man determined to make the best of the rest of his life."

—*Booklist*

"This novel strikes me as the American version of *The Fall* by Camus. Dahlie writes elegantly and beautifully, which does not prevent him from dramatically delving into the raw terrain of the male psychology."

—Josip Novakovich, author of *Infidelities: Stories of War and Lust*

"No fly fisherman can help but love this brilliant first novel. *A Gentleman's Guide to Graceful Living* is filled with ungentlemanly hilarity and ungentlemanly low-jinx, with poignant irony, uncommon wisdom, and shrewd insights into love and fly fishing clubs."

—Nick Lyons, author of *In Praise of Wild Trout* and founder of The Lyons Press

"Almost no one could be less prepared for the vicissitudes of modern upper class divorce and dating than the retiring Arthur Camden, and watching him navigate these tricky waters is both touching and hilarious. *A Gentleman's Guide to Graceful Living* is a reader's guide to intelligent delight."

—Margot Livesey, author of *The House on Fortune Street*

"Michael Dahlie has written a wholly pleasurable and surprising book . . . a triumph of humorous restraint. He's created an unlikely but endearing hero in Arthur Camden, and we cannot help but laugh and shudder and cheer as Arthur blunders his way through his rarefied world, which Dahlie renders in sly and pitch perfect detail. It is rare to find a book that is so funny—usually at the expense of its hapless main character—and yet so compassionate as well."

—Sarah Shun-lien Bynum, author of *Madeline Is Sleeping*

"A book as fine as this doesn't come along often. *A Gentleman's Guide to Graceful Living* is very funny, yes, but it's also tender in a way that amounts, at last, to a kind of elegy. Arthur Camden may get into a muddle, but he is a gentleman, and graceful too. That such rare men can have faith (or at least go on being patient with the rest of us) is the hope this book holds out. That such men still exist is what it seems to propose."

—Louis B. Jones, author of *California's Over*

"Michael Dahlie's unusual and wonderful new novel, *A Gentleman's Guide to Graceful Living*, is a tour de force that manages to combine mellow wisdom with wicked cleverness. The tragicomic adventures of his hero show a feckless Everyman trying to do the right thing, but constantly stumbling against an unreceptive world. Dahlie is an impressive new writer who walks a fine line between compassion and irony, optimism and despair. There were moments when I didn't know whether to laugh or cry, but I never wanted to stop reading this absorbing book."

—Lynne Sharon Schwartz, author of *The Writing on the Wall*

"[A] witty and intelligent comedy of manners."

—Janice Harayda, oneminutebookreviews.com

"A reader will love Arthur at some times, will want to shake him at others, will roar with laughter at some of the situations he finds himself in, will treasure Arthur's son, will want to shoot some of his friends, and will marvel at Arthur's patience and what I guess is best described as his fortitude."   —*Springfield Republican*

"Mr. Dahlie is such a compassionate writer."   —bookslut.com

"[A] charming, laugh out loud novel."   —popgoesfiction.com

"[A] funny, moving debut novel."   —booksandauthorsblog.com

"Dahlie clearly has a knack for distilling a situation and getting right to the heart of a matter. . . . perhaps [the book's] greatest achievement is that Dahlie elicits sympathy from the reader for a character whose social class does not easily elicit such feelings. Although Arthur is a wealthy, white American male, many readers can appreciate a character who illustrates that the struggle for self-confidence is arduous and lifelong."   —mostlyfiction.com

A GENTLEMAN'S GUIDE TO

GRACEFUL
LIVING

A NOVEL

MICHAEL DAHLIE

W. W. NORTON & COMPANY
New York • London

Copyright © 2008 by Michael Dahlie

For information about permission to reproduce selections from this book write to Permissions, W. W. Norton & Company, Inc., 500 Fifth Avenue, New York, NY 10110

For information about special discounts for bulk purchases, please contact W. W. Norton Special Sales at specialsales@wwnorton.com or 800-233-4830

Manufacturing by Courier Westford
Book design by JAM Design
Production manager: Anna Oler

Library of Congress Cataloging-in-Publication Data

Dahlie, Michael.
A gentleman's guide to graceful living : a novel / Michael Dahlie. — 1st ed.
p. cm.
ISBN 978-0-393-06617-3
1. Upper class—Fiction. 2. Life change events—Fiction. 3. Self-actualizations (Psychology)—Fiction. 4. Self-realization—Fiction. 5. New York (N.Y.)—Social life and customs—Fiction. 6. Psychological fiction. I. Title.
PS3604.A344G46 2008
813'.6—dc22   2008011983

ISBN 978-0-393-33635-1 pbk.

W. W. Norton & Company, Inc.
500 Fifth Avenue, New York, N.Y. 10110
www.wwnorton.com

W. W. Norton & Company Ltd.
Castle House, 75/76 Wells Street, London W1T 3QT

1 2 3 4 5 6 7 8 9 0

IN MEMORY OF MY FATHER

PAUL DAHLIE

ACKNOWLEDGMENTS

The author wishes to thank Chris Bannon, Erin Belieu, Jill Bialosky, Samantha Choy, Dave Cole, Moira Crone, Anne Dahlie, Elizabeth Dahlie, Susan Dahlie, Joseph J. DeSalvo, Jr., Deborah Eisenberg, Wayne Fields, Seth Fishman, Sarah Frisch, Gary Goldberger, Emily Hazel, Rosemary James, Louis B. Jones, Kathrin Kollmann, Frederick Mendelsohn, Christopher Miller, Charles Newman, George Nicholson, Lynne Sharon Schwartz, Doug Stewart, The Pirate's Alley Faulkner Society, Paul Whitlatch, David Wimberly, James Yaffe, and Allison Lynn.

A Gentleman's Guide to

Graceful
Living

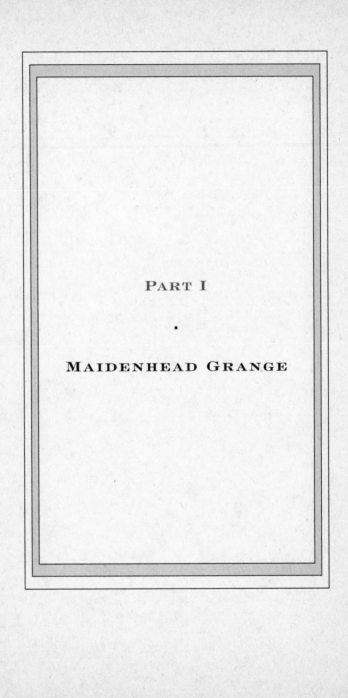

PART I

·

MAIDENHEAD GRANGE

1

By the time of their April meeting in 1998, it was well known among the membership of the Hanover Street Fly Casters that Arthur Camden's life had fallen apart. The collapse of his import and export business, founded by his grandfather in 1902, had left Arthur not only in financial jeopardy but also disgraced among his extended family, many of whom had a stake in the firm and had never wanted him to take over in the first place. There was even talk of a lawsuit over Arthur's failures, although the firm's demise was due mostly to Arthur's incompetence and it was decided that this was not really a thing they could sue over. It was Arthur's other and related misfortune, however, that sent him into the depression that was now so evident to his fellow Fly Casters. His wife of thirty-two years had left him for a former boyfriend she had not seen since she was seventeen. The couple had been unexpectedly reunited that fall at a benefit held at the Pierre and before the night was over (as the now-famous story goes) they escaped from Arthur and checked into one of the hotel's expansive suites. It was well known that Rebecca Camden had always cheated mercilessly on Arthur. But at this point in their marriage she no longer felt the need to keep holding things together. Instead of crawling into bed later that evening with stories of how she had spent time catching up with an old friend, she met Arthur only at breakfast the following morning, back at their apartment, to say that she was at the end of her tether and that she could not possibly stay with Arthur for another day.

Members of the Fly Casters heard about Arthur's humiliation long before their April luncheon at Sprague's. They all knew that Arthur had been seen at various times and by various people in assorted states of depression and anxiety. One of the Fly Casters—Charlie Feltham—had run into him several times at the Geographers Club, where, as he described to friends, Arthur was always as white as a sheet and entirely incomprehensible. None of the Fly Casters, however, expected the kind of display that Arthur finally presented at lunch that afternoon, where, after the soup was served, he began weeping openly, saying that the ten men at the table were the very best friends he had ever had, and that in the face of his recent difficulties, he took great comfort from knowing every one of them.

"Despite the difficulties I've recently faced," he said, "I want you to know that I'm still hanging on, and the reason I'm still hanging on is because I love every single one of you."

It was a strange and awkward moment, and when the members bumped into each other at various times over the next few weeks, it was all they could talk about. There was, of course, pity from everyone. They all said they could hardly imagine going through what poor Arthur was going through. All the same, each of the members agreed that such an emotional display was a little beyond what they had expected. The sad fact was that none of the members had ever really counted Arthur as much of a friend.

2

Two weeks after the Fly Casters' luncheon, Arthur flew to Steamboat Springs, Colorado, to visit one of his sons, Patrick, who had been inviting Arthur out for an extended stay ever since he heard about his mother's infidelities. Patrick was a venture capitalist of sorts in the high-tech industry, and had bought a ranch with money he made from several careful investments in Taiwanese microchip manufacturers. The ranch consisted of about four thousand acres and had been part of a large cattle operation for nearly ninety years. Patrick bought it when the ranch owner was packing in the business and moving to San Diego, his sons having moved to New York to pursue careers on Wall Street instead of following in their father's footsteps. Patrick wanted nothing to do with cattle, although he tried to retain the cowboy feel of the land, and erected a sizable new ranch house for his family. He also put up two guest cottages, one of which he specifically designated for his parents, although he now insisted that it belonged exclusively to his father. Patrick had a decent relationship with his mother, and he even felt a tiny amount of sympathy for her when she left Arthur that night at the Pierre. Still, Patrick felt like there was no possibility his mother would ever come to the ranch for more than a long weekend. His father, however, might be tempted out for at least a month or two. "Frankly, I'd like everyone I know to come live out here," Patrick had told his father when he was first discussing his construction plans. "I'll just keep building and hope everyone shows up."

Arthur had seen the ranch in various stages of construction, but he had yet to view the ranch in its final glory, and he was looking forward to seeing how his son's plans had materialized. In fact, the entire trip gave him something other than his own troubles to think about, and he found he was somewhat relaxed as he spotted Patrick on the other side of the security divider at the small Steamboat Springs airport. Patrick and Arthur had, of course, spoken on the phone many times since Arthur's business failed and Rebecca left him. Patrick insisted that he had sufficient financial resources to help his father if he needed it, although the truth was that Arthur had managed to protect a fair portion of his personal net worth, and he countered his professional bankruptcy with sufficient retirement funds for a man who lived in a pleasant apartment on Park Avenue. Patrick had even offered something of a bailout for the business, but by the time Arthur was forthcoming with the company's problems, there was really nothing left to bail out. Importing businesses like Arthur's were generally little more than a front man and his relationships, and Arthur had dissolved almost every business connection he had by the time his company went under. This fact was not overlooked by Arthur, and when he started making the calls to tell everyone what was going on, he felt as if he had sullied every relationship (social and financial) that he'd ever been part of. But he had always been close to Patrick.

That night at dinner, Arthur continued to unwind, and after a few glasses of wine and the steaks that he and Patrick grilled, he even found himself forgetting about Rebecca and his failed business. Patrick's two daughters, Sarah (three) and Katie (two), sat on his lap through dessert, as Patrick's wife, Marina, fed him cake and poured him coffee and listed the numerous things at his disposal on the ranch.

"I just put sheets on your bed," she said. "On all the beds in the cottage, actually, but I figured you'd want to sleep in the master bedroom. But you don't have to. Wherever you'd like to sleep. There's towels, a fridge full of food and cold drinks, and we just got satellite television installed, so you can keep up with whatever it is you like to keep up with."

"I hated to get the satellite thing," Patrick added. "But the dishes are so small these days. You can hardly even see them."

"Everything sounds perfect," Arthur replied, trying to balance Katie and Sarah on his knees as he ate his cake.

"I bet it will be nice to be away from New York for a while," Marina said. "After three years out here, I'm still recuperating." (She and Patrick had lived in New York together for five years before moving west.)

"It will be nice," Arthur replied. "It will be nice to be around so many friendly faces."

They continued to talk over other matters, mostly having to do with family, although they avoided specific reference to the impending divorce. They talked about Arthur's sister, and his other son, David, who lived in Boston, and his recent engagement to a so-called art historian from London. Everyone agreed it was a perfect match, David being far more bookish than Patrick. And they talked some about fishing. Patrick had become involved in a local conservation group that protected rivers in northwest Colorado, and he told Arthur quite a bit about what they were doing.

In these somewhat blissful surroundings, Arthur enjoyed thinking about life outside the bounds of the social world he normally inhabited in New York, with all its mysterious customs and protocols. Patrick seemed to accept Arthur without condition or expectation, and Arthur felt the same from Marina as well. She even said something along these lines later that night. Arthur had gone upstairs to help tuck in Sarah and Katie, and on the way back down, Marina leading the way, she started telling him how much she appreciated him. At first it made Arthur just a bit nervous. Was he now such a basket case that people needed to work so hard to pick up his spirits? Still, it was clear that Marina was sincere.

"I really couldn't ask for a better father-in-law," she said. "You don't get a guy like Patrick from nothing. Patrick's one of the most kindhearted men that I know, and I only say 'one of' because you're the other one. Really."

Arthur hardly knew how to reply. As they came to a halt at the bottom landing, all he could do was stare at his feet. It really was a sincere compliment, and it was, after all, a compliment that he could somehow believe. When people said things like, "You've got a great sense for business, Arthur, so you're sure to find your way into something else!" it seemed so patently false (even when said with genuine compassion) that it only made him feel more depressed.

"Well, that's extremely nice to hear, Marina," Arthur finally replied. "I could hardly have had better luck than to have a son like him." Then he added, "But it's probably more you than me. The wrong kind of person might have got her hands on him, and then where would I be? Not out here, in such a beautiful place, with such a wonderful daughter-in-law."

This last part came with just a bit of awkwardness. Arthur was never good at this sort of intimate moment. Still, he managed to check his desire to flee the landing and spend the rest of the night in bed. All the same, as he got to the end of his reply, he concluded, with a forced tone of excitement, that he had heard there was some kind of special cognac that she and Patrick had bought for the evening.

"You know what a big fan I am of cognac," he said.

"I know, Arthur," Marina replied, now smiling. "We got it just for you." Then she led him off toward the living room.

Arthur, Patrick, and Marina sat by the fire for another hour or so, drinking the cognac and talking about various matters before Arthur finally stood up and said he was tired and that it was time for him to get to sleep. His cottage was nearly a quarter of a mile away, and Patrick offered to shuttle him over in his pickup. But Arthur refused. "I need the exercise," he insisted.

As he began his walk back, Arthur considered that he was certainly a lucky man to have access to all this, to have such a good son who had done so well for himself. When he looked at life from this perspective, things actually seemed all right. But after five minutes of thinking how fortunate he was, he slipped back into the peculiar despair that had been haunting him recently, and spent the remaining ten minutes of the journey focusing on what a disaster he felt his life had become and wondering how things could have turned so bad so quickly. Most on his mind was how nice Marina was to him, and how rotten Rebecca had turned out to be. What puzzled him most, though, was where Rebecca's coldness and disloyalty had come from. Had she always been that way? Was she even really that way at all? Arthur hated to think about it, but an argument could be made that she was simply no longer in love with him, and that she needed to do something different with her life. These were depressing thoughts, and as Arthur finally arrived at the cottage, the best solution he could come up with was to open a beer, turn on the satellite television, and fall asleep to CNBC.

And the following morning, after thinking things over further, Arthur finally decided that all that family happiness the previous night had, after all, probably been too much for him. He called his travel agent and changed his ticket, deciding to head home the next day. He hadn't expected this change of heart, but he suddenly determined that he was still in the "picking up the pieces" mode of his life, and that this was no time to be hiding out on his son's ranch, basking in the happiness of someone else's family, no matter how closely related he was. It didn't make him happy to return. But then again, it wasn't going to do him much good, in the end, to stay. Arthur decided a number of other things that morning as well. He would seriously consider investing money in a friend's restaurant proposal; he would join a gym; and he would spend more time fishing at the Fly Casters' camp in the Catskills—a few of his fellow Fly Casters were supposed to be heading up that weekend, and he would make a point of joining them.

"Are you really sure you want to go back already?" Patrick asked as they stood again by the security barrier at the airport.

"Oh, I don't know what I'm doing anymore," Arthur said. "But I'm not really sure if what I need right now is a vacation. Seems to me that I need to get back to the city and see what's going on there."

"Well, we'll keep the cottage heated in case you return."

"Ha. Good. I'll be back for a longer stay soon enough."

Arthur hugged Patrick and said goodbye once more and then headed toward his gate.

3

On the Friday following his return to Manhattan, after making a few phone calls and running several errands, Arthur headed out of the city and north to the Catskills for a weekend of fishing at the Fly Casters' camp. He was looking forward to getting out on the stream, but he was also excited about spending time with friends. He wasn't sure who was going to be there, but several members had said they would go if they could get away. It actually seemed more fun this way, not knowing who would be there and taking a head count as members arrived.

The Hanover Street Fly Casters was founded in 1878 by twelve men, including Arthur's great-grandfather, Peter Camden. The men all had their hands in the business and financial world of New York City, and all had offices located on Hanover Street in lower Manhattan. They also shared a love of fly-fishing and a certain belief that America offered as much as Europe in the way of top-notch angling. The founding of the club was an attempt to "really put American fly-fishing on the map." It was also established at a time when much of New York was banding up in clubs of one sort or another, and the men decided that fly-fishing was the best possible reason for like-minded men to throw their lots together.

Since its founding, the club had grown in prestige, although not in size. The Fly Casters had a strict limit of eleven members. Twelve members had founded the club, but one of them, a commodities trader named Jonah Houseman, had been expelled after a gross violation of the rules. He had been caught showing the club to his wife and, after an hour-long emergency meeting, was promptly removed, with the additional provision that no one be allowed to replace him. It was a sad day for everyone. Jonah was well liked. But it was decided that if the Fly Casters were to have any sort of integrity at all, this was a breach of trust that could not be overlooked. And the constant threat of expulsion did, in fact, succeed in keeping other members in line. Most would rather have faced censure from the SEC or the American Board of Physicians than lose their membership to what was quickly being regarded as the most exclusive club in New York.

Membership in the Fly Casters was hereditary, passing from father to eldest son at the time of either the father's death or his abdication (usually early enough for the next generation to enjoy membership before his own old age and infirmity took over). If there was no son, then the member could designate an heir, but only on the condition that the heir be unanimously approved by the rest of the members. Because many members remained in the club into their seventies and eighties, new members were often already in their fifties by the time they joined, although the heirs all knew each other and were generally on familiar terms before taking on the Fly Casters mantle. They were also able to fish together at sporadic father-son weekends.

The Catskills property encompassed a confluence of hallowed trout streams that everyone agreed was the main reason membership in the Fly Casters became so coveted. According to those who knew about such things, the Fly Casters' three miles of water was one of the two or three best fishing beats in North America, although few people had ever been permitted the privilege of fishing there. To be invited to fish by the members was extremely rare, and at the time that Arthur's wife left him, no outsider had been allowed to fish the Fly Casters' water for nearly fourteen years.

But the Fly Casters' property consisted of more than just pristine trout streams. Instead of finding club space in the city (as did the much larger Geographers Club, for instance, when they purchased an entire floor of mahogany-paneled rooms on Fifth Avenue), the Fly Casters used their capital to build one of the most impressive sporting lodges in the Catskills—better even than the camps belonging to the famous Catskill Angling Club and the Manhattan Rod and Reel Society. The Fly Casters built their camp in 1881 using lumber harvested on their estate and stones gathered from their riverbeds, constructing something very similar to the boyhood summer home of one of the members—Friedrich "Dicksie" Kollmann—who had grown up in Austria. The camp had eleven large bedrooms (Jonah Houseman's having been converted to storage) and each member furnished and maintained his own quarters. In addition, there was a library, a billiard room, a main sitting room, a formal dining room, an expansive kitchen, and staff quarters, which, by the time Arthur's generation took over, were generally only occupied once a year, when the Fly Casters had their annual Meeting-in-Full in October. The camp also had a full-time caretaker, although he lived off-premises. The caretaker was left with strict instructions to keep all nonmembers off the land, and was expected to guard the property with the same jealousy that the members themselves felt for their camp.

The camp was named Maidenhead Grange, and had been so named during a time when it was fashionable to give grand houses in the country British-sounding titles. The trend lasted for some time and more well-known examples included the Meredith house in Litchfield (Westminster Long Barrow), the Purse house in Dorset (Kitsgate Meadows), and the Vacheron house in Lambertville (Abington Heath). The phenomenon was baffling to most contemporary observers, although the general theory was that it stemmed from the earlier and more specific trend of romantic matriarchs naming their country homes after locations in Brontë novels. In the case of the Fly Casters, alcohol was also involved. According to Fly Caster lore, Maidenhead Grange was named after a prolonged drinking binge following the death of founding member Tully Mason, who had grown up fishing on the Maidenhead River.

Drinking, of course, was a large part of the culture of the camp, and as Arthur arrived, he was already thinking about his first martini. Arthur was not a big drinker, but, as much as he hated to admit it, alcohol had provided some relief in the time since his wife had left him.

There was no one at the camp when he got there, although he had called ahead to Sam Kendall, the current caretaker, and it had been opened up by the time he arrived. It occurred to Arthur that it would probably be some time before anyone else showed up, seeing that it was the afternoon and most of the members, after all, still had jobs. At about four-thirty, however, just as Arthur was unpacking, he heard a noise downstairs, and when he went to investigate, he found two fellow Fly Casters, Ken Fielder and Jim Fordyce, loading liquor bottles into the extensive liquor cabinet and talking excitedly about what they were going to have for dinner that night.

When the men saw each other they all smiled, shook hands, patted each other's backs, and said how happy they were to be there. After chatting for a few moments, Ken finally suggested that since it was already four thirty it was certainly time for a drink. "Four thirty is close enough to cocktail hour for me," he said.

"Me too," Jim replied. "Arthur?"

"I'm in," Arthur said.

By seven o'clock, the three men were very nearly drunk, and were laboring in the kitchen with sweaty brows and rolled-up sleeves preparing dinner. No one else had arrived, but they cooked enough for eleven, just in case, and decided that they wouldn't complain if others didn't come because they were each hungry enough to eat for four. The cooking was not complicated, but the gin had affected their motor skills, and small tasks such as crushing garlic and sautéing spinach were done with a sort of daring and flair that reflected not the nature of the tasks but the state of their minds. Indeed, by almost any measure, everything happening in the kitchen represented a serious safety hazard.

Ken Fielder was coordinating the efforts, having taken several cooking classes over the years with his wife, Lauren. Jim Fordyce relinquished command in order to act as the meat specialist, and grilled the steaks with an imaginary kind of precision, producing a large platter of nearly raw meat by the time the table was set. Arthur simply took orders from the other two, and was in charge of handing Jim and Ken utensils, cleaning up after them, and making sure their drink glasses were full.

By eight, the three men were seated at the dinner table, trying to keep together some kind of conversation as they bolted their steak and spinach. Arthur thought how happy he was to be with Ken and Jim, although, as dinner progressed, it occurred to him that he had never been particularly close to either of them. He certainly liked them. They had the sort of healthy and contented charm that most of the Fly Casters had. But he had never struck up any sort of tight friendship with them, and his knowledge of them, while extensive, seemed to be fixed on what might be called the general facts of their lives. He knew, for instance, that Ken Fielder had been a successful banker, and that he had launched his wife's interior design business—the now-famous Lauren Fielder Interiors—with a series of large bonuses from the bank where he had worked. (They were now mostly supported by Lauren's business, Ken doing only occasional consulting work.) As for Jim, Arthur knew that he was a sort of financial analyst at Holt & Pruitt, although he had inherited most of his money: he was the grandson of the industrialist Sam Fordyce, who had been instrumental in expanding the Fly Casters' land by four hundred acres. Aside from the basic details, however, he was not actually very close with these two men.

At any rate, after they had finished their first helpings of food and had slowed their eating somewhat, the conversation became more lively, touching on numerous issues, mostly those dealing with business matters and current events. Finally, however, when the men were left only with their empty plates and their wineglasses, Jim moved the discussion to more personal matters. Specifically, he asked Arthur how he was doing in regards to his impending divorce, or, as he put it, "all that mess with your wife."

Arthur said that he was fine, and that he was ready to get his life started up again. "I visited my son and his family last week in Colorado," he said. "The trip was relaxing, but it also made me realize that there are plenty of reasons for me to be happy that I'm in New York."

"You know, there's a new crop of divorcées in town these days," Ken said, smiling. "Were I in your position, I might think that this was a wonderful time to be single again."

Arthur blushed. Although finding someone new had crossed his mind, it was really the least of his worries. Furthermore, going out with women was something he felt mostly incapable of negotiating, having never been much of a ladies' man in his younger days, and having never been much of a flirt in later years.

"Actually," Ken continued, "if you're interested, my wife has a pretty close friend who might be just the thing for a guy like you. Divorced a few months ago, but separated for more than a year now. Very charming woman, and, to be absolutely honest, quite a dish." As Ken said this, the three men burst into a sort of nervous laughter, unsure of how to navigate this kind of conversation. Finally Ken picked up where he left off. "So what do you think?"

"Oh, I don't know," Arthur said. "I'm not sure I'm really ready for that kind of thing."

"What are you talking about?" Ken said. "Of course you're ready for that kind of thing. Who isn't ready for that kind of thing? I know things have been rough on you. I mean it. I don't think I'd be doing half as well if my wife left me. But you've got to remember that there are plenty of men who are a bit envious of you. On your own again. Free to do as you please." He paused. "Out whoring around." Again the men burst into nervous laughter, mostly unpracticed in this kind of conversation and unsure if this was really the way men in their late fifties and early sixties ought to be talking. The laughter came to a sudden halt, however, when Ken added, with a terrible sense of timing, "And after all, your wife certainly isn't waiting around."

Arthur had already been blushing, but now he turned bright red. He wasn't angry or even particularly insulted, but was, rather, merely shocked by the kind of awkward misstep Ken had made. Each of the men seemed to feel this way, and were all so stunned that they couldn't quite figure out how to change subjects, how to get back to the cheery conversation they had just been having. Finally Ken said, "I didn't mean it like that, Arthur. I just meant that you shouldn't worry about propriety or appearances. Things are pretty different from when we all first got married."

"Almost unintelligibly different," Arthur said, after a pause. Then, because he honestly felt bad for Ken for saying something so potentially wounding, he added, "Anyway, you're absolutely right about my wife not waiting around. Seems like I ought to make a point of enjoying myself rather than indulging in so much self-pity."

The conversation ended not long after that, although the suggestion of a date with the friend of Ken's wife stayed on Arthur's mind as he mounted the stairs and prepared for bed. It seemed impossible that he could manage such a thing, he thought as he brushed his teeth and washed his face, but he also realized that he had better start doing something to work his way out of his bind. After all, he couldn't keep bursting into tears at Fly Casters luncheons.

And the idea of a blind date stayed on his mind through the following day, as he fished and prepared dinner and sat up late with Jim and Ken again, drinking cognac at the dining room table. The next morning, the issue was still on Arthur's mind, although Ken had not brought up the matter again, as Arthur had hoped he would. So after a large breakfast, as they were saying their goodbyes by their cars, when Ken still didn't address the issue of the date, Arthur said (trying to appear as casual about the whole thing as possible), "Well, let me know if your wife's friend is interested in meeting me."

Ken looked slightly confused by this, but then quickly said, "Of course. I'll try to set it up as soon as I get home."

The men all shook hands, said they'd be in touch back in the city, and then said goodbye.

4

It took three weeks for Ken Fielder to arrange the meeting between his wife's friend, a woman named Angeline Holland, and Arthur. After some hesitation on Arthur's part, it was decided that the best way to introduce the two would be at a dinner party at Ken's apartment.

Ken and his wife owned a fairly impressive duplex on Fifth Avenue—not far from the Met—which was decorated and redecorated by Ken's wife, Lauren, according to the latest designing trends. It seemed to bother Ken that the interior of his home changed every other season, but his wife was a driven businesswoman, and felt that it was essential that her home act as a sort of showcase for her work.

Lauren was especially known for her kitchens, many of which had appeared in prominent architectural magazines. They were great fun for the amateur gourmet, but they were mostly designed for the sort of entertaining that was done with hired chefs and caterers. Lauren's work was well known among the private chefs of the city and it was considered an unusual luxury to be asked to cook in one of her productions.

Arthur arrived exactly on time on the night of the dinner party, and was the first to arrive by twenty minutes. Ken and Lauren were still dressing, and Arthur amused himself in the Fielder living room with a glass of white wine and an impressive platter of cheese. Lauren and Ken popped in and out, straightening their clothes and checking on one thing or another, and Arthur did manage to talk to Lauren for just a bit and found, happily, that she had a very calming effect on him.

After another half an hour, all the guests had finally arrived, including Angeline, who wore what Arthur thought looked like a prom dress, although she wore it with a nonchalance that seemed to suggest that prom-style dresses were the very latest thing and she was dressed exactly as she was supposed to be. Angeline also happened to be very attractive, slim, and had elegant streaks of gray running through her long dark hair, which Arthur found very appealing.

Lauren introduced Arthur and Angeline inconspicuously among other introductions, and as the guests drank their cocktails and ate hors d'oeuvres, the two said nothing directly to one another. They were able to interact more when they sat down to dinner, Lauren having placed them next to each other, and they spent quite a bit of the meal talking. Arthur described his son's ranch in Steamboat, his association with Ken through the Hanover Street Fly Casters, and even talked some about the difficulties of running an importing business. Angeline listened intently to all this and then talked quite a bit about her work with the New York Society for the Prevention of Juvenile Diabetes, insisting that Arthur come to the charity ball they held every year. "It's mostly people our age," she said, "which I happen to like, since when there's a younger crowd, they always seem to have all the fun."

After dinner, Angeline and Arthur parted cordially as they exited with the other couples, telling each other that they were happy to have met one another and that they hoped they would see each other soon. Two days later, as Arthur was debating when he ought to telephone Angeline and what exactly they ought to do on their first date, he got a call from Ken, who, after a few general remarks, finally said, "Well, I guess it didn't work out so well with Angeline, huh? I guess that's the way these things go. Always a crapshoot. But don't worry. My wife's got a list a mile long."

It wasn't that Angeline was disinterested that bothered Arthur as much as it was that her disinterest seemed to be the sort of obvious fact that Ken could freely talk about, as though Arthur couldn't possibly have come to any other conclusion. Arthur quickly tried to replay the events of the evening, but he could come up with no obvious point when Angeline seemed to lose interest, although he had never really understood such interactions.

"I'm afraid I'm not very good at this sort of thing," Arthur finally said in reply to Ken's remark about his wife's list. "Perhaps we should just take all this slowly."

"Well, you only get a few days to rest, Arthur," Ken replied. "I've got four tickets to the opera this Saturday night, and Lauren is determined about all this. For some reason you made some kind of impression on her the other night. She described you as 'sweet and vulnerable,' which I guess is some kind of compliment. Anyway, I'll tell her to get busy, unless you have someone in mind."

"No, no one in mind," Arthur said, puzzling over Lauren's remark. "I guess best to let Lauren handle it."

The evening was another failure, although again there was no sort of egregious incident to conclusively rule the match out of order. Things passed pleasantly and two days later Arthur got another call from Ken telling him not to get discouraged and that it was all a numbers game, that it was all about "increasing your odds by placing more bets."

Over the next several weeks Arthur went on quite a few more arranged dates, with Lauren and Ken as occasional chaperones, and all were as uneventful and unsuccessful as the first two, each time leaving Arthur more bewildered than before as to what exactly he was doing wrong. And by the time the Fly Casters' next luncheon rolled around, Lauren's mile-long list seemed to have been exhausted.

"Just what exactly are you saying to these women?" Ken said, smiling, as he and Arthur sat down next to each other at Sprague's. Arthur was not offended by this and, in truth, welcomed it, because he was fairly embarrassed by his poor showing, and Ken's gentle teasing seemed to lessen his shame.

"I can't say that I really know," Arthur said. "I suppose I'm a bit out of practice, and even when I was in practice, I wasn't very good at all this."

Arthur smiled as he said this, and was even slightly amused by his failures, but he also thought, simultaneously, that all this was just the beginning of what was sure to be a very lonely time for him.

5

Arthur had never figured himself as the sort of man who would take his sexual conquests (or lack of them) as much of an indication of anything, but as he was walking home from a dinner party one evening, where he had met several divorcées who seemed entirely disinterested in him, he wondered just where all this mess was headed.

In the midst of this brooding, something else happened to complicate his thoughts. He was passing by a new restaurant called Albertine, located on Madison Avenue in the Sixties, when the restaurant's door flew open and out walked his soon-to-be (legally) ex-wife, draped in a flowing cream-colored wrap and followed by a tall, obviously European man—not the former boyfriend she had run off with, but clearly the man she was with that evening.

To Rebecca's credit, she quickly stopped looking so completely happy and greeted Arthur solemnly but warmly, and introduced him to André (a Belgian man, of all things), and then asked how everything was. Arthur had actually been thinking quite a bit about Rebecca that day. The divorce was nearing its final negotiations and he had just received a letter from her lawyer that morning, detailing their proposal. The truth was that Rebecca was not looking for any sort of unfair settlement. She had brought to the marriage several million dollars and that, plus the substantial interest it had accrued over the years, was what she wanted to leave with. She let Arthur keep the apartment on Park Avenue, having already moved into a new apartment of her own about three blocks away, and in exchange she wanted to keep the summerhouse in East Hampton, which Arthur had never cared for much anyway.

"I heard from your lawyer today," Arthur finally said, forcing a smile. "Looks like everything is going through smoothly. I think the end is at hand."

"So it is, Arthur," she said with a tone of sympathy. "But let's not talk about it here or now. Not that I wouldn't love to talk to you. Perhaps you'd agree to meet me for an early dinner one day next week?"

Arthur did agree. It seemed to him to be a terrible idea, but he felt it might alleviate the immediate awkwardness, and in a few moments he was happy to be walking swiftly away from his wife and her Belgian escort.

It was strange, he thought, how he was working through all this. He couldn't help but recall his most recent visit to Colorado and the thoughts he had had about the wonderful life that his son had established with his wife, Marina. Again, Arthur tried to figure out if Rebecca had always been the sort of cold and carefree woman she appeared to be now, or if she had changed over the years. Arthur knew little of what everyone else seemed to know about Rebecca's infidelities, so it was hard for him to judge. Still, he suspected that her most recent affairs were not the first. But he couldn't help but think that there was a time that she had loved him the way Marina seemed to love Patrick. He could remember dinner parties when his wife was just as eager to feed his friends and entertain their guests and, in a certain respect, share some of the happiness that she felt with Arthur.

That his marriage might once have been happy, might not have been a total wash, suddenly made Arthur feel very sad. He had been clinging to the "one big lie" explanation of his dissolved marriage as a way of somehow dealing with his loss, but as he approached his apartment, he determined that Rebecca had once been every bit as charming as Marina, had blissfully clung to him as she was now hanging on to that Belgian man, and he couldn't help but wonder if he hadn't somehow destroyed everything, turned her against him, not unlike the way he had ruined his grandfather's business. Given how things were all unfolding, this explanation seemed very plausible, and because of this, he became even more depressed about the string of disastrous meetings he'd had with the eligible women he was introduced to. Clearly Rebecca was a woman that men wanted to be around, while he was attractive to no one.

The following day, after Arthur returned from a game of squash at the University Club with an old prep-school friend, he found that Rebecca had left a message on his machine proposing a light dinner that Wednesday. He had seen Rebecca exactly four times since she left him, all under controlled circumstances, escorted by lawyers, or at family functions where they absolutely had to be together, so this dinner promised to be a fairly unnerving experience for Arthur. Still, he returned Rebecca's call that afternoon, leaving a message of his own that said Wednesday would be fine. When she called back that evening, they quickly agreed on a time and place without bringing up any other, more difficult, subjects.

They met at six thirty at a new restaurant called Beaudant. It was not far from either of their apartments, although it was reasonably neutral, neither of them having been there before. They were both prompt, and when they saw each other, they kissed hello and sat down together as though there were nothing at all odd about their meeting. In some ways, Arthur felt more comfortable now than he had with any other woman in the past months, although the truth was that he was sitting across from the source of much of his misery. This didn't necessarily make him feel miserable at that moment, but it did make him a bit apprehensive, as though at any instant the direction of the meal might take a very unpleasant turn. And this apprehension was not unjustified. Not long after their food arrived, Rebecca launched into a long monologue about how Arthur was truly a wonderful person, and that she meant none of the harsh things she had said to him, but that she had changed over the years, that she was now a different woman, and that there were certain things she needed from a relationship that he couldn't quite give her.

"You are really a wonderful man," she kept saying. "So sweet and kind. But all that is precisely what makes our being together impossible."

"You like villains and scoundrels now?" Arthur said, not really pleased with Rebecca's praise.

"No," she replied. "That's not what I like. But I do like to stay out late. I like to travel. I like to have fun of the sort that you don't particularly like to have."

Arthur began to deny all this. He liked to have as much fun as anyone, he told her. Whether or not this was true, Arthur wasn't sure. He felt it might be true—it might be true that he liked to do fun things—but the reality was that it was mostly irrelevant. As Arthur realized, the reason they hadn't done more fun things together wasn't because he didn't like to have fun. It was because Rebecca didn't particularly want to do these fun things with him. In a strange way, what Arthur vaguely wanted was to be included on this new adventure that Rebecca had embarked on. It all seemed fascinating to him. But Rebecca clearly wanted to go it alone. Arthur hadn't held her back from all this excitement because of his personality. He had held her back because she was no longer in love with him.

All the same, Arthur continued to protest that he was just the sort of man that liked to have lots of fun, and she kept telling him that he wasn't being true to himself and that he knew, as well as she did, that he'd much prefer to spend his time on his son's ranch in Colorado or fishing in the Catskills than staying out late in New York City or spending weekends in Paris.

"I mean, we had an entire lifetime to do those things," she said, "and you never seemed interested."

"Neither did you," Arthur said. And this was true. Rebecca had never been the bon vivant that she was now.

"Well, I always wanted to," she replied. "I always wanted to."

"Well, maybe I wanted to as well."

"Oh, Arthur. Nonsense. You're just saying that. We both know that's not your way of living."

The whole argument was mystifying to Arthur, but he was ultimately unable to express himself because he also felt that he couldn't bear to hear Rebecca say in clearer and more concrete terms that she absolutely no longer felt any kind of love for him. To put an end to the faulty logic of Rebecca's "we're different people" argument would have forced her into a "you still love me but I no longer love you" argument, and this seemed to be more than Arthur could stand to hear.

The dinner ended with Arthur feeling slightly exasperated and Rebecca acting as though it were virtually impossible to deal with a man as repressed and confused as Arthur. They did manage to move to a discussion of their sons to take the edge off the direct discussion of their failed marriage, and they left each other quietly, with promises of staying in touch.

Arthur was relieved to get away from the frustration of that conversation, but the relief was only momentary, and by the time he arrived at his apartment he found that his frustration had been replaced with a sort of bitter loneliness and anger. For all the confusion that he felt, one thing was perfectly clear to him: Rebecca was thrilled by the new arrangement, by the fact that their marriage was over, while he hated it. Furthermore, Rebecca was good at her new life. He was a complete failure at slipping solo into the social world, while Rebecca seemed to be more pleased than she had even imagined she would be.

As Arthur prepared for bed, putting on his pajamas and brushing his teeth, he stared with a sort of revulsion at himself in the mirror. His graying hair and gaunt frame seemed to be closer to that of an old man than ever before. He remembered once, as a boy, seeing his great-grandfather without a shirt on and how horrified he had been by the incredible atrophy that had taken place. Was his the sort of body that would horrify a young person? He calculated his age and realized that, at that point, his great-grandfather was a full twenty years older than he was now. But as he looked at his sagging skin and eroded muscles, he could already see that body starting to appear. And as he continued to calculate years and ages, he came to another striking conclusion—he just might face at least another twenty years of this demoralizing rejection and loneliness, all the while descending into his great-grandfather's shattered physical state. As far as Rebecca was concerned, he had already arrived, at least as far as his personality went. A dreary personality and a body to match, he thought, as he dried his face and put on his pajama top. The worst thing of all was that he could see no way to resolve his problems. They just seemed to be increasing, and as he got into bed he couldn't help but feel like he had been unfairly singled out for a particularly cruel kind of punishment that had been spared everyone else.

6

Over the next several weeks, Arthur did what he could to restore some kind of optimism to his life. He went out to lunch, took long walks in Central Park, made numerous phone calls to both his sons, and went to the Catskills to fish, spending time with various members of the Fly Casters. None of these trips matched the kind of fun he had had with Jim and Ken. They were calmer visits, where the men shared dinners, but spent most of their time on the stream, or sleeping, or relaxing in the library. One of the weekends Arthur even found himself entirely alone, which he didn't mind, although it did give rise to the kind of troubling introspection he was working to avoid. Because Maidenhead housed a shrine of sorts of his male forebears, he couldn't help but think about growing up surrounded by such robust and successful men, and it kept striking him that he didn't measure up very well. Furthermore, such conclusions were continually matched with difficult and puzzling memories, one of which, concerning a weekend away when he was young, came very forcefully on Sunday morning as he was standing hip-deep in a pool just north of Maidenhead Grange.

When he was ten, Arthur's family took a weekend trip to the Equinox in Vermont, joined by another family which included a girl named Alice, near in age to Arthur's sister, and a boy named Kip, who was about Arthur's age. The plan was for the males to spend the weekend fishing on the Battenkill while the females rode horses. The trip started off well but in the end added up to a certain kind of personal catastrophe for Arthur. That is, Arthur observed in fairly vivid and compelling detail just how capable he was of completely exasperating his father, leading the elder Camden into wild and colorful expressions of frustration coupled with halting and failed attempts to rein himself in. Of course, Arthur had seen this in small glimpses before, but never to this extent and never in such repetition and fluidity. Especially disturbing (Arthur concluded as he slowly moved up the stream above Maidenhead) was that all of it was so clearly his own fault.

The troubling day began when Arthur mentioned to his father, quite reasonably as far as he was concerned at the time, that his waders were way too tight and that they were hurting his feet, perhaps dangerously cutting off his circulation. He followed this with several other observations, pointing out that he was extremely cold—certainly too cold to fish—that he was entirely exhausted, that he was starving (he had refused to eat the salmon sandwiches they brought for lunch), that his fishing vest pinched him terribly under his arms, and, finally (and this Arthur did realize might be crossing the line) that he would have much preferred to go horseback riding with his sister and mother than fish on that particular day. (All of this set against the foil of Kip, who happily bounded over rocks in his waders, gobbled down his salmon sandwiches with reckless appetite, boldly took off his jacket and sweater midday, and, when Arthur mentioned that he wished he was riding horses, declared that he recently got into a fight with a kid who went horseback riding because he hated "that kind of crap.")

Throughout Arthur's complaints, his father did his best to talk him into being a bit hardier, a bit more accepting of the challenges and the imperfections of life. And had an outsider observed the scene, he probably would have concluded that Arthur's father was actually doing his best to encourage him to embrace a more virtuous outlook on life and not simply berating the boy. But the truth was that, despite his somewhat sympathetic parenting techniques, it would also have been perfectly obvious to anyone that whatever toleration he was showing was out of some sense of paternal obligation and that underneath it was a stunned disbelief that his son could be quite such a complainer. And he did manage to lose his temper a few times, saying things like, "I mean, my god, Arthur, you act like you're in Siberia. It must be fifty-five degrees out. How cold could you be?" and "You ate a salmon sandwich last time we fished and you loved it. What's the problem? You're acting like we deliberately decided to punish you."

The matter of food, in fact, came up again that evening when the families were out to dinner at the more formal of the Equinox's dining rooms. Arthur insisted that the only thing he wanted to eat was lobster Newberg. He'd had it before, he said, and it was his favorite food, and, since he had to go without lunch, he'd really like to have something that would make up for it. It cost the same as the steak, he pointed out—the steak was what Kip and the two men were having—so there wasn't any financial reason not to. And, after all, lobster was a popular dish and probably very good for you.

Initially, Arthur's father fervently refused, insisting that he knew Arthur too well for this and that he was positive that Arthur was going to hate lobster Newberg.

"But I've had it before," Arthur pleaded, "and I love it. It's my favorite food and I never get to eat it."

The debate went on for some time, and at last (and not without precedent as far as this kind of thing went) Arthur's father relented. And the truth was that he seemed to do so not entirely out of desperation but with at least an attempt at a change of heart, at last declaring that this was supposed to be a happy weekend and that if Arthur was so sure he wanted lobster Newberg, then why not.

Of course, when the lobster Newberg arrived, Arthur was astonished to discover that he had never seen anything like it before, and that the idea of lobster cooked in such a thick, white, creamy sauce was an even more horrible thing than the salmon sandwiches. He knew that the stakes were now very high, and that he'd really better eat it despite how revolting it obviously was. But after he distracted himself by eating three pieces of bread and poking his dinner several times with the end of his knife, his father finally saw what was happening and yelled, "You see! You see! I knew it. I knew it. I knew you wouldn't like it. Why don't you ever listen to me?" at which point Arthur burst into tears, realizing that the day had been a total disaster and any attempt to tough anything out now was entirely useless because he was entirely to blame.

His mother tried to make him feel better. And his father did actually look quite remorseful as he saw his son crying. But there was no way out now, and eventually Arthur asked to be excused, and left the table and the families for his room, which (almost too awful for Arthur to think about on that solitary Sunday morning at Maidenhead) he was sharing with Kip.

The events of that day came up again when the family arrived back in the city. It was Sunday evening and Arthur found himself in the kitchen with his father, looking out over the deep courtyard behind their Park Avenue apartment as they ate bowls of ice cream together. Arthur's father brought up the matter of the trip first and said that he was sorry that he had made his son cry. "You're a great kid, Arthur," he continued. "In so many ways. But you've got to understand that life is full of difficulties. Sometimes our waders don't fit. Sometimes we're a bit unhappy with the weather. Sometimes we're served salmon sandwiches when we don't want them. But we've got to accept what we have and move on. Believe me, Arthur, you're going to face a lot worse than unappetizing sandwiches in your life, and I really think you need to learn to be a bit tougher and embrace the world a bit more."

Arthur nodded and said he understood. They were eating a brand of butter pecan ice cream that Arthur didn't particularly like, but he decided he might do well to listen to his father at this point in time and keep this to himself. It seemed like a lesson that was probably very important. And the truth was that the lesson lasted longer than just that night. In the years that followed, Arthur did what he could to hide his fears and disappointments whenever it was possible. But he was never very good at it. That was a fact. And there was the other matter that despite his father's small moments of kindness, Arthur couldn't help but somehow grasp that he wasn't very much like his father, and that, perhaps, were it not for the fact that he was his father's son, his father might not actually like him very much at all. This last particular notion, however, though strong, was something Arthur never quite faced head-on.

The remarkable thing was that Arthur did eventually grow to love fishing, and he became quite good at it, as far as these things go. He wasn't quite sure how or why this happened. But he really did love it. He loved the mechanics of casting. He loved the look of the gear—the split-cane rods he grew up with, the antique fly boxes, the click of the Hardy Perfect his grandfather had given him when he was fourteen. And, just as important, in this setting he had somehow learned to suffer tight waders and cold temperatures without opening his mouth too much. Fly-fishing, rather than being an occasion for his disgrace, became something he could do with some competence and even with just a bit of bravado, as far as bravado is possible in fly-fishing. But again, he really did like it for reasons other than that it was simply an opportunity to fit in and do what he was supposed to, although as Arthur stood in the stream that morning thinking about possible reasons for his affection for fishing, he couldn't come up with much more than that it was just one of those things a person unexplainably likes to do. It was very difficult to make sense of it all. Just as he was thinking his way through this particular matter, however, a fish rose to his fly, bringing him swiftly back to the task at hand, and soon Arthur was totally absorbed in reeling in what would surely be, Arthur was positive (judging from its strength and the force of the rise) a very impressive trout.

By the time he was bringing the fish to his net, however, Arthur did, in that instant, wonder once more how much he had really changed since his boyhood. Was he still a kind of complainer, as his dad put it, unable to face even the simplest problems in life? He hoped not. The point was, though, that he should work hard not to be this way. He did not want to be that sort of person. He wanted to be more like his father. And if he really worked at it, surely he would be able to find a way to keep his more unappealing tendencies at bay.

7

Fortunately for Arthur, about this time (in the midst of this particular introspective period) there was a thing-in-the-world, so to speak, that did begin to buoy up his spirits, namely, the not-too-far-off Fly Casters' Meeting-in-Full. The meeting always happened over Columbus Day weekend and it was generally the highlight of Arthur's year. The weekend was never subdued, never really relaxing, and consisted of lavish dinners, long nights of cards and cigars, and serious fishing. Arthur had actually signed up to organize the event this year, feeling he had the time and energy to spare. He had done it once before, twelve years earlier, although at that time it had been somewhat difficult to manage—his business was still afloat, although starting to founder, and his wife and sons were still very much in his life. This year he was happy that he had sufficient time to devote to the event, and he began making lists and assigning small tasks to members well over a month before the Meeting-in-Full was scheduled to occur. The truth was that this was the kind of occasion where Arthur always felt he shined, where he could prove that he was not the timid, boring man that Rebecca and others seemed to think he was. The event always had a bacchanalian spirit to it (as much as eleven older men from Manhattan are capable of that sort of thing), and the scotch and steak and creamed spinach, combined with the vigorous and well-rehearsed storytelling, always made Arthur feel as though he were involved in something very deep and very human.

The membership generally considered it very bad form not to come to the Meeting-in-Full; only a few times in recent memory had there been absentees. But there was always the danger of cancellations, and there were the more equivocating members who couldn't commit till the last minute, saying that they would be there so long as they didn't get tied up with work or family matters. This particular year, Arthur wanted to make sure that everyone came, and called members repeatedly, trying to confirm their participation. He did this under different guises, including the assignment of various duties, the arranging of rides, the pinning down of arrival times, and other such things. In other instances, he called for no other reason than to nudge members to commit, assuring them that they'd regret not going or that they had a duty to the other Hanover Street men. He knew he was being pushy, but he felt that it would all pay off in the end, when all the members were gathered together, drinking liquor, smoking cigars, and talking.

There was only one member who seemed particularly annoyed by Arthur's assertiveness. This was Casper Moore, a stockbroker under investigation for securities fraud. He was a well-liked member, who (according to other Fly Casters) had been unfairly singled out by grudge-bearing rivals, and Arthur did his best not to put added pressure on him with Meeting-in-Full preparations. All the same, Arthur did feel it was his job to make sure Casper attended, and he also felt a sort of personal responsibility toward him, having suffered such terrible business problems of his own in the past year. Generally, when Arthur brought up the matter of the meeting, however, Casper simply replied, "Look, Arthur, I'll do my best to be there, but I can't say right now if it's going to happen." Arthur always wanted to say more, to tell Casper that Maidenhead was just the thing to take his mind off his troubles, but he was never quite able to do this.

He did finally press the point one morning, however, following a night that Arthur determined was one of the worst times he had faced since his wife had left him. Just days earlier, Ken had given Arthur a long lecture on the importance of a man taking the lead in romantic situations. "If you don't," he said, "they'll think you're not interested." This prompted Arthur to consider whether or not all his recent failures with women had been because he had seemed too removed, too aloof. So, during an awkward pause in conversation at the Bristol Hotel's bar with a fifty-something blond woman named Trisha Hammond, Arthur leaned forward and tried to kiss her. Trisha's reaction was not one of rejection so much as utter horror, and she immediately slid her chair back from the bar with a look of panicked confusion.

Arthur, in an attempt to smooth over what had suddenly become a very awkward moment, quickly told Trisha how much he liked and admired her, and then, shockingly, tried to kiss her again. Needless to say, his second attempt was fended off with even more astonishment, and the date ended moments later with Arthur seated alone, staring off into space and wondering just how long this particular misstep was going to haunt him.

It was in the midst of these feelings—feelings that now had extended into the following morning—that he called Casper Moore. Arthur hadn't planned anything specific, although it was in the back of his mind that he might try to reach out to Casper as he encouraged him to attend the Meeting-in-Full. Casper, however, initially seemed so annoyed that Arthur was calling, yet again, that Arthur became extremely nervous and suddenly launched into a long explanation about how he understood exactly what Casper was going through, and that he was there if he ever needed to talk, and that there was nothing like a little fishing and quality time with close friends to help face one's troubles and misfortunes.

Casper's response was quite a bit more hostile than Arthur had imagined it would be. He started by saying he didn't need anyone to talk to and that his problems would be solved soon enough, and then he began saying that he and Arthur were nothing alike and that he resented any comparison. "Our problems are totally different," he snapped. "Mine stem from the fact that I've got enemies at the SEC. Yours stem from the fact that you're an incompetent idiot."

Arthur was, of course, fairly insulted by this, although even now he managed to extend some sympathy to Casper, assuming that he really was overwhelmed by all the pressure. But Casper's invective continued. "Do you know that everyone in Manhattan makes fun of you, Arthur? Everyone makes fun of you. Dinner parties, benefits, we all laugh at you behind your back. All your stupid crying over how sad you are. You should hear people laugh about all your botched dates. It's the first story anyone wants to hear anymore. So since you're giving out advice, I'll return the favor. Stop trying to organize fishing trips and start working out what to do with your miserable life."

The phone call ended quickly after that. Arthur didn't hang up on Casper. He said goodbye. But he didn't offer any specific response. He was too embarrassed by the thought of people telling stories about him to be able to think of anything to say. Arthur had seen other people become the butt of jokes among his social circles, and in particular at the Fly Casters, and he shuddered at the idea of everyone in New York (or his broader set, at least) now laughing at him. He remembered crying in front of everyone at Sprague's—how he hadn't been ashamed at all, and how he now felt like some sort of simpleminded rube, unable to control his emotions. Worse, there was the matter of his romantic life being such a topic of conversation. Arthur's recent loneliness had seemed to him a sort of quiet, private problem that he could endure. Now it was more of a public disgrace—another one in a long string of public disgraces.

About five minutes after Arthur hung up, the phone rang. It was Casper again, although now he quickly offered a detailed and (Arthur thought) sincere apology. He said that he was, to be honest, under lots of pressure and that it had been completely deplorable to speak to Arthur that way. He also said that many people liked Arthur a great deal, and that the stories of Arthur's life weren't really told with any kind of malice. Rather, he pointed out, the stories were delivered with affection more than anything. And he repeated several times that he hoped Arthur could forgive him for his outburst.

Arthur was still confused by the whole exchange, but he said that Casper was of course forgiven. Arthur did feel it was a sincere apology, although he was unclear whether the apology was for what he had said or what Casper actually thought about him. In general, however, the apology was mostly irrelevant. Arthur was now painfully aware that his life had become a source of amusement for certain people, no matter how much affection they may or may not feel for him.

But the truth was that after he and Casper hung up for the second time, Arthur oddly began to feel a new sort of firmness come over him, a firmness and a feeling of determination. Arthur started pacing his apartment and muttering to himself that it was time for him to stop all his wallowing. It was all ridiculous, he told himself. It was time for him to accept his problems without so much complaint and do what he could to begin his life again with a sort of strength that had been utterly lacking in recent months. He wasn't going to dwell on his misery, and he certainly wasn't going to complain (let alone cry) to friends in the Fly Casters again. He had become a laughingstock. And he was not a laughingstock because he was disliked. He was a laughingstock because his life had, in fact, become entirely ridiculous. This ridiculousness, Arthur resolved, was exactly the thing that he had to end.

And over the next two weeks, Arthur did manage to maintain a certain amount of the strength and equilibrium he was trying to effect. It took effort. It was a conscious struggle. But when Arthur began to think about how unlucky he was to have lost his business and his wife, he did what he could to force his mind on to other things. He looked into taking a trip to Europe. He spent time on the phone with his sons. He called the friend who was thinking about opening a restaurant to reiterate that he "really might be interested in putting in some money." He also continued to organize the Meeting-in-Full, although now with a more businesslike attitude and without the unfounded and slightly desperate optimism.

Arthur even went on two more dates. The first didn't go very well, but Arthur refused to feel bad about it when he ended up alone, back at his apartment again. On the second date, however, he actually found that he connected with the woman. He felt a certain sort of initial attraction that he had not really felt with most of the other women he had gone out with, although this date would prove to be the most catastrophic of all.

The woman's name was Rixa Corbet. She was fifty-seven, and was friends with a man Arthur knew from college. Arthur resolved to plan the date out as little as possible (there was to be no more hand-wringing or anxious strategizing), but there was a Wednesday concert at Lincoln Center that he wanted to see—now just two weeks before the Meeting-in-Full—and he decided to give Rixa a call at the last minute to see if she would like to accompany him.

They met beforehand for a drink, and, as far as Arthur could tell, they seemed to get along very well. Rixa's father had made a living importing agricultural commodities—mostly cocoa beans and kola nuts from West Africa—and she was interested in hearing all about Arthur's life in the import and export business. More importantly, her father's business had also closed down, and she insisted that it was the kind of business that always went under one way or another and that the important thing was to build up enough reserves to survive after disaster strikes.

"You seem to have done very well," she said. "You seem to have set yourself up very well."

Arthur did not exactly agree with Rixa's analysis of his situation, but just the idea that someone looked at it in any sort of positive light made him feel good, and by the time Rixa and he were taking their seats at Lincoln Center, he was thinking that things were progressing very well.

After the concert, which was an assortment of arias performed by young Spanish sopranos, Arthur suggested they get dinner, and before long they were seated at a corner table at a restaurant called Epi Dupin, leaning in to each other and, although Arthur felt he was not qualified to identify it as such, flirting. Arthur told Rixa about his sons, his separation from his wife, and his plans for the Fly Casters' Meeting-in-Full. Rixa shared similar information, but kept turning the conversation back to Arthur, being most intrigued by the Fly Casters, and particularly the camp.

"Of course I've heard of Maidenhead Grange," she said. "Who could forget something with a name like that? I hear it's supposed to be stunning."

Arthur said that it was, and after he'd described it in some detail, and after they'd had a few more drinks at the restaurant's bar, Rixa began to insist that she'd like to see it one day.

"I'm afraid that's out of the question," Arthur replied.

"How far is it?" she asked.

"With no traffic, you can get there in about two hours."

"I think you should take me there."

Arthur smiled. "It would be absolutely forbidden. Or it would require a members' review that would take thirty years."

"Well, then take me there in secret."

"I'm afraid that really would be impossible."

This kind of playful interaction continued for some time, Rixa ordering more drinks and softly touching Arthur's arm, and insisting that she be allowed to see Maidenhead. And just before midnight, in a state of confusion (and questionable sobriety), Arthur found himself in his car, driving across the George Washington Bridge, headed toward the Fly Casters' camp.

"This is a terrible idea," he kept saying, but by this point he and Rixa had kissed and were holding hands (when it was possible for Arthur to take one off the steering wheel), and he was so thrilled by the entire situation that he couldn't help but think, simultaneously, that this was the best idea he had ever been a part of.

This was Rixa's argument as well. "I think it's a wonderful idea," she kept repeating. "You sneaking me up to your men's camp to seduce me. What could be more fun than that?"

This was, in fact, precisely the logic that she had used at the restaurant when she first proposed that they go up that night and, as far as Arthur was concerned, the logic was entirely flawed. But he kept thinking (in his state of confusion and panic) that if there was really any truth to his resolution to behave differently and to somehow defeat the nervous and depressed man that he had become, this was an opportunity he should take. It had all the elements of what he was struggling to find. He was seducing a woman he felt was beautiful, and he was doing it in secret at the hallowed camp of his forefathers. This, ultimately, was what gave Arthur license to act in this way: part of the appeal was, in effect, a certain vague fantasy of being caught and expelled from the Fly Casters for daring sexual exploits. Arthur had never had anything close to what might be considered daring sexual exploits, let alone gotten in trouble for them. All the same, Arthur had no intention of getting caught. It was a Wednesday night and he was sure no one was scheduled to be there, and in the very unlikely event that someone was there, he'd see the car from the camp's long private road and simply turn around. The only chance he was taking was with Rixa's discretion, although he repeatedly swore her to secrecy—something she greatly enjoyed swearing to. "I swear," she kept saying. "I swear I will tell no one. It will be our great secret." And she said this again as they drove up the Fly Casters' gravel road and once more when they walked in the front door of Maidenhead Grange. "It will be our great secret," she said.

Arthur was actually slightly worried as he turned on the lights and began to give Rixa a tour. If there was sex to be had, it would begin soon, and he was, by all measures, completely out of practice. But Rixa hung on him affectionately and stopped to kiss him every so often—in the Billiard Room, in the upstairs hallway, in the kitchen—and slowly Arthur began to relax. It crossed his mind that perhaps they should go right to his bedroom, but he then decided that the night ought to begin in the living room with drinks and a fire. He ought to do this right, he thought, otherwise they might as well have stayed in the city.

Arthur made himself a scotch and soda, and Rixa opened a bottle of wine, and as she sat on the large camelback sofa to the right of the fireplace, Arthur lit a pyramid of kindling and newspaper, and after a few moments put two large logs on top. After the fire was burning, he grabbed his drink and sat on the couch next to Rixa. He began to talk in a slightly nervous and scattered way, but Rixa quickly put an end to the conversation and began kissing Arthur. And they kissed for several minutes before Arthur pulled back a little to ask Rixa what she thought about the famous and highly secret Hanover Street Fly Casters' camp.

"I'm very impressed," she said, smiling. "Perhaps you'll show me your bedroom soon."

"Of course," he replied, thinking how easy all this was. Perhaps he was the sort of person that was good at this after all, he thought, and then proceeded to kiss Rixa again, just exactly in the way he imagined a confident and successful man was supposed to.

After a few more minutes of such kissing, Arthur began to think that it was finally time to escort Rixa upstairs. He considered what might be the most elegant way of doing this, although it was clear that he was not going to be rejected. Still, he was going to great efforts to play a certain role that evening, and he didn't want to do anything to detract from it. But just as he was thinking the matter over, he began to notice a strong smell, and when he cast his eyes to the fireplace, he noticed that the smoke was not entering the chimney correctly. He started to get up, but Rixa pulled him back, and he decided that the flue hadn't quite heated up yet and that it would start to draw properly in a little bit. And he rehearsed this logic for the next few minutes as the smoky smell increased. He tried to get up once more, but Rixa only giggled and pulled him back, and Arthur didn't have the will to refuse. Finally, though, after continuing to smell the smoke, he decided that the flue ought to have been adequately heated by now (if such a thing really needed to happen) and that the smoke wasn't going away.

"I'm sorry, but I just have to check this," he said, now coyly pulling Rixa's arms off him.

He stood up, walked to the fireplace, and started to adjust the brass handle that stuck out from the stone facade. It didn't seem to help things, but just as Arthur was trying to peer into the chimney opening, there was a sudden roar and the smoke began flowing up the chimney again. Arthur couldn't figure out what was happening, although he was relieved that the fireplace seemed to be drawing well now. Still, it seemed that something was not quite right, and after hearing a loud cracking noise coming from the chimney, he decided he'd better take a look outside to see if everything was in order.

He first went back to the couch to give Rixa a quick kiss, but, after an instant, pulled himself away again and said that he had to run outside for just a moment.

"I'll be right back," he said, as Rixa tried to look pouty on the couch. What exactly Arthur was looking for, he wasn't sure, but it didn't take long for him to realize that there was, in fact, a serious problem with the chimney. High orange flames were now pouring out of it. The fire was just coming from the chimney, which was stone and not really flammable. Arthur imagined that perhaps a raccoon or something similar had built a nest there, and that it would burn itself out. Still, it was a fairly alarming sight, and Arthur quickly ran back in the house to attend to the fire in the fireplace. He first ran to the kitchen, filled a large pot with water, and returned to put out the fire in the fireplace. Then he closed the flue, cutting off the jet of oxygen that was rushing up the chimney. That would help some, Arthur thought, and then he headed back outside to check on the chimney. As Arthur went back out, he was most concerned with how to keep the mood up with Rixa. He was feeling that this whole chimney incident was terrible luck, although he kept telling himself that the seduction was already a success and that it wouldn't take too much effort to begin again where they left off. When Arthur got outside, however, he realized that any kind of trip to his bedroom was now out of the question. Although the flames from the chimney had died down, the roof was now on fire.

Arthur stood for a moment, staring bewildered at the burning roof. Of course, it immediately occurred to him to call the county fire department. But as he calculated their probable response time and the damage that could result from a burning roof, his mind quickly flashed through other solutions, such as putting the fire out himself, or fleeing before he was discovered. All of the possible scenarios, however, involved furious members of the Fly Casters and the notion that it would be nearly impossible to explain himself. Finally, as he seemed to come to the end of his examination of the spectrum of actions and consequences—all done in an impressively thorough manner for a time span of sixty seconds—Arthur ran back into the camp and dialed 911.

The county's volunteer fire department was spread thinly through the area, and it took some time for them to finally reach the camp, located, as it was, far from the fire department's headquarters. When they arrived, Arthur was standing outside with Rixa, continuing to stare in disbelief as he watched the fire now envelop the house.

It took some time for the firefighters to make any headway, and it was quickly clear to Arthur that at the very best, Maidenhead Grange would suffer extensive damage. If the rooms were not burned to a cinder, then they would surely suffer from the smoke and the firefighters' water. Arthur slowly considered all that would now be lost. Since each member of the Fly Casters took care of his own quarters, each room was a sort of time capsule of treasures and heirlooms extending back to the original members. Ancient fly rods, volumes of sporting diaries, personal souvenirs from past Meetings-in-Full, and numerous other items would now certainly be destroyed. At first, Arthur took some comfort from the fact that his room was closest to the chimney and that he'd get the worst of it; his guilt was somehow addressed by the idea that he stood to lose the most. But this relief slowly gave way as he realized all the rooms would certainly succumb to the fire.

He began to feel another kind of shame as well, as he thought about his grandfather and his father and how he had slowly ruined everything they had ever built. He thought about their long lectures over the years on issues such as family responsibility and stewardship, how he had been carefully instructed on matters of the family business and the legacy of Maidenhead Grange, and how he seemed to have subverted every lesson he was ever taught—and subverted them in such ridiculous fashion. Had all this been caused by an untended cigar or an overworked stove, he might have been able to retain some sense of dignity. Instead, he set fire to the camp while trying to seduce a woman there. The whole thing was mind-boggling, and the only thing Arthur could do was burst into tears, although he eventually managed to control himself.

When the fire was finally out, the roof and the entire second floor were gone, and the first floor seemed damaged beyond repair. As the crew chief began to question Arthur as to his identity, the origins of the fire, and who the property belonged to, Arthur could barely speak. He answered quickly and in staccato, unable to say anything more than the basic facts.

Rixa was also questioned, although in a friendly manner. The firefighters were full of sympathy and not at all angry. But as the chief wrote down Rixa's answers, it occurred to Arthur again that he had acquired a daunting set of new problems. After he and Rixa had finished supplying the chief with details, as Arthur continued to stare at the destroyed building, Rixa came up alongside him, grabbed his hand, and said, "I'm afraid our secret might get out."

Arthur looked at her. "Yes, I'm afraid it might," he replied. He then looked back at the smoking timber, and the firemen winding up their hoses, and began to think about just what he ought to do next.

8

On the drive back to Manhattan, now seven in the morning, Arthur silently considered various ways of structuring the letter of resignation that he would certainly have to write to the Fly Casters. In some ways, such a letter would be a sort of relief to him, given the trouble he now felt he faced. There would be no review, no disciplinary action, and no hiding if he was immediately forthcoming and showed enough contrition to resign. He had no doubt that the Fly Casters would immediately accept his resignation— not because of the fire but because the fire had started after he had brought Rixa there. That was the unpardonable offense. It did occur to Arthur—at brief moments, in the midst of his shame— that maybe all this secrecy and fear of outsiders was ridiculous, and that he shouldn't feel so bad. All he did was bring a potential girl-friend there. Should that really be grounds for dismissal? Perhaps, he thought, the Hanover Street Fly Casters was an entirely outdated sort of organization and Maidenhead's bylaws were nothing more than bizarre artifacts from eleven repressed businessmen at the end of the nineteenth century. Arthur thought about this over and over, but these ideas kept giving way to another stark conclusion—the Hanover Street Fly Casters were, despite all contrary arguments, very important to him. For whatever imponderable psychological reasons, they were very important to him. And he had now grossly violated the spirit of the Fly Casters and of Maidenhead Grange by sneaking in a stranger—a possible girlfriend, no less—and then setting the camp on fire. It was a terrible feeling, and it now made the prospect of the resignation letter almost unbearable. The letter might help him save some face and avoid some trouble, but he could hardly bear the thought of no longer being one of the Hanover Street set. This thought again brought him to tears, although he managed to hold back from any overt sobbing—Rixa, after all, was in the passenger seat next to him.

When Arthur arrived back in Manhattan, however, things unfolded a bit differently than he expected. Arthur spent the entire morning thinking about the fire and his resignation letter. He got no sleep and was only able to pace around his apartment. He even started on a draft of the letter, although he decided that it could wait and that what he really needed to do was call a few of his fellow Fly Casters to let them know what had happened. They would probably be finding out that day anyway, and Arthur felt that he really ought to be the one to tell his cohorts about the fire. When he started making calls and passing along the news, however, Arthur found that he began telling a slightly altered version of the story. He didn't intend to, but as he described the events of the previous night, he found he couldn't quite confess to everything. That is, he excluded Rixa entirely from the matter. He told the story of going up the previous day, of being a bit chilled, of starting a fire, and of suddenly discovering that the chimney was ablaze. He didn't intend to lie. He intended to be entirely honest. But, almost against Arthur's will, he not only removed Rixa from the tale, but also began thinking that there was a good chance that no one would ever find out about her. And, to Arthur's surprise, as he repeated his story to various members, he found that there was quite a bit of sympathy for him, many of the members saying things like, "It's terrible news, but it's hardly anyone's fault," and "It's amazing that something like this didn't happen years ago." Thus, by the time the Fly Casters convened an emergency meeting four days later—to talk about what was lost and how to rebuild—no one had any sense that there had been a woman with Arthur at the time of the fire, and the matter of his resignation was not even discussed.

The emergency meeting took place over lunch at Sprague's, where the men talked gravely about the catastrophe, and the funds they would need to rebuild, and how they should modernize and fireproof the new building. They also talked about the great historical legacy of the Hanover Street men, the terrible fate that Maidenhead Grange had suffered, and what sorts of personal effects had been destroyed. Arthur also told his story again: that he had happened to have been up for the day, that he had lit a fire in the fireplace, and that an uncleaned chimney had caused the roof to burn. Arthur, of course, felt sick about withholding the other details of the night, but it was too late to do anything at this point.

And as the lunch progressed, members continued to treat Arthur sympathetically. Everyone said it was an act of God, and could hardly have been avoided. There was nothing wrong with lighting a fire in the fireplace, everyone said, and it could have been any one of them. Despite the sympathy, however, Arthur continued to apologize throughout the meal, barely touching his fish, and feeling a strange mixture of shame and sadness. He felt terrible about what had been lost in the fire. He felt bad for what he had lost and he felt bad about what others had lost as well. He was entirely humiliated that he had been the cause (in one way or another) of the whole thing. But he felt worse because he was now in the midst of a sort of terrible betrayal, lying as he now was about the evening.

As the lunch concluded, the members once again expressed their determination to rebuild Maidenhead, and they all agreed that whatever the insurance policy didn't cover, they would pay for out of their own pockets. In this way, the Fly Casters were able to part with some sort of optimism. It was decided that that year's Meeting-in-Full would be canceled, but maybe they could have construction done by October of next year, and that the next Meeting-in-Full would celebrate the ongoing strength (the rebirth, even) of the Hanover Street Fly Casters. And as they stood up from the table, the members told Arthur to buck up and face the future bravely, clearly addressing the fact that he looked to be in a state of near collapse.

As Arthur left Sprague's and got into a cab going uptown, he continued to consider the meeting and the sort of problems he always seemed to get himself into. He was beginning to feel relief over his successful concealment of Rixa's presence, but also a new sort of dread at the prospect of having to keep this new secret. When he got home, he paced through his apartment for some time, finally deciding to call his son Patrick to say that he might head out to Steamboat for that "extended stay" very soon. "I really think I'd like to spend more time with you and Marina and the kids," he said. Then he paused for a moment. And then he began to tell his son the terrible thing that he had done to Maidenhead Grange, and how awful he felt, and how he would probably never get over it. Despite the honesty of the discussion, however, he still couldn't quite confess that there had been a woman involved.

For the next week, Arthur avoided interacting with anyone, only leaving his apartment for food and newspapers. He didn't want to face anyone, and, with a kind of magical logic, he felt that by being physically absent and mentally removed from everything, his problems might go away. He thought that his terrible feelings of guilt might fade, and that the matter of Rixa's presence would somehow disappear. Nearly ten days after the emergency meeting, however, still in the midst of his despair, Arthur received an unexpected phone call from Ken Fielder early in the morning, and realized then that hiding facts about the fire would now be an absolute impossibility.

Ken sat on the Prudential Committee of New York City's Episcopal Church, and because he had some experience handling the finances of not-for-profit organizations, he had been put in charge of wading through all the paperwork that follows things like catastrophic fires. As the phone call commenced, Ken began to tell Arthur how much he liked him, and how much he respected him, and he even said that he had really enjoyed getting to know him better over the past summer. "But I'm not sure you've been entirely forthcoming about this fire, Arthur," he said finally, his voice now becoming a little nervous. "I'm looking over these insurance and fire reports and I'm just wondering who this Rixa Corbet is. It seems she was up there with you?"

Arthur hesitated. Even now he wondered if there was a way out. He considered saying something like *I've never heard of her* or *We all know these rural officials aren't much for paperwork.* But as his mind turned over the various options, Arthur could only conclude that at this point there was no way out, and he finally revealed his entire idiotic story, and his endlessly stupid seduction plans, and how he felt that there was nothing left for him to do but resign from the Fly Casters. Arthur vaguely hoped that Ken would try to talk him out of this course of action, that he might suggest that all those bylaws and all the Fly Casters' secrecy was nonsense. *This could have happened to anyone*, Ken might say. But no such reply was forthcoming. After a moment of silence, Ken said, "I hate for it to come to that. But I think we both know there's hardly any other way to handle it at this point. Especially because you kind of kept this fact from everyone. The way the Fly Casters are, you know. In some ways I think you should stay. In this day and age, I'd say that maybe it should be forgiven. I'd forgive you. I would. I do. But I'm not sure the others will. All the tradition and all the old men who believe in that sort of thing. I guess I can keep this under my hat for a while, but people will find out soon enough. They always do. It might be better to take care of this now. With a little grace and dignity."

These things, it occurred to Arthur, were precisely what he lacked most in his life. He even said this to Ken. "Well, you know," he said, "dignity seems to be the very thing that I lack most in this world." He paused. "But, of course, you're right about all that," he finally said. "I'll start working on the letter today."

Ken and Arthur talked for a little while after that, and Ken even suggested that he'd still be keeping his eyes open for available women. Then, in what Arthur regarded to be a very kind act, Ken brought up the idea that Arthur must have been doing pretty well for himself to be sneaking women up to the camp. "I think you've been keeping secrets from me, Arthur," Ken said. "Here I am all worried about your love life and you're carting women around the Catskills."

Arthur began to blush, and said that he had only just met her, but then said that he had had a bit of luck with this one.

"Is she good-looking?" Ken asked.

"Yes, I'd say so," Arthur replied, "and she seems to like me." Arthur laughed nervously as he said this, and then, as he thought about what had transpired in the past two weeks, he was overcome with a terrible feeling of sadness. "But at this point, I'm not sure it's headed anywhere," he continued after a pause. "I actually don't think I'll probably see her again anytime soon. I'm planning to head to Colorado soon. For a long stay. At my son's ranch in Steamboat. Ride some horses. Stay there for the ski season and hope my knees hold out. So we'll see what happens."

"Steamboat sounds like a good plan," Ken replied. "That sounds like a good plan."

After talking a little more, Ken and Arthur hung up, promising to stay in touch, despite Arthur's impending resignation.

That afternoon and evening, Arthur drafted his resignation letter, feeling slightly relieved. He wrote that he was planning to spend most of his time now in Colorado and that perhaps it was time to pass his membership on to some new blood. "And, of course," he said, "because of recent incidents, I feel that grace and dignity require some kind of act of contrition and sorrow. In the same way that a captain goes down with his ship, I feel the best thing for me to do is to vanish with the fire. If you'll forgive the drama, I'm sure all of you know that this is the thing that I must now do."

After finishing the letter, Arthur ordered dinner from a nearby Italian restaurant that delivered, and then called Patrick to discuss again his plans for coming out to Steamboat. "I might stay for the whole ski season," he said.

"The whole season would be great," Patrick replied. "You can stay out here forever. Marina, the kids, and I would love it."

Arthur said that "forever" was tempting but that he still wanted to keep some sort of life going in New York. As he said this, he wondered to himself if he might be able to talk Rixa into coming to Steamboat for a visit. He considered asking Patrick if this would be all right, but then decided to wait until he got settled first and got a sense of how his life would be there. As he wrapped up his phone conversation with Patrick, he thought that perhaps he had been trying to rush things over the past year, and that in the end it might now be best to proceed with more patience. But he decided that if it was possible, he would like for Rixa to visit and that perhaps she would enjoy herself on his son's ranch. Still, that was some ways off, and as Arthur set out a knife and fork for his dinner, his mind turned to the problems of what he ought to pack, and how he ought to leave his apartment, and just how long he would, in fact, end up staying.

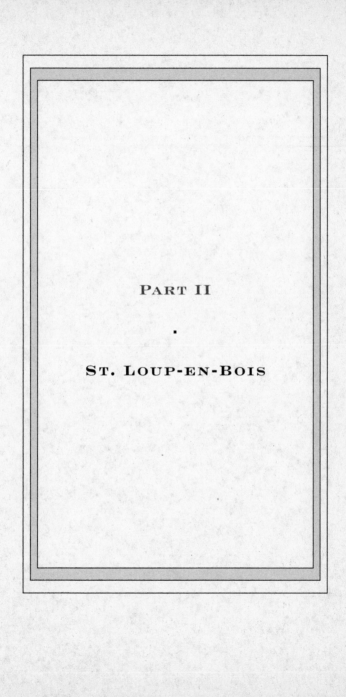

PART II

.

ST. LOUP-EN-BOIS

1

Gap was hardly the place Arthur had imagined he'd be spending a summer. He was, after all, from Manhattan, so foreign travel and foreign living ought to be done in places like Paris or Rome, or in some small village in the Vaucluse that no one had ever heard of. Spending time in the outskirts of a mid-sized city that boasted neither fame nor obscurity seemed slightly ridiculous to him. But he had a friend who was living there, who had been there for nearly two decades, and seeing that Arthur was looking for something close to anonymity for a while, Gap was a fairly appealing place.

Arthur had decided to fly in to Geneva, which was a little over two hours north of Gap. Lyon might have been a little closer, but he got a better deal on his rental car at the Swiss airport. This surprised Arthur as he was first making arrangements, seeing that everything in Switzerland was always so expensive. But luxury was more commonplace there, and while renting a Mercedes for a month or two in Lyon was grossly overpriced, in Switzerland it was just a reasonable increase over the regular rates. Of course, Arthur rented what he considered to be a modest Mercedes. "It's nothing at all flashy," he had told several people back in New York when he was describing his trip. But seeing that he planned to do quite a bit of driving in mountainous terrain, it seemed appropriate that he should have something comfortable and reliable to travel in.

But it was also true that Arthur was happy to fly into Geneva because he loved Switzerland. (Arthur was now thinking about this matter while inspecting a rack of mints at one of the airport news-agents, just beyond Swiss customs.) He had traveled to Switzerland as a young man, and had later done a fair amount of trade with various Swiss food companies when his business was still on its feet. And the truth was that he always felt that Swiss people liked him—unlike his Portuguese clients, for example, who canceled all accounts with him within six months of his taking over his family's business. One of these companies actually went so far as to explain its decision by saying that Arthur was "completely and totally impossible to deal with."

As Arthur thought about this, he finally decided on a small green box labeled *Astralmenthes*, and paid a somewhat shocking five Swiss francs for it. "Thank you very much, sir," the cashier said with a heavy Slavic accent.

Arthur said, "Thank *you*," smiled, and continued to the rental car area.

It was puzzling to Arthur, though, why he seemed to get on with the Swiss so well. After all, ask any person in the import and export business and they'll tell you that the Swiss are a silent, dry, and entirely inscrutable people. Few would describe them as pleasant and affable, as Arthur would. He wondered if this said something about him. In a flattering way it could be a sign of how well he got along with others, no matter who they were. On the other hand (and much less flattering), it was not impossible that Arthur had a general and instinctive tendency to mistake distance and an absence of malice for affection. This was a slightly disturbing idea to Arthur, and (ironically) just as he was thinking about what was now a very profound and confusing question, he happened to pass by Air Portugal's check-in counter, and suddenly wondered if, in fact, he ever really knew how to get along with other people at all. The decorations surrounding the Air Portugal counter included several pictures of the sun, the ocean, beachgoers, and large platters of shellfish, and everyone in the queue looked relaxed and happy, as though they were headed off to some sort of wonderful and exotic vacation. As Arthur looked at all this, he suddenly wondered if maybe his summer would have been better spent in a place like Portugal. Maybe he'd be able to conquer his current malaise by spending time in warmer climates with people known for passionate music and spicy fish. For a moment Arthur had a vision of himself in a loose-fitting white shirt unbuttoned to the waist, sandals, and linen trousers, sitting at some sort of dockside bar in Lisbon and drinking green wine. As absurd as this image seemed to Arthur, the reality was that it was also fairly pleasing. He even put his bags down for a moment and stared at the ticket counter. How hard would it be to change plans right there? Arthur's mind slowly turned over the possibilities. He was free of most professional and personal duties. There was not a thing in the world stopping him. And who wouldn't want to spend time in Portugal? Arthur stood there for several moments, thinking about how enriching and therapeutic such a trip would be. He could even extend it beyond the summer and perhaps, if he liked it enough, make Portugal a sort of second home.

Arthur considered these things for some time. And they were very pleasant thoughts. All the same, Arthur finally picked up his bags and continued toward the rental agency. He carried on with a tiny bit of ambivalence. But the truth was that at the end of his moment of introspection, Arthur came to grips with the fact that he generally disliked seafood, he never knew what to do when he was at the beach, and he could not really believe that he'd be happy sitting in dockside bars listening to sad music—and wearing linen, no less. In the end, Arthur concluded that the Portuguese were a wild, seafaring people, and there was really no way that he'd ever feel comfortable among them. Maybe this was exactly the same sort of verdict the Portuguese companies came to when they broke off relations with him, so perhaps their decision wasn't so insulting after all. Not every place is suited for every person.

2

It was interesting how Arthur had, in effect, chosen to go away that summer. He had been at a sort of family gathering to celebrate a nephew's birthday. He was standing next to his cousin (whose son was having the birthday) when Rebecca walked in the door with the man she had now been seeing for some six months. Arthur had never been introduced, but he knew that the man was extremely wealthy, clearly handsome, and always a hit at social events because he told such funny stories. Arthur was a little surprised to see Rebecca and him at this specific party (it was given by his relatives, after all). But it wasn't completely unexpected. Rebecca had been friends with this particular cousin for years, and they were still close, despite the divorce.

Arthur tried to be brave about it all. He told himself that he was just going to have to get used to this type of thing. Immediately after Rebecca had passed off her coat to the caterer who was working the door, Arthur even went so far as to walk directly up to her, smile, kiss her on the cheek, and say, "Hello, Rebecca. It's so nice to see you here."

"Arthur!" she said, returning the kiss and seeming very happy that he was being so gracious. "It's so good to see you here too." Then she turned to the man she was with and said, "Arthur, this is Stephen. Stephen, this is Arthur. Arthur Camden."

The two men's eyes met and they shook hands and Arthur immediately tried to effect a kind of carefree ease with the whole situation, as though "life is filled with many journeys, and while some come to an end, others are always beginning"—something he read in a book about getting over a divorce. It was a bit trite, but Arthur figured that looking carefree and in touch with "life's journeys" was better than bursting into tears. But then, in that brief instant, just as they were concluding the handshake, Arthur saw something just a bit disturbing in Stephen's eyes. It wasn't malice—a thing that Arthur not only expected but also vaguely hoped for. Rather, it was a kind of noble pity, as though Stephen had just beaten Arthur in a prep-school boxing match and he wanted his defeated opponent to know that, even though he was the lesser man, he still respected him.

Arthur felt his carefree facade quickly give way, and in the next moment found himself hurrying down one of the apartment's long hallways to the den, where the young people were watching a baseball game.

"Who's winning?" Arthur said as he came in. But he said it quietly, almost under his breath—or this was what he had no choice but to believe, because no one even looked up to respond. He thought about asking again. After all, these were people he was related to, and they had always seemed to like him. After another minute, though, Arthur decided he ought to just return to the world of the adults, and was soon telling the bartender that he'd like a glass of scotch. Arthur could only conclude that it was going to be a difficult night.

But Arthur had already had many difficult nights since the divorce, and after his first sip of scotch, and a handful of almonds, he calmed down somewhat. He again reverted to a kind of willful negation of his pain, and told himself over and over that seeing Rebecca was no problem at all. But then he heard an unexpected and happy-sounding commotion coming from the other side of the large, formal living room, and it quickly began to reverberate. It seemed that Rebecca and Stephen were in the middle of it, although Arthur couldn't quite figure out why. They had now only been there for about five minutes. Then Arthur heard a single chilling sentence from the crowd: it was spoken by Heidi Straenhof, who, after calling her husband's name several times, said, "Come over here right away and look at Rebecca's ring!"

Arthur knew very quickly what that implied. Still, he tried to remain calm. It could be any kind of ring, he thought. But then Heidi yelled, "When did this happen?" and Rebecca replied, "He just asked me yesterday. I didn't want to say anything—I didn't want to take away from the birthday. But I couldn't not wear my ring, could I? Isn't it beautiful?"

To Rebecca's credit, she was not shouting this. On the contrary, it seemed to Arthur that she was speaking several notches below her normal volume. But Arthur was well acquainted with the sound of her voice, and given the nature of this news, he couldn't help but hear every terrible word, including the final declaration that she and Stephen were thinking of "a wedding in St. Kitts some time in the fall."

Arthur put down his scotch and headed for the door. So much for a stiff upper lip, he thought. He did feel bad, though, running away like that, but toughing it out would simply be too painful. The likely consequences would be something of a scene—a scene with Arthur weeping angrily as he listed Rebecca's past cruelties and infidelities—and there was simply no way he was going to come out on top with that kind of behavior.

Soon he was on the elevator, trying to keep calm in front of the man who was operating it. He succeeded, and when they arrived at the lobby, it took him exactly ten more seconds to escape into the cool spring air that was now flowing down Fifth Avenue. It felt better. Being outside was better. Still, Arthur hardly knew what to do next, or how he was going to get through what would obviously be a difficult stretch of time for him.

It was on the following day that Arthur decided he needed to go away. Arthur didn't have to think long about where—or, at least, he was psychologically incapable of considering too many possibilities. He thought about his son's ranch in Steamboat, but he had made several trips there in the last few months, and anyway, his son would be in contact with Rebecca, and he wanted to stay away from any talk of the wedding. Arthur also thought of the other obvious destinations (again, Rome, Paris, and, in a moment of bohemian excitement, the Vaucluse), but somehow these ideas seemed very indistinct, and also very lonely. He knew people there, but no one he was particularly close to.

Arthur finally arrived at Gap for the simple reason that over the past several years—or decades, rather—a boyhood friend named Prentice Ross had repeatedly invited him to visit. Prentice came back to New York about once a year, and when he and Arthur would bump into each other—usually at the Geographers Club—he always told Arthur he should come and stay with him. "I have a huge place," he would say, "and there's a beautiful guest cottage I'd put you up in. You'd have plenty of privacy, so neither of us would be underfoot, and it's a great entry point for traveling the French and Italian Alps. You could stay for as long as you liked. Really! You have to take me up on it."

Arthur always promised to come, but never gave the idea much thought. He never seemed to have the time. He had always been slightly curious, however—he never really understood what Prentice was doing in Gap in the first place. And as Arthur thought about Rebecca, the day after he had found out about her engagement, he decided that Gap might be his best choice.

After coming to this decision, Arthur went to the bookstore to buy books on alpine France and northern Italy and even visited a few clothing stores to see what he might like to bring with him, if he actually did make the trip. It was only after a day or so of this kind of initial thinking that he finally called Prentice. They had known each other since they were eleven, so on a certain level, Arthur felt completely comfortable with him. Still, Arthur found that he was more nervous than he expected when making the call. They had just seen each other over the most recent winter holidays, and the offer was again extended. But they hadn't talked much then. They had only spoken for a few moments at a charity ball for wetlands conservation where Prentice mostly told Arthur how sorry he was to hear about him and Rebecca. Still, even though their conversation was short, he and Prentice had been friends forever, and Arthur was sure that all his offers were sincere. So he called him up, thinking that the only thing he should feel bad about was that he hadn't done this years earlier.

The phone rang several times before a woman finally answered. "*Allô, oui?*" she said. For some reason, this surprised Arthur. He was calling France, but he somehow didn't expect to have to speak French, seeing that it was Prentice's house. He knew some French— from college and from business—but after he fumbled through a few phrases, the woman finally replied in a thickly accented English, "Yes, I find him."

Prentice got on the phone a few seconds later, and soon Arthur was explaining that he needed to get away, and he'd like to spend time with an old friend, that he'd never really visited Prentice's part of France before, and that he was thinking now was the perfect time to do these things.

Prentice was just a bit surprised at first. He didn't seem reluctant to host Arthur, but it was clearly not anything he had expected. Prentice finally declared, however, that it would be fun to have "a pal from the old country" visit and that he and his "newish girlfriend" Delphine would be happy to have some company.

"Do you have a sense of when you'll come?" Prentice asked. "Or how long you'll stay?"

"I'd like to come next week, if that's possible," Arthur replied. "I was hoping to stay a month, but would be willing to make it two, perhaps, if that works."

"Two months?" Prentice said with what sounded like a fair amount of surprise.

"Well, one month," Arthur said. "But perhaps two. I'm not really sure yet. You said that you had a guest cottage, so I'm assuming that would be okay. You said that neither of us would be 'underfoot.' "

There was an alarmingly long pause, and during that terrible silence, Arthur just about hung up the phone. Finally, though, Prentice said, "Why not? It'll be great. The cottage is always empty, and I'd love to have you."

Arthur felt a great deal of relief when he heard this, and went on to thank Prentice several times, telling him that he'd be in touch just as soon as he arranged his travel plans.

"That's great, Arthur," Prentice finally said. "I'll really be looking forward to it." After that, they hung up the phone and Arthur began making preparations for his journey.

3

In 1959, Prentice Ross astounded his parents by enrolling in aviation school instead of going to Yale. Of course, being generous and humane people, Prentice's parents didn't have anything against pilots per se. It just happened that they had never met one, nor had they ever even thought of how a person became one. In fact, they knew not a single person who drove any machine at all (for a living, that is), so they were at a loss when they tried to imagine what their son's future would be like. But it was the late 1950s, and even though Prentice could have easily taken a number of lucrative jobs after finishing his degree, there was, in fact, something a bit romantic about becoming the captain of some sort of huge commercial airliner.

But even that was not a thing that Prentice pursued. He trained on seaplanes, and was soon running small cargo shipments between Anchorage and various mining and timber operations around Alaska. He did this for nearly five years, and then went on to do similar jobs in numerous other locations, although he spent the largest part of his time flying in Algeria and Morocco, giving up the difficulties of flying and landing seaplanes for the hazards of dust and heat and wind.

The interesting thing about Prentice (as far as Arthur was concerned) was that he was never the sort of double-fisted adventurer one might imagine embracing this kind of life. He was tall and athletically built, but he was also somewhat bookish, and as a teenager his interests included things like botany and assembling shortwave radios from Sears and Roebuck kits. Prentice's whole pursuit of aviation actually seemed largely intellectual, as though landing in a narrow lake two hundred miles north of Juneau were a kind of thought problem as much as it was an act of physical bravado. It was something like assembling a radio, although the variables and the stakes and the physical challenges made the puzzle much more complex and much more fascinating.

This kind of technician's outlook seemed to carry on throughout his career. Prentice began running his own cargo operations, and hiring his own pilots to deliver shipments in war-torn jungles and budding dictatorships all across Africa, approaching it all with that same mathematical outlook—he took a great deal of satisfaction from manipulating the course and destination of people and machines through very complex environments toward a specific and measurable goal.

As for Prentice's current career—what he was doing in Gap—Arthur's understanding was still unclear. He owned an airfield that had some kind of commercial function, but Arthur didn't know much more than that. As Arthur passed the exit for Courchevel in his modest Mercedes, and continued along the auto route toward Gap, he considered that the only real description Prentice had given of his current occupation was that it was his retirement job, although he had now owned the airfield for nearly twenty years.

At any rate, the drive to Gap took just under three hours. But getting to Gap was the easy part. While the airfield was technically within Gap's borders, Prentice's home was set farther in the country, near the village of Faverney. The maps Arthur had were entirely useless, since they didn't have any of the smaller country lanes marked. Arthur assumed that somewhere in the world there was a map with these lanes. But the state-sponsored rest stops sold maps that were only useful for broad campaigns from one end of France to the other. There was nothing that seemed to describe the rural outskirts of Gap or the village of Faverney with any kind of practical detail.

Of course, Arthur did have directions from Prentice, and these were what he relied on as he turned down small streets that went in and out of the small settlements surrounding Gap. The directions almost seemed as if they came from some sort of underdeveloped nation in the Southern Hemisphere, things like abattoirs and nail factories making up most of the relevant milestones.

It had seemed to Arthur that Prentice was feeling rushed when he was giving directions—or perhaps he was just too tired to talk. He kept saying things like, "I have no idea what it's called. It's just a chicken farm. You'll see it. When you do, go left." Arthur tended to like exact instructions with this sort of thing, so perhaps he was being a bit difficult himself, but as Arthur came to what looked like a chicken farm and there was no left to be made, he wished he had been a little more insistent with Prentice.

Finally, however, after nearly an hour and a half of driving (and nearly an hour of deciphering the agricultural geography of the area), Arthur came to what looked like the front gates to St. Loup-en-Bois—the somewhat regal name of Prentice's property. Arthur looked at his notes and recalled Prentice describing the two big stone pillars and iron gate that were now in front of him.

Still, Arthur stopped to get out and see if he could spot anything else that indicated that this was the place. He couldn't see the house from the road, and he felt slightly nervous just driving onto someone's property, especially when there were no house numbers to suggest that this was actually Prentice's property. But as Arthur peered up the gravel road and tried to see if he could recognize any other relevant landmarks, he looked to his right, just at the bottom of one of the pillars, and saw the words "St. Loup-en-Bois" etched in simple lettering into the bottom stone.

"I guess this is it," Arthur said to himself. In the next instant, he was back in his car and headed up the gravel road. It took some time before he arrived at anything that looked like a home, but when he finally did see what could only be the main residence, he at last understood the nature of Prentice's estate. St. Loup-en-Bois looked more like a hotel than a home. It was three stories high with a complex dormered roof, twelve columns of windows from end to end, and, according to Arthur's calculations, was about the size of the Vanderbilt's mansion on the Hudson—a place he had once visited on a tour with his sons.

It did look just a bit more institutional, though. This was true. And as Arthur would later find out, it had been built as a high-end convent for disgraced noblewomen, so it had been a sort of institution. But it was an institution built on a very grand scale, and as Arthur brought his car to a halt next to what must have once been a sort of stable and carriage house, he wondered how Prentice had come to find this place. But before Arthur could think about this question for too long (and just as he stepped out of his car and began straightening his sports coat and shirt) a thin, elegant, dark-haired young woman stormed out of the front door and toward a Range Rover that was parked at the far side of the large open driveway. Arthur followed her with his eyes (still smoothing out the lapels of his jacket) and even thought about calling out to her so he could introduce himself. Just as she opened the Range Rover's door, however, she burst into loud, angry tears. Arthur looked away as she got in and turned the ignition, now wanting only to give her some privacy, and as he cast his gaze back toward the house, he saw, for the first time, Prentice, standing in the doorway, looking slightly embarrassed.

"I'm sorry, Arthur," he called out as the woman tore out of the front courtyard and down the drive. "Delphine and I are having a bit of a fight. But nothing to worry about. Probably my fault. I always say the wrong thing." Prentice was clearly not feeling as relaxed as he was trying to let on, however. His hair was a mess and he looked somewhat flushed.

Arthur called back, "I'm that way with women too, so I've seen it all before." As Arthur thought about this, however, it occurred to him that no woman had ever stormed away from him in tears. Their hostility was almost always expressed as bored disinterest. Before Arthur could add some sort of statement to clarify this to Prentice, however, Prentice said, "Well, you've got to be tired. Why don't you come in?"

Arthur again ran his hands along his lapels. "Perhaps I'll leave my bags in the car? Get them later?"

"Okay. Whatever you like," Prentice said.

With that, Arthur walked to Prentice, shook his hand, and followed him into the house.

4

Arthur imagined a tour was now in order. After all, it was an expansive house, and Prentice was clearly proud of it—or, at least, he obviously took meticulous care of it. The paint was all new, the floorboards looked like they had just been restained, and there were even fresh flowers in the long entryway Prentice led Arthur through. But when they got to the end of the hallway, they made a right and stepped into a huge kitchen, at which point Prentice simply sat down at the enormous kitchen table and asked (somewhat preoccupied) how Arthur's trip was.

"My trip was excellent," Arthur said. "I slept on the plane for nearly five hours."

Prentice still looked distracted. "That's good," he said. But then, as though through an act of great will, he sat up straight, smiled, and added, "Well, I'm really glad you're here. It's good to see you. It really is. As you can tell, I'm a bit out of sorts. Delphine. Always difficult with her. Mostly because I love her. But issues with my ex-wife get her down. I guess it can't be helped. But it's good to see you. It really is."

There was something of a sense of obligation behind these final words. But there was a sincerity as well—enough of a sincerity to calm Arthur a bit. "It's good to see you too, Prentice," he said. "I can't tell you how happy I am to be here."

"Can I get you something?" Prentice continued. "Something to eat or drink?" At this, Prentice stood up and walked to a cabinet and took out two small glasses. The kitchen was clearly built for the purposes of feeding at least fifteen disgraced noblewomen, so Prentice had nearly twenty cabinets to chose from. There was also a large wood-fired oven, a wall of French doors that looked out to the back gardens, a gigantic wooden butcher block near the stove and the cabinets, and a large stainless steel refrigerator, which was exactly like the one Rebecca had bought just before leaving Arthur. Arthur, in fact, suddenly remembered the day the refrigerator arrived (along with three confused contractors), just a week after Rebecca had announced her intentions to divorce Arthur, and what a horrible day that was. It seemed shocking that there was anything left of his psyche at all, as far as Arthur was concerned, and when he saw Prentice open up a bottle of red wine, Arthur said, "I'll have some of that, if that's what you're going to have."

"I shouldn't," Prentice said, halting for a long moment before he began to pour. "But what's the good of living in France if you can't drink wine in the afternoon?" Prentice then shrugged his shoulders and poured out two large glasses.

As Prentice sat down, Arthur looked at the glass of wine and wondered for a moment if he should actually start drinking so early. It was only four o'clock, and while Arthur certainly had nothing against drinking that early in general, it was not always the best thing for his moods to start before five o'clock, especially when he was so easily jarred into sorrow by things like familiar stainless steel refrigerators. And the fact was that he was, by now, starting to feel the effects of jet lag, despite all the sleep he got on the plane. All the same, he was at the beginning of a sort of adventure, so he concluded that perhaps this was a good way to begin.

It took exactly an hour for the two men to finish the bottle of wine. Prentice put out some olives, bread, a large wedge of French Comté (which Arthur's business had once imported), and a dish of salted herring. And as soon as Arthur finished his third glass, helped with several pieces of bread and salty fish, he decided it had, after all, been a very good idea to start drinking, and soon he was recounting in some detail the events that had led up to and then followed his divorce, complete with his disastrous dates, and his run-ins with Rebecca, and various gripping descriptions of his other numerous humiliations.

Prentice was a good listener. He laughed at the right moments, looked serious when he needed to, and when Arthur described what had happened at the recent birthday party where he found out that Rebecca was engaged, Prentice even put his hand on Arthur's shoulder and said, "That must have been very hard, Arthur."

Prentice talked too about his own divorce and the two children from his marriage, both of whom lived in Gap with their mother. This was not something that Arthur knew much about, although he had heard bits and pieces over the years. And as Prentice opened a second bottle of wine, he began to talk about the impossibly complicated custody procedures in France, and how the courts and his ex-wife had established him as something of a monster, and how they had severely curtailed his visitation rights.

"It wasn't that hard for them to do," Prentice said. "I've lost my temper a few times. I was caught, ridiculously, in possession of an illegal handgun—an American antique I've had for years. And they also went to great lengths to prove I have a drinking problem."

Prentice looked down at his wine as he said this. "Of course, they may have something there." He laughed, said, "Not really," then picked up his glass and drank what remained. Then he poured himself another, and suddenly launched into a highly animated and quite astonishing description of how furious it made him that the "fucking French government" and his "fucking ex-wife" had the right to tell him ("The father!") when he could and when he couldn't see his own children.

"It makes me so fucking crazy," he said over and over, but also added several times (a little more calmly), "It's just so deeply, deeply wrong. It's just so immoral. I don't know how much longer I can take it."

Prentice repeated this description of his ex-wife's sins and the corruption of French domestic code several times in the hour or so that their discussion lasted. Throughout this time, Arthur's lack of sobriety felt more and more uncomfortable—almost as if he had accidentally drunk too much at a business dinner and could no longer speak coherently to his clients. Mostly, Arthur wanted to say something to Prentice to comfort him a bit—or to talk him down. Prentice was beet red and gripped his wineglass so tightly that Arthur was sure it would break.

"It is wrong," Arthur quietly said several times, growing more and more nervous about Prentice's anger. "No one should keep family members apart."

Finally, after Arthur said, "It's just very wrong, what's happened to you," for the third or fourth time, Prentice jumped up and began pacing around the kitchen. "It's this whole fucking country," he said. "But I can't leave, because I want to at least be near my kids. But what's the point if I can't see them when I want to? They need that. My kids need it as much as I do." Prentice suddenly opened a closet near the back door and pulled out a leather jacket. He slowly put it on, now looking much more pensive. He then looked up at Arthur, still with a kind of fury in his eyes, and said, "I'm afraid I need to go out for a little while, Arthur."

Arthur stood up. He wasn't sure what to say, but when Prentice picked up a set of car keys and then grabbed another bottle of wine, he felt obliged to make the point that Prentice shouldn't be driving in his condition. "Especially with all these curving roads up here," he said.

"I know these roads like the back of my hand," Prentice yelled. "Besides, this is important."

Arthur again started to speak, but before he could say more than "Prentice, I'm just not sure you should be driving," the back door was slammed shut and Prentice was running toward a small, separate garage at the back of the house.

As Arthur watched this, and then as he watched an old Jaguar XK12 tear out of the garage and around a small gravel road that led to the front drive, he concluded that this was perhaps a new side of Prentice that he had never really seen before. Of course, it was a hard thing, being separated from your family. Arthur felt he knew something about that. Still, he had a hard time integrating the wild anger that had come over the bookish radio assembler that he remembered from boyhood. The scene was all extremely puzzling. It was now seven-fifteen. Everything was dead silent. He was in a strange house. And he was all alone. It was still light out, but the sky had begun to dim. All Arthur could think at this point was that this was not quite what he expected on his first evening at St. Loup-en-Bois. He hadn't even been shown to the so-called guest cottage. If it were earlier, he might go look for it himself. But the sun was already going down, and he didn't really want to be wandering around Prentice's estate with no sense of where he was. And anyway, maybe Prentice wanted him to stay in the main house that night. It wasn't as if he were a renter and had some rights in the matter. He'd have to take his cues from his host. He'd wait for Prentice to return.

By midnight, however, there was no sign of Prentice. Arthur had passed the time by flipping through French architecture magazines, reading cookbooks, watching half an hour of a rugby match, and eating more herring. He even had a small glass of whiskey because he was feeling a little hung over now and wanted to take the edge off, as it were. But Prentice was nowhere to be seen.

At this point, Arthur decided to find what might serve as a temporary bedroom for that evening. He was now exhausted. But as he started up the stairs to look for a room, the phone rang. Arthur's first inclination was to ignore it. It wasn't his house, and maybe it was best to let the answering machine get it. But after thinking for another moment, he quickly descended the stairs and picked up the phone in the kitchen. As Arthur had suspected, it was Prentice, and, thankfully, he sounded much more sober. But what he said was somewhat alarming to Arthur. "If the police come by," Prentice said rapidly, "don't tell them what happened this afternoon."

"What happened this afternoon?" Arthur quickly said. "Nothing happened this afternoon."

"I know, I know. But I'm not supposed to be drinking. And I wasn't supposed to try to see my kids this evening. Being drunk will make it a million times worse. I know my ex-wife is going to report it, and the cops will be over there soon enough to check me out. I mean, it was perfectly obvious that I was drunk. But if you say we were together this evening and we didn't have any alcohol, what can they do? I'm going to a hotel for the night—just to make sure everything's out of my bloodstream. I'll see you tomorrow. But remember, you're my only alibi, so we didn't have a thing to drink. Not a drop. Got it?"

Arthur hesitated just an instant too long. "Do you understand?" Prentice yelled. "I need to know if you'll do this for me."

"Yes," Arthur said. "I understand." But as he said goodbye and then hung up the phone, he wondered what he had agreed to—if he had, in truth, agreed to anything—and Arthur concluded that he really did not know what he'd say if the police, in fact, came to St. Loup-en-Bois.

5

And the police did come by, although not until much later that night. It was two A.M. and Arthur was fast asleep when he heard the doorbell ring several times. Eventually, he got out of bed and went downstairs to see who it was. He could see the peculiar black French police hats through the windows, and that dapper uniform that (as Arthur remarked to himself) looked as though it were straight from some 1960s French detective movie.

Arthur walked quickly to the door, played with the rather confusing system of French locks, opened the door, then said, "*Allô?*" Actually, he also tried to say, "Can I be of any assistance to you?" but his French was so unclear that neither of the police officers had any response.

After a second, one said, "American? You speak French?"

Again, Arthur answered in what he imagined was French—a long sort of answer about his college years, and the youthful and romantic dreams of a young man. But again, the police were at a loss. They looked at him for another moment and said, "Monsieur Ross?"

"He's not here," Arthur said, again in his own kind of French. Then, because this too didn't register, he shortened the sentence and said, much louder, *"Pas ici. Pas ici."*

The police officers nodded and then walked right past Arthur into the foyer.

Arthur didn't exactly know what the custom for this type of thing was. Were the police really allowed to walk into your house uninvited? They looked around again, then one said (in English that Arthur couldn't imagine was better than his French), "Questions? Yes? Later. We find *traducteur*?"

"A translator," Arthur corrected him.

"Yes. Yes. Translator."

At that moment, one of the officers started walking up the stairs. As Arthur watched his ascent, the other took the opportunity to poke his head in the living room. "Drink?" he said, looking back over his shoulder. *"Boire?* Drink tonight?"

Arthur had not forgotten his instructions. He had, however, never lied to a police officer before. Nor had he lied to anyone of any authority, for that matter, and he couldn't quite adjust to this sudden and new moral problem. The officer stared at him some more, then said again, "Drink? *Avec* Monsieur Ross?"

Arthur paused again, but then, in a burst of loyal feelings for his old friend, finally said, "Absolutely not," thinking that good lies are delivered with enthusiasm and force.

The police officer stared at him for a moment, then said, *"Traducteur.* Translator. Yes." And then he turned and walked toward the kitchen, leaving Arthur alone again in the front hall.

And he was alone for longer than he expected. At first he thought the police would return immediately. But they didn't, and Arthur wasn't quite sure what was expected of him. Finally, just as Arthur decided to walk to the kitchen to offer his assistance, that particular officer came back to the foyer holding two empty wine bottles.

"Drink?" he said again.

"Me," Arthur said, now feeling like he must be blushing terribly and absolutely pegged as a liar. But he pressed on. "Me," he said again. "I drink. Alone. *Moi. Seul.*"

"Two *bouteille*?"

"I'm an American," Arthur said in English, although, realizing how stupid this sounded, added, "and I love to drink. We all do."

The officer looked at him carefully, then said, again, "Translator. Later." He then called up to the other officer, spewing long and impossibly difficult sentences which Arthur could not decipher at all. The other officer called back in similar fashion, and in the next minute was coming down the stairs. He was still talking, and Arthur now gathered that he was saying that he didn't see any sign of Prentice upstairs, although Arthur concluded this mostly because the officer was shrugging his shoulders and twisting his lips in a way that suggested that they might as well be off.

In any event, the two police officers were there for a total of about ten minutes, just long enough to show Arthur (and whoever may be in hiding) that they were in charge. Then they tipped their hats and left, taking the empty wine bottles with them.

"We call you," they said. "Later. In this week. Goodbye."

As Arthur shut the door behind them, he suddenly had the idea that an English-speaking officer would come eventually, and that he would have to continue with his lie, although he didn't know if it would be so easy in the presence of someone who could actually understand what he was saying. Still, he was too tired to think any more about the matter. He'd face these moral dilemmas the following morning, after he'd had a good night's sleep.

And Arthur did sleep quite well, although he woke up early, seven A.M., which he thought wasn't bad given the potential for jet lag. But Arthur had always been able to sleep reasonably well—even in the hardest times of the past few years—so waking up after sleeping nearly seven hours (minus the interaction with the French police), didn't actually surprise him too much.

Arthur had planned to make some coffee that morning, and to sit in the kitchen and read through his guidebooks as he waited for Prentice to return from his hotel. But when he arrived in the kitchen (in the same robe and slippers he used to travel through his own apartment in Manhattan) he found Delphine sitting at the kitchen table, dressed in a sequined evening gown, high heels, and smelling of liquor and a horrible perfume.

"Where is he, Prentice?" she said as Arthur appeared.

Arthur wasn't quite sure how to respond, and all he could come up with was, "Excuse me?"

"Where is Prentice?" she asked again.

Arthur paused for a moment. He didn't know if his instructions to deny everything to the police might apply to Delphine as well, and he thought he should just keep his mouth shut about the whole thing until Prentice returned, or called again with more detailed instructions. The drinking might not be a problem with Delphine, but the idea of Prentice tearing off in a wild rage to see his old family could cause some trouble. Finally Arthur said, "Oh, don't worry about Prentice. He's as good as they come. I'm sure he's somewhere safe." Only after he thought about these words for an instant did he realize how ridiculous he sounded.

Delphine looked like she thought the same. But she didn't say so. "Please, feel at home," she finally said. "Maybe you look for breakfast? Can I get you coffee?" Delphine laughed at this last question, apparently to make it crystal clear that this was not a serious offer. All the same, Arthur treated it as such.

"Oh, no. No," Arthur said. "I never drink coffee. Or not usually, really." Then, not sure what to do next, he sat down at the table, picked up an apple that sat atop a bowl of fruit, and took a large bite.

"This is delicious!" he said, after chewing for a moment.

Delphine glared at him. "You do not know where Prentice is?" she said again.

"I'm afraid not," Arthur replied. "I'm surprised he's not here right now."

Delphine groaned, then said a few phrases in French, which Arthur gathered were something about getting coffee for herself. This was confirmed when she stood up and poured herself a cup from an elegant and very European-looking insulated coffee decanter.

It struck Arthur that he didn't know what Delphine's arrangements were as far as the house went. In fact, he knew almost nothing at all about anything, as he was slowly discovering. But as Delphine sat back down at the kitchen table, the matter of where she lived, or what kind of rights she wielded at St. Loup, seemed to be the most pressing gap in his understanding. Arthur wondered if he was somehow impinging on something she wanted to be doing, although he couldn't imagine what. Nevertheless, who likes to have a strange man in a bathrobe sitting in your kitchen? Maybe she wanted to walk around naked—there was, after all, no telling what the habits of the French were, and this French woman in particular. At last, Arthur decided that he might as well ask. "Delphine," he said, still holding the apple. "I know so little about you. I was just wondering if you live here, if you're the lady of the house, so to speak."

"I live in Gap," she said, "and also here. I have apartment in Gap. But I share a bedroom here. And I have a small studio in a shed. Here."

"Well, your English is certainly excellent."

"My aunt is American. Prentice seduced me as she try to seduce him. You are positive you don't know where he is?"

Arthur paused. "I'm afraid not. But I'm sure he's got an excellent explanation. Again, he's as good as they come."

Delphine looked like she was on the verge of asking another question, or restating the one she had now asked twice, when Arthur abruptly stood up and said, "Well, I think I'll get dressed. I'm a bit embarrassed to be sitting here in my bathrobe." Arthur hesitated, and then determined that what he most wanted was a cup of coffee. "You know," he added, "perhaps I'll try to learn to like coffee now that I'm in France. Maybe I will take a cup."

Delphine hesitated, then stood up, pulled a coffee cup out of one of the cabinets, and put it on the counter, leaving Arthur to pour the coffee for himself. Arthur was now quite sure that he had been permanently linked to whatever problems Prentice was causing in Delphine's life, and that he was pegged as a new and inconvenient ally to her paramour. As Arthur poured his coffee, he thought he'd drink it black that morning. He didn't think he could manage to be around Delphine for the time it would take to add milk and sugar.

Arthur took only five minutes to get dressed, and another ten minutes to pack up his bag. He decided he'd try to find his way to the guest cottage and set up there as quickly as possible, although he didn't know exactly where the cottage was located. He was not anxious to talk to Delphine again, but he concluded that she might be pleased to let him install himself outside the main house so he wouldn't be around when her fight with Prentice began. Arthur recalled how much he hated it when Rebecca picked a fight with him in front of friends. It was a common sort of technique she employed to ensure that she would carry her point. Arthur never launched a full-scale defense to her complaints when others were around, but rather just nodded and apologized for whatever crime he was supposedly committing.

Delphine seemed to know something about this sort of strategy as well. "Don't you want to stay to watch the fight?" she said after Arthur asked for directions to the guesthouse.

Arthur laughed, trying to treat this comment as though it were some kind of pleasant joke. "I'd just like to move myself in, at the moment," he said. "Perhaps you can give me a report of it later?"

"You will get a report," Delphine replied. "But not from me."

Then Delphine looked at Arthur for a perplexing and awkward instant, and what Arthur saw in her was something a bit like regret, as though she weren't acting the way she normally liked to act. Delphine quickly looked away, opened a drawer beside the stove, and pulled out a pad of paper. She smiled weakly, grabbed a pen, and said, "It is near the road that you came in. It is another road. A few minutes with car." Then Delphine began to sketch out a map, still forcing a smile and, as far as Arthur could detect, at least making an effort to be more civil, and, perhaps surprisingly, Arthur found the whole thing just a bit touching.

"I really appreciate this," he said. "I'm so looking forward to my stay here."

Again, Delphine forced a smile. Still, it was real enough. Or it at least seemed to say that the next time they met, she might not be in such a foul mood. All Arthur could think was that he hoped this would be true.

6

But, after all, he had lied to her. Arthur could hardly blame Delphine for being angry with him. As he drove away from the main house and toward the little road that would take him to the guest cottage, he couldn't help but wonder what kind of trouble his duplicity would lead to. However, he was now most thinking about the various problems that might ensue from lying to the police, especially since they were going to return with a translator. Or so they said.

As Arthur approached the guest cottage, he remembered that only two days ago he had imagined this particular morning beginning with something like poached eggs and champagne in the company of Prentice and his charming lover, who would certainly be eager to make a good impression on Prentice's old boyhood friend. In fact, Arthur wondered if striking up his old friendship wasn't the main point of the whole trip—Arthur had been feeling so friendless of late—and he was beginning to feel a bit disappointed and lonely. But as Arthur brought his car to a halt along a low stone wall and finally saw the cottage where he'd be staying, he started to relax a bit. It was a very charming one-story stone building that sat beneath several large poplar trees.

The windowsills were newly painted, the front door had a basket with a fresh bouquet of flowers in it, and an old bicycle was parked out front which would be perfect for idyllic trips around the countryside. The bike even had a basket, in which (Arthur imagined) he would carry things like fresh eggs and loaves of bread. The scene was exactly what you'd find in an American novel about a recent divorcé building a new life in provincial France. This was more in line with what Arthur had hoped for, and as he got out of his car, he concluded that coming here was probably a very good decision after all.

The front door was open, and as he walked in he found an envelope on the front table with his name written on it. Inside the envelope he found a set of keys and a brief note from Prentice saying that he really didn't need to lock the door unless that was the sort of thing he preferred. It then said that he (Prentice) couldn't be more excited to have an old friend staying at St. Loup, and that he looked forward to many pleasant adventures.

As Arthur read the note, he wondered why Prentice had written it. Had he expected to get drunk, harass his kids, and then hide out in a hotel while Arthur was left on his own in the house of a stranger? Perhaps it was more that Prentice wanted to emphasize Arthur's independence—that he was a guest, but that he could come and go as he pleased—and so he might not even be there when Arthur let himself in.

Whatever the reason, Arthur soon dropped the matter and began to look around. The house before him wasn't quite as picturesque inside as it was out. It smelled a little of mold, although this didn't really bother Arthur, and it was not very light—the trees provided quite a bit of shade. But it had pleasingly wide-planked and crooked wooden floors, rows of bookshelves with out-of-print paperbacks from the 1950s and 1960s, a small fireplace, a long ragged couch, and a leather wingback chair where Arthur assumed he'd drink his cognac in the evenings—something like Somerset Maugham, in a state of gentlemanly inebriation as each day ended.

Arthur walked through the rest of the rooms. The kitchen was rather small and old, although Arthur quickly recognized the colors and spirit of the room from the hundreds of Upper East Side kitchens that had tried to duplicate it. There was a small eating room, which couldn't quite be called a dining room but was also not really part of the kitchen. There was a bathroom with a large cast-iron tub but no shower. Or, as Arthur soon discovered, it had a so-called French showerhead with a long hose attached to it. But there was nowhere high to position it, and there was no shower curtain, so Arthur concluded that he'd be cleaning himself while reclining for the next couple of months.

And there was a small bedroom in the back decorated with maps of various French martial campaigns. It had a large closet and a large dresser, and when Arthur saw all this, he decided that it was time to unpack. He put the house keys and the note on top of the dresser, and then headed back outside to collect his bags.

It was a fact that packing and unpacking were two of Arthur's greatest pleasures. It stemmed, he imagined, from a kind of boyhood desire to be entirely self-sufficient, or at least to be completely prepared for any kind of disaster. This was something of a psychological stretch. After all, he would hardly need so many pairs of socks in the event of a meteor strike or a nuclear catastrophe. All the same, the idea that he could fit all he needed into a couple of bags gave him a great deal of satisfaction.

As Arthur unstrapped the leather bindings of his suit bag, now on his new bed, he remembered a gift he got when he was eleven and had just joined an Upper East Side chapter of the Boy Scouts. The gift was a variety of jackknife that had a spoon and a fork that folded into the casing. It also had a crude can opener and a flathead screwdriver as well as the actual knife, which was sharp enough to whittle thin branches that Arthur collected from Central Park. But it was the spoon and the fork that he was most excited about because they gave him (like the act of packing a suitcase) a sense of total readiness, as though he could one day jump on a boxcar bound for New Mexico and always be perfectly prepared to eat dinner at any moment. The gift was from his father, although he seemed to regret giving it to Arthur almost from the moment Arthur opened it. He appeared to be bothered by Arthur's unnatural attachment to it, as though Arthur had completely misunderstood the jackknife's usefulness.

"It's functional," his father said. "There's no doubt about that. But trust me, a compass and a box of matches are going to get you farther in the wilderness than a foldable spoon."

Still, Arthur didn't care, and he began taking the knife with him wherever he went. He even took it to school, where such things were obviously forbidden, although he always kept it safely in his pocket. The thing that bothered Arthur's father the most, however, was that he began eating his meals with it, and this led, night after night for nearly two weeks, to a kind of difficult bickering between his parents. It was the kind of argument his parents often had. Not unlike the outrage over Arthur's distaste for salmon sandwiches and lobster Newberg, Arthur's father was often worried "for the boy's own good" about one thing or another that he felt made Arthur look absurd. His mother would reply that Arthur was young and that if he wanted to eat his soup with his jackknife, that was just fine. Arthur was never sure what was worse—his father's worries that he was behaving foolishly or his mother's defense that he was just a boy and therefore entitled to be as foolish as he pleased. But he loved eating with his jackknife and even paternal humiliation couldn't sway him.

As Arthur hung his suits in his closet, he wondered if what he really enjoyed was winning the argument. He wondered if he wasn't happy to hide behind his mother because this was the surest way to win out over what he regarded to be his father's attempts to improve him somehow. Still, the truth was that his father did have a point. As Arthur smoothed down the lapel of the tuxedo he had packed (for exactly the kind of unexpected event he enjoyed anticipating while packing), he remembered what did eventually cause him to lose his affection for the jackknife with its foldable fork and spoon. He had signed up for a three-day camping trip with two other scout troops in the city, ones from Carnegie Hill and Sutton Place. He placed the knife in his backpack with great enthusiasm and proudly brought it out that first evening in the Poconos when he was served a plate of grilled knockwurst that had been cooked over a large open fire. But despite the entirely obvious practicality of a device that contained a fork, and a knife, and a spoon all in one, it was not, in reality, that practical for eating a thing for which you had to use a fork and a knife at the same time. At home, if he absolutely had to, he could use a kitchen knife or fork in conjunction with the jackknife. But out here, he had decided to use only his jackknife in the spirit of self-sufficiency and self-reliance. This meant, however, that he had to fold in the knife and fork as he went, using them alternately and then closing them back in their case. That is, he pressed the knock-wurst down with his fingers, cut it, then folded the knife back in so he could use the fork.

He had eaten like this before, so he was experienced in this method. But for some reason, it now appeared to be much more clumsy than previous times. This was mostly, however, because of another and newer problem, which seemed far worse. Somehow, in the previous several months, with his own troop and with the boys from Carnegie Hill and Sutton Place, it had become fashionable to own a sheath knife—the nonfolding kind of hunting knife that comes in a leather sheath and which has no spoon or fork attached.

And, as was appropriate to their backgrounds, each of the boys' knives seemed more like family heirlooms than scouting equipment. Some had mother-of-pearl handles. Others were made of etched steel from top-notch metalworkers. But all of them had long blades that not only deftly handled knockwurst, but looked as though they could quickly gut a deer, or take care of some kind of wandering criminal they might meet while traveling through the forest.

As Arthur looked at their knives, and then looked at his own, his father's declaration that he looked ridiculous all at once rang true. It was almost as though he had brought along a stuffed animal or a doll on the trip, and Arthur became completely disgusted with himself. He fought this feeling. He told himself that there was no reason to be embarrassed. He was an individual, after all, and there was nothing wrong with being different. But this last-ditch effort to bolster his ego quickly fell apart when a member of the Sutton Place troop, Terrance Gibson, an older boy who was also several inches taller than anyone else, suddenly said, "Take a look at Arthur's spoon knife. What do you use that spoon for, Arthur? Shoveling shit?"

On the face of it, of course, the comment made no sense. It wasn't clever or funny. But it was the intention and the malice that counted, that was funny, that made everyone laugh, especially when it came from such a dominating member of the group. As everyone laughed and repeated Gibson's witty "shoveling shit" remark, and as the scoutmasters told everyone that cursing was not allowed, even in the wilderness, Arthur had the urge to throw the jackknife away as quickly as possible. He did not throw it away, however. He simply buried it in the bottom of his backpack that night, and didn't take it out again until he got home, using utensils brought by the scoutmaster for the rest of his meals. The boys teased him the next few nights. "Are you going to be shoveling any shit tonight, Arthur?" they said. But Arthur neither retaliated nor stuck to his guns. He simply ignored the taunts as much as possible, and even found himself thinking about what a funny guy Gibson was. When he returned home, he went so far as to wage a campaign to get a sheath knife of his own, telling his father and mother (repeatedly) that he was the only one on the trip not to have one. Finally, before the next monthly scout meeting, Arthur's sympathetic maternal grandfather bought him a knife, and, much to the annoyance of Arthur's father, Arthur began bringing it to every meal, eating with it as he had the jackknife. "My god, it's always something different with you," his father groaned the first night Arthur brought it to dinner.

"Leave him alone," his mother said. "His grandfather bought it for him. We should be happy he likes it so much."

As Arthur completed his unpacking that day in Gap, he wondered if there wasn't a profound lesson to be learned here, or at least some kind of valuable route into his hidden psychological tendencies. He closed his second suitcase, shoved it under his bed, and sat down to think about it all. But he was soon distracted by the problem of where his sheath knife was now, until he finally remembered it had been lost (or it had melted) in the fire at Maidenhead Grange, and Arthur suddenly felt that the knife now had double the power of humiliation. It occurred to Arthur, as it had many times, that he was most glad that his father was not alive to witness his disgrace with the Fly Casters, although he also imagined that his father would have forgiven him. He always forgave Arthur. That, Arthur thought, was one of the good things about his father. He could always overcome his annoyances and eventually learn to live with whatever was troubling him. All the same, tolerance and acceptance are not exactly the things that a son wants from his father. That is, acceptance is not the same as causing your father to feel actual pleasure. Arthur concluded that he had probably never brought his father much of that.

7

Five days passed before Arthur saw the police again. During this time he had established the locations of various essential places, like the gigantic wholesale-style supermarket at the edge of Gap's city limits, and the smaller bakeries, butchers, and grocers in the nearby village. He had even taken the bike out one morning to buy some bread and half a kilogram of air-dried beef, although the trip hadn't been quite as peaceful as Arthur expected. The ride to the village was mostly downhill, and this leg was magnificent, but the uphill ride home was entirely unbearable. Arthur walked the bike halfway, and the whole trip took him four and a half hours. The blisters on his feet burned all the way through the fourth hour of the journey (and through the third day of his stay at the cottage) and he was, in fact, soaking his feet in a large squared tin bucket filled with hot water when he heard a knock at the front door.

Arthur had been vaguely expecting Prentice. They had talked once in the past few days, when Prentice called the guest cottage from a new hotel, somewhere in the city of Annecy. Prentice explained to

Arthur that he had to get his "head on straight," but that he'd be back soon.

"Well, I'm fine here," Arthur said. "It would be great to see you, but we'll have plenty of time for that. It's always important to take time to reflect. Why do you think I'm in France?"

"Well, Arthur, I should probably tell you that I do think I have a small drinking problem. I mean, I don't think that should be held against me where the kids are concerned. But I think it's true and I need to figure out what to do about it. I've done programs before. But they never seem quite right for me. We live near Switzerland, though. That's a good thing. If there's one thing the Swiss are good at, it's running rehab centers. It's like the Minnesota of Europe."

Prentice then asked Arthur about the police, and if they had been by.

"They have," Arthur replied. "They came that first night."

"What did you tell them?" Prentice said.

"I told them that I had gotten drunk alone while you were somewhere I didn't know about."

"Great. That's great, Arthur. Thanks a lot. I know that was probably hard on you, seeing how you've always been so aboveboard."

"It wasn't that hard. I can't say I'm that afraid of French police." This, of course, was not entirely true.

They talked for a little while after this, and Prentice assured Arthur that he'd be back when he could think more clearly, when he didn't have Delphine breathing down his neck, and when the police went away. So when Arthur heard the knocking at the door (again, while he was soaking his feet), he assumed that Prentice had returned and popped down to say he was back.

"I'm coming," Arthur called out, placing his wet feet on a towel he had spread out on the floor. He dried his feet off as best he could, and then stood up and walked quickly to the door, opening it just as he heard knocking again.

It was not, however, Prentice. Rather, it was the police again. Two of them once more, although Arthur didn't recognize the second one. He was a tall, distinguished-looking, gray-haired man in street clothes, but appeared to be the one in charge. This impression was borne out when he stepped forward and said, "Hello, I am Inspector Laurent. You are Arthur Camden?"

Arthur hesitated, but then realized that denying this would certainly lead to trouble. "Yes," he said. "I am."

"I am very pleased to meet you," Inspector Laurent said with enthusiasm. "I love Americans, and, above all, Americans coming to Gap. We are just at main house and look for Mr. Ross, and now we decide to come to say hello to you."

The inspector's accent was extremely puzzling. It had a thick Frenchness to it, but the English side of the sound was as though he were trying to mimic some sort of upper-class character actor in a BBC miniseries.

"Well, I'm glad you decided to pop in," Arthur finally said. He then added, "Where did you learn to speak English so well?"

"I spend two summers in Kent when I was young," Inspector Laurent replied, smiling and putting his right hand against his chest. "Also, I study criminology at University of Nottingham for one year. I am not translator by profession, but, sadly, Mr. Ross has given us trouble in the past. And the father of his ex-wife is my friend, and he ask me to examine this recent problem. Personally."

"Yes," Arthur said, not really wanting to acknowledge anything at this point.

"And now I have just a question. My colleagues say to me that they ask if you and Mr. Ross drink together six nights ago," the inspector continued. "Is this true?"

"Yes," Arthur said.

"And you say Mr. Ross did not drink?"

Arthur paused. And the pause lasted for just a bit longer than it probably should have. Arthur unexpectedly had the feeling of very much wanting to tell this man the truth. For a police officer, he seemed like a very friendly man. But before he could add anything, Inspector Laurent interrupted Arthur's train of thought and said, "Would you like to tell me something?"

"What?"

"Would you like to tell me something?"

"Well, no, not really," Arthur said after a moment.

"But how did you make your answer?"

"Answer?" Arthur replied.

"The question. About you and Mr. Ross drinking."

"I said yes," Arthur replied. "Or, I said yes that I had been drinking," he continued. "But I also said that Mr. Ross had not. He had not been drinking."

"And did you say you drink two bottles?" the inspector continued. "Yourself alone?"

"Yes, yes I did say that. I had two bottles. I guess I got a little carried away since it was my first night on what I hope will turn out to be a wonderful stay in your part of France."

"I hope so too. But two bottles. A lot of wine for drinking alone, and I say that as Frenchman."

"Well, I drank them over a long period of time. Over an afternoon and evening."

At that the inspector took a deep breath and nodded. He looked down at his feet as though he was thinking it all over, and then finally put out his hand. "Well, that is all for now," he said. "I just want to come by to hear for myself."

Arthur shook the inspector's hand, now greatly relieved that this was coming to an end. It hadn't been that hard, after all. Arthur even felt like something of a rebel. "I can only tell you what I know to be true," Arthur added with a sudden poetic flourish.

"Well, of course, I believe exactly what you say," the inspector replied with sincerity. But then he took things in a new direction that Arthur found quite alarming: "But this is serious. I'm talking about Mr. Ross. His anger. His drinking. There are children. The office of Gap police will need to ask you these questions again in formal setting."

Arthur wasn't quite sure what this meant, but he could feel the blood draining out of his face.

"At the police headquarters," the inspector continued. "With our prosecutor. In about ten days. Also we will place you under oath. It is formality. It assures us that you are not perjuring yourself. Me, I know you are not. Really. I believe you entirely. But family law in France is strict. Especially in this case. Violent behavior. Children. Safety. Someone could be hurt. It is very dangerous. A perjury conviction is very grave in France, so we ask all witnesses speak under oath in important cases like this. But again, it is just formality. Me, I believe you. One hundred percent."

"Thank you. I understand completely," Arthur said, now desperately trying not to look worried. He then added, "I myself am a great believer in the rule of law."

"Americans usually are," the inspector replied. "And this is why I'm such a great admirer of your people."

"Thank you," Arthur said, nodding solemnly.

They all stood there now for just one more second—the inspector, Arthur, and the silent accompanying officer—but finally they said goodbye, and the inspector and the officer turned and walked toward the driveway. Arthur watched for only a second and then quickly shut the door. He suddenly had a terrible image of being locked up in a French prison, and Rebecca and her new fiancé and numerous other people he knew in New York all discussing Arthur's fall from grace and his involvement in a scandalous French domestic abuse case. He would have to talk to Prentice to sort this out. Who knew what sorts of penalties he'd pay in France for perjury, especially since this Inspector Laurent was now personally involved? The situation was almost too much for Arthur to think about.

8

For the next week, Arthur did his best to keep his mind off his impending legal dilemma by occupying himself with small distracting projects and outings in the area. He began by visiting a series of public parks in Gap, all of which he found to be very impressive. They were perfectly maintained, lushly appointed with various plants and shrubs that he was sure he had never seen before, and they each had immaculate public restrooms—a thing that New York City inexcusably lacked.

He also visited various museums in the area, including a toy museum, a museum of Savoyard military history, and the very imposing and austere Museum of French Protestantism. In addition, Arthur visited a large slate quarry just outside of Gap, which he heard gave tours. He rode up a small funicular to a low indentation in the foothills overlooking Gap and followed an ancient bald man around the grounds, listening to French that he couldn't understand at all. The sun was strong that day, and the sky a deep blue, and as Arthur stood listening to the old man talk about god knows what, he surveyed the city below, and the high peaks in the distance, and decided that he very much liked this area, and he was glad he was there to explore it.

In this spirit, Arthur went to a bookstore in Gap the next day and bought field guides to the flora and fauna in the area, with the intent of keeping a kind of catalog of the various living things around the grounds of St. Loup. Additionally, in a continuing celebration of French regionalism, he visited a liquor store and bought a dozen bottles of local wine, all recommended by the friendly and nearly toothless proprietor, who spoke slowly, tolerated Arthur's halting French, and resorted to English as Arthur made his choices by whispering, "This is a masterpiece!" Arthur also bought several local liqueurs from the man. He purchased a liqueur flavored with pine needles, a liqueur flavored with assorted wildflowers, and a honey-flavored liqueur made by the wife of a very good friend of the shopkeeper.

But, of course, finding amusements was only part of what was on Arthur's mind. His activities and distractions only moderately masked what was slowly becoming a more intense fear regarding the French police. Part of him was able to dismiss the threat. What were French police to him? What real power did they have? At the very worst, if he did get into trouble, it would be a minor inconvenience for some low-level American embassy worker to sort out. It could hardly be in France's interest to prosecute friendly American retirees. Anyway, it would all make for a good story. As Arthur sipped his third large glass of the wildflower liqueur one night, he found himself reversing his earlier fears and actually fantasizing about news of his problems with the French police finding its way to New York. With the right shading, he might come off as a sort of Henry Miller, drinking all night, lying to the police, and finding himself in jail for bamboozling French officials. Of course, the nature of these fantasies took him far away from reality. As he reached the bottom of his glass, he imagined himself being arrested in a brothel, punching a French policeman in the nose, and associating with bona fide European criminals.

But the fact of the matter was that he had to make a decision. About a week after the police stopped by, he got a call from Inspector Laurent to arrange a day (at Arthur's convenience) when he could come in to produce an affidavit. They settled on a day five days from the date of that phone call, leaving Arthur yet again with a very real problem to work through.

"All you have to do is tell me exactly what you say when we met," Inspector Laurent said several times. "It is nothing to worry about. You will be under oath, and I must say to you that perjury in this country is punishable by jail. But me, I know that is not a problem with you."

"Of course not," Arthur said, but he was naturally thinking something very different from this. It obviously was a real problem with him. What Arthur most wanted was to talk all this over with Prentice. Maybe they could work out some kind of compromise. They could agree on a half-truth: Arthur thought the wine had been non-alcoholic; or Arthur wasn't actually sure if Prentice was drinking or not, and wanted to confirm it with the now-absent Prentice before he said anything. At the very least, Arthur wanted to get their stories in sync before his lying continued. The insignificant details and the minor odds and ends were where police always caught a man lying. Or this at least was what Arthur gathered from the police and courtroom dramas he had seen on television.

But, of course, all these discussions were impossible so long as Prentice was off getting his "head on straight." It occurred to Arthur, however, that perhaps he had left word with Delphine about where he was and when he was returning, and so, about half an hour after hanging up with the inspector, Arthur decided to go up to St. Loup to see if she was around.

At first Arthur thought he would drive, but when he stepped outside and realized what a beautiful day it was, he decided to walk. It would take about fifteen minutes, but Arthur thought it might help him think. And it did, to a certain extent. Or it calmed him down, at least, and by the time Arthur began feeling some bit of mental relief, he arrived at St. Loup and saw that Delphine's car was in the large stone driveway. Arthur rang the doorbell and then waited for several moments. Then he rang the doorbell once more, but again there was no response. Arthur wondered if he could just go inside and call out to Delphine. He was a guest, after all. Maybe he didn't even need to ring the doorbell. But then Arthur recalled that she had a small art studio out back in one of the old outbuildings, and so he walked around the house and headed to a small renovated shed that had a trail of smoke coming out of a center chimney—a kiln chimney, it seemed to Arthur. In another second, Arthur knocked on the door, and then entered without waiting for a reply. Delphine was in there, and appeared to be in a deep discussion with a very strong man with ash and soot stains all over his arms and neck. Arthur smiled, trying to look friendly. Then he quickly said, "Hello, Delphine. Good to see you."

Delphine didn't look pleased that Arthur was there. But she seemed to be an acerbic woman in general, so Arthur could hardly take her bitterness personally. "Hello, Arthur," she finally said. "Is it something I can find for you?"

"No, no," Arthur said. "I'm fine. I was just wondering if you've heard from Prentice."

"No," she said. "Not in past several days."

At this point, Delphine turned to the man she was talking to and said, "This is Nicolas. He take care of the gardens."

Arthur nodded and smiled, and Nicolas did the same in return.

"So, no sense when he'll be back?"

"No, none at all," she said. "Can I help with something?"

"No. No. Just something I wanted to discuss with Prentice. But it can wait. But can you tell him to either call me or come down to the cottage as soon as he gets home?"

Delphine nodded, then said, "I gave your telephone to a police officer. I hope it is all right?"

"Of course. Just fine. A bit of a snafu going on. But nothing serious." Then, because Arthur felt as though he wasn't wanted, he said, "Well, I'll leave you now. Good luck with the pots. And with the gardening, Nicolas."

Nicolas smiled again and nodded, although Arthur was sure he had no idea what he had said.

As Arthur walked back to the cottage, he wondered why he felt so awkward around Delphine. She wasn't particularly nice to him. That was a good reason. But Arthur couldn't help but wonder if he wasn't missing the boat on this trip somewhat. After all, he really was trying to turn things around for himself, and this was hardly going to happen if he continued to be so shy and deferential.

After thinking this over for nearly ten minutes of his return walk, Arthur came to an abrupt halt and turned around, resolving that he'd invite Delphine down to his cottage for dinner that night, because he was all alone, and because she was so close to Prentice, and because perhaps he needed to start making a little more effort with all this. Hiding out wasn't what he came to France to do. Relaxing, getting his "head on straight," maybe, but why should that happen in solitude? Arthur had always liked the company of others, even when he couldn't always navigate the social worlds he was part of, and there was absolutely no reason why Arthur couldn't have a perfectly pleasant evening with Delphine. Maybe she'd even let him practice his French with her.

It took another ten minutes to walk back up the hill to Delphine's studio, and by the time Arthur arrived, he had managed to buoy up his enthusiasm and decided he wouldn't take no for an answer. He'd absolutely insist, telling Delphine that he was an excellent cook and that he was longing to hear more about her life in France.

And with all these firm conclusions, Arthur softly knocked on the studio's door and entered. The knocking was really little more than formality, of course. It was an art studio, a potting studio, and why would anyone need to knock in the first place? But when Arthur opened the door, and even got through the words, "You know, Delphine," he decided he had made a terrible, terrible mistake. Delphine was entirely naked, as was Nicolas, and they were in a sort of knot of sexual frenzy that Arthur found extremely shocking. What struck Arthur the most, though, at that exact moment, was the scene's total lack of ambiguity, its overwhelming bluntness. This was not a suspicious stroke of someone's shoulder or a suggestive squeeze of a forearm. This was, in fact, the least ambiguous example of human interaction that Arthur had ever seen.

"I'm so, so sorry," Arthur quickly blurted out, which was a mistake because neither Delphine nor Nicolas had seen or heard him, so absorbed were they in their carnal activities. When he apologized, however, they quickly jerked around, and before Arthur could even step back out the door, Delphine was on her feet and charging him. Quite wisely, Arthur stepped back, pulling the door shut behind him, and was bounding backward by the time Delphine threw open the door again.

"You stupid prick-sucker," Delphine yelled, obviously employing an English insult she imagined she had once heard, and then the French came, which, thankfully, Arthur could not understand. At this point, Arthur was now also running, and he had shoes on, so Delphine quickly gave up. He looked back several times. Delphine stood back at the door, naked, still screaming unintelligible French insults. But soon Arthur was down the driveway and behind a row of hawthorn bushes, and far away from that very surprising scene.

Halfway back to the cottage, Arthur slowed to a walk. He was very out of breath and, needless to say, very confused. He wondered what he should tell Prentice, if, indeed, he told him anything at all. On the one hand, it was none of his business. On the other, Prentice was an old friend and Arthur couldn't stand by while he was betrayed. Of course, there was also the possibility that Prentice and Delphine had a type of open relationship, and maybe sleeping with the gardener was well within the rules of their normal interaction. Who knew how relationships in France were bound together? Certainly not Arthur, who was feeling, yet again, that he was missing some crucial bit of knowledge that absolutely everyone else seemed to possess.

As Arthur finally arrived at his cottage and opened the door, he decided that he'd have to lay low for a while, and certainly couldn't risk another uninvited trip to the main house. All he could hope for was that Prentice would return soon, or call to give him some idea of his plans.

9

But Prentice didn't call. Nor did he appear at Arthur's door. Nor did Delphine come by to let him know that Prentice was on his way, although this was obviously a relief to Arthur. So Arthur simply minded his own business, staying far away from the main house at St. Loup and descending into an even more introverted life. He went on long walks, read detective novels that stood on the book shelves to the left and right of the fireplace, and filled the pages of his so-called naturalist's catalog with pressed flowers and dried leaves, each with its Latin name written underneath. The catalog took up quite a bit of time, which Arthur was happy about, although it was also extremely depressing. The fact was that Arthur had really never had the patience for this kind of thing, and after a while he finally concluded that he didn't really care all that much what was growing around him—or he didn't care enough to collect samples of everything. He also had terrible penmanship and, because he had decided he ought to do all his writing with a fountain pen (in keeping with his romantic notions of the gentleman naturalist), many of the words were badly smudged. It was simply not a very appealing record of his increasingly odd visit to France.

One of the activities that Arthur did enjoy, however, and was very proficient at, was sampling the alcohol he bought. His favorite (by far) was the pine-needle liqueur. He decided that he'd bring a few bottles back with him, and even wished that he had known about it when he was running his business. He concluded that he could have made a killing selling it in the States. But just as quickly he decided that it was exactly this sort of decision—how to introduce America to some sort of foreign oddity—that had brought an end to his company. The truth of the matter was that Arthur never knew what would sell and what wouldn't. The only thing Arthur knew for sure was that his tastes were always at odds not only with Americans in general, but with the highbrow New Yorkers who supposedly had made up a big part of his market. Arthur even began to wonder if the pine-needle liqueur was really as good as he thought it was. Maybe the toothless man at the liquor store was pulling a fast one on the gullible American. It was just so delicious that it was very hard for Arthur to tell whether or not he was actually supposed to like it.

Finally the day came when Arthur had to appear at the police station to retell his story. Arthur drove to the Gap central police headquarters and presented himself at the front desk, intending to continue on with the charade, sticking to the plan that Prentice had presented to him on the telephone on that peculiar night when he had first arrived.

"Inspector Laurent, *s'il vous plait*," Arthur said, trying to keep things simple. However, he didn't understand anything the police officer said in response. He was just beginning to formulate a reply— something along the lines of, *You'll have to forgive me because I was just a young man when I learned your beautiful language*, when, from across a sort of plastic and fabric barrier, Arthur saw Inspector Laurent's head and heard him say, "Mr. Camden. You are on time. So unlike a Frenchman."

"Hello," Arthur said. He actually felt good for a moment. Inspector Laurent seemed so friendly that Arthur experienced some relief. But just as quickly, the goodwill started to sting. He was now preparing to lie yet again to this man—a man that Arthur actually felt he liked quite a bit.

Inspector Laurent quickly walked around the barrier, extended his hand, and smiled broadly. "I hope you have many good things to eat since I have seen you. Gap is not known for food, but it is as good as anywhere in France. I promise this. That includes Paris."

"Oh, yes," Arthur said. "I've discovered a pine-needle liqueur that I'm really very impressed with."

"It's a specialty, but sadly you find it is specialty of every mountain region in Europe. I like it too. Not quite champagne. But I like it."

As Inspector Laurent came to the end of this endorsement, he became silent and simply stared at Arthur. Arthur wasn't sure if he was supposed to pick up the conversation at this point, especially because the inspector seemed to be looking him over more than anything else. He felt as if he had just returned from college and his father was sizing him up, looking to see if he'd grown or filled out any. Finally, Arthur decided to once again affirm his affections for this pine-needle liqueur when Inspector Laurent said, "Well, I am sorry we make you do this. Once more, I trust you completely. But it is French law. And it is important case. And so we must start."

The questioning happened in a small windowless room that had several audio and video recording devices mounted on the walls. A lawyer was present ("a deputy prosecutor") as well as a low-level officer who seemed to be in charge of turning things on and off. He was also probably there as a precaution against the more violent and unpredictable suspects, although Arthur was sure that no one expected any sort of sudden physical outburst from him. It was true, though, that Arthur was feeling extremely nervous, and couldn't quite predict how all this would play out. And as the officer turned on the video recorder, and Inspector Laurent smiled and told Arthur to relax, Arthur wondered yet again if he shouldn't tell the truth. But at this point it seemed to be a rather different proposition. After all, if he had wanted to make a clean breast of things and get himself out of trouble, the best opportunities had surely passed. It would have been one thing if he had taken Inspector Laurent aside when he arrived and said that because of friendship and loyalty he had lied and that he was now not prepared to perjure himself before the French justice system. But here, in this setting, Arthur felt that any such confession would be extremely difficult and extremely humiliating, in large part because it would all be on video. Arthur had a terrible image of Prentice at a custody hearing watching footage of Arthur tearfully telling the French authorities how his friend had asked him to lie and that Prentice was completely drunk when he left that night. On top of that, it was not impossible that he had already committed a crime by lying to the police, and a recorded retraction would be pretty conclusive evidence, if it was, in fact, a crime to lie to the French police while not under oath.

The truth was, however, that despite these flights of imagination, Arthur had made up his mind. He was going to continue with the lie. He couldn't help but think that he somehow owed it to Prentice. He still had a feeling that he had lost track of who Prentice was—he could not remember such rash outbursts and unpredictable behavior in his teenage friend—but Arthur felt bonds of loyalty with so few people at this point in his life, and he really felt that a primal kinship was driving him forward at this point.

But as he steeled himself to carry on, now seated in a very uncomfortable metal chair, he realized that his heart was thumping forcefully, and that he had broken a sweat. He wondered for a moment if they'd strap him up to a lie detector, although this seemed unlikely. This was more a deposition than an interrogation, and it wasn't him that was accused of a crime. Still, Arthur was convinced that even the most poorly trained police officers could tell he was lying at this point, given the sweat and what he believed must be visible effects of his heart rate. But he carried on. He nodded and said, "Yes," when he was read the oath, and then, over and over, he simply repeated that as far as he knew Prentice had not been drinking during the night in question.

"Not even a glass?" Inspector Laurent asked.

"He said he didn't drink anymore," Arthur replied.

"Do you know where he is now?"

"I'm afraid I have no idea. It's upsetting to me as well."

"Did you suspect him of drinking that night? While you were not watching?"

"He seemed perfectly sober to me."

"Do you often drink two bottles of wine, all alone?"

"That was my first day in France. I started drinking early. I got carried away." All at once, Arthur felt a very uncomfortable moistness across his chest, and several drops of sweat actually slid across his forehead and down the end of his nose.

"You are discomfortable?" the deputy prosecutor now interjected with a heavy accent. "Tell us the truth. You protect your friend? If you lie, you go to prison. I make sure. Women and children."

"I'm just not used to this sort of thing," Arthur quickly replied. "I can't say I feel very comfortable at all. But it's just the surroundings."

"Of course," Inspector Laurent said quickly, flashing something of an angry look at the deputy. "Do not feel afraid. We just have a few more questions."

Inspector Laurent repeated the basic questions one more time to make sure that all of Arthur's answers were clear, and then he stood up, smiled, and told the junior officer to turn everything off.

As Arthur stood up, he felt sure that he would soon be hand-cuffed and led off to jail. He thought of the French's notorious belief in occult things like handwriting analysis and imagined some sort of quasi-psychologist describing perspiration patterns and unusual eye motions that always show up when a person is lying. He was now so nervous that he wondered if he'd even be able to walk out the door. But he managed well enough, and after saying goodbye to the now-stone-faced deputy prosecutor and the diligent junior offi-cer, he started looking forward to a large glass of the pine-needle liqueur. Inspector Laurent, on the other hand, seemed very relaxed, as though everything had gone as planned and that this had been just another routine deposition of a thoroughly honest gentleman. In fact, as they walked together toward the front door of the police station, he put his hand on Arthur's shoulder and (quite astonish-ingly) said, "You know, I hope this is not wrong. I think I am not supposed to do this. But I will do it anyway. I wonder if I invite you to dinner if you come. My wife is excellent cook. She speaks some English. But I never have the chance to practice my own, especially with an American. Gap is not popular place for tourists. And when we do have them, they are mostly British. Me, I love Americans and I would love to have you for dinner."

Arthur, who was now feeling somewhat cold because of his wet shirt and damp hair, simply smiled and said with a bit of relief, "That would be wonderful. I'm actually feeling a bit lonely at the moment."

"How about next Wednesday? A week from today."

"Next Wednesday sounds perfect." Arthur did notice a small quiver in his voice as he said "perfect." But the truth of the mat-ter was that this invitation did relax him some. Or it relaxed him until he got to his car and started his journey home, at which point Arthur began to revert to his paranoia and anxiety. What if they found out he had lied? Inspector Laurent might be his friend, but the deputy prosecutor didn't seem to like him very much. He had mentioned prison, after all. Arthur wondered just how long a prison term for perjury was in France, and what French jails were like. He imagined wasting away in an overdesigned Le Corbusier prison cell and thought for a moment that he'd almost rather suffer a kind of decaying Portuguese prison than endure the spic-and-span order of French institutional life. Mostly, Arthur began to picture Inspector Laurent as he slowly figured out that Arthur had lied, and the kind of gross disappointment he would most likely feel. Here they were quite unexpectedly becoming friends—exactly what he wanted out of his summer in Gap—and Arthur had let him down in a very egregious way.

About this time in Arthur's thought process, just after he turned into the entrance of St. Loup, he spotted Delphine. She was walking along the road with a basket that seemed to be filled with wildflowers. Arthur's first inclination was to step on the gas and accelerate past her as quickly as possible. But then he thought that this chance encounter might actually be a good way to normalize their relations. He could roll down the window, offer a friendly hello, and as she said the same, they could both ease into some type of compact to pretend as though nothing had happened the other day, as though she hadn't been caught naked with that robust and highly masculine gardener. However, as Arthur rolled down his window and smiled as broadly as he could, Delphine turned, gave him an icy glare, and said, "Fuck you, you prick-sucker. You prick-sucker."

Arthur slowed for a moment to let what she had said sink in. "Prick-sucker" was such a mysterious turn of phrase. Then, in the next instant, as it was clear that Delphine would enter into no sort of compact, Arthur resorted to his first plan, and stepped on the accelerator and sped past her, unable to think of anything else to say. Once again, Arthur was finding his only solace in the promise of a glass of pine-needle liqueur, and he could hardly wait to get back to his cottage.

10

But perhaps the worst was behind him. He had given his statement, and there wasn't too much more the police could do, so long as his story held up (and there was no reason it shouldn't). Furthermore, although Delphine clearly hated him, it was she who would be on the defensive, given what Arthur now knew about her. They'd never be friends, of course, but Arthur could live with that so long as they mostly stayed apart and behaved with restraint around Prentice, if he ever returned. And as Arthur poured himself his second glass of liqueur that night—now the honey-flavored kind—he took out his guidebooks with a bit of relief and began to look for places he might take overnight and weekend trips to.

That night and the next day, Arthur distracted himself from his worries about potential French legal problems by laying out a fairly elaborate agenda of the things that he'd like to do in the coming weeks. He found several castles that he'd like to visit, built by various colorful dukes and august princes from the region. He figured out how to get to Turin and where to stay, and he thought he might even tour more of northwestern Italy if he could chart an interesting trip. He also investigated trips to various caves and mountains and lakes in the area that his guidebooks recommended. Finally, by Friday evening, he was going through the pleasing ritual of laying out what he might need on his first overnight trip—a visit to the medieval fortress city of la Roche St. Foron—thinking again about just how much he liked to pack. This ritual was interrupted, however, because it was that evening, that Friday following Arthur's deposition on Wednesday, that Prentice finally returned. He showed up at Arthur's cottage at about six o'clock without calling, and Arthur was extremely surprised to see him when he opened his front door.

"You've resurfaced!" Arthur said, smiling.

"I've resurfaced, yes," Prentice replied, nodding and then stepping into the house. "Sorry about leaving you like that," he continued, "but I figured you'd have everything you need." Prentice looked around for a moment, and Arthur followed his gaze. There were a few books opened on the coffee table, and an empty wineglass sat next to them. But other than that, the house looked exactly as it had when Arthur first arrived.

"I love this little place," Prentice finally said.

"It's been very comfortable," Arthur replied.

Prentice walked past him. "I'm glad, Arthur," he said, walking to the large couch beside the fireplace and taking a seat. "I've really felt like a terrible host. But there's plenty for a stranger to do around here. On his own, that is."

Arthur smiled and agreed that this was true. "Even little trips to the grocery store have been interesting enough to keep me going," he said. "And I'm keeping a sort of journal of all the wildlife and plant life I've spotted."

"Good, good," Prentice said, still looking around the room. He suddenly looked distracted, and as Arthur took a seat across from him, he glanced up and said, with something of a look of sorrow,

"Arthur, look. I have something difficult to bring up, and I'm not sure it can wait. I actually got in this morning, and when I talked to Delphine she told me something that I found to be just a little upsetting."

Arthur didn't know quite how to react to this, although he did decide that a look of confusion was the best response at this point. He didn't want to let on more than he had to. Still, he was not at all prepared for what Prentice said next.

Prentice paused, ran his hand across his face, opened his mouth, hesitated once again, and then said, "Delphine said you made a pass at her. She said that you came upstairs in my house and made a pass at her. Is this true?"

Arthur was so shocked at hearing this that the best he could say was, "What? She said what?"

"She said you made a pass at her," Prentice replied. Strangely, he looked more perplexed than angry. And just after Arthur said, "I assure you that nothing could be further from the truth," Prentice said, "Well, I can't say that it sounded much like you. But she's pretty adamant that you did it. I asked if she could be mistaken, if maybe she misinterpreted something. But she said you tried to kiss her and told her that I'd never find out. She said you said you wanted to, quote, 'Fuck her silly.' "

Arthur was startled at this last claim. But in that same instant he now understood that this was all a preemptive strike to prevent him from telling Prentice about the groundskeeper—or to undermine his plausibility if he did tell him. All the same, he wasn't sure what to do. He had already resolved not to tell Prentice about Delphine's affair, mostly because Prentice seemed to have so much to worry about already. This still seemed true, but the more important matter at this point was that even if Arthur did tell Prentice what he saw, would he be believed? It would certainly look like he was the one making up things to get out of a bad situation. Arthur could only stammer once more that the story was entirely ridiculous. "It's completely ridiculous," he said.

"Why would she make it up?" Prentice asked.

Arthur paused. "I don't know. I don't know," he said. Again, it flashed through Arthur's mind to tell Prentice what he had seen in Delphine's art studio. But just as he was again rehearsing the argument against this (and rapidly changing his mind), Prentice finally said, "Well, my opinion is that I think she must be mistaken. I mean, that's how I'm going to look at it." He laughed a little, and then said, "I just can't imagine you doing it. Or saying anything like that. You of all people. Fuck her silly. Delphine can be a bit flighty. I guess I'm not going to believe it."

Prentice looked up at Arthur with a strange kind of sincerity, like he wanted to say something that he really needed Arthur to understand. "But I'm in love with her, Arthur," he said at last, "and I've got to try harder to make it work. That's something I realized while I was away. I'm not always such a devoted boyfriend, and, frankly, and I hate to say this, for some reason she's got it in for you, Arthur. She wants you to leave, and I'm afraid that I have to go along with what she wants, even though I'm a little mystified by this story she's telling me, and I hate to have to ask a guest to leave, especially an old friend, and one I invited to stay as long as he liked."

Arthur was stunned. "You want me to leave?" he said, in a pitch that sounded much more wounded than he would have liked.

"I'm sorry, Arthur. But it's not as if you're destitute. You're in a great part of the world, and there's some great hotels you can stay at. You could even rent a chalet. Maybe in a place like Chamonix. It's not like you're some kind of pensioner that I'm putting out on the street. You have an apartment on the Upper East Side, for Christ's sake. You don't need this cottage."

Arthur didn't respond. He could not get his mind around the idea that he was being asked to leave, and for hitting on Delphine, of all things. In his wildest dreams he would never be able to hit on someone like Delphine, and now he was having to put up with this kind of accusation, and from Prentice, no less. Arthur felt very deeply hurt and very much betrayed. He thought about how much sleep he had lost over lying to the French police, and how he had perjured himself for the sake of this friend who was now kicking him out because his tramp of a girlfriend made up a lie about him. In fact, the matter about what to say next was settled. He would definitely tell Prentice about what he had seen happening between Delphine and the gardener. Still, he wasn't quite sure how to actually go about this. It would be fairly shocking information, after all, and probably very painful for Prentice to hear. But at last (still determined, though, to tell on Delphine eventually) Arthur merely said, "I really never did anything like what Delphine is saying about me. It's not at all how things really are."

Prentice looked at Arthur, then looked over at the fireplace. "Well, I'm sure that's true, Arthur," he said. "I am. I just need to get everything in my life straight. I spent a week at a small treatment facility in Lausanne, and I'm going to go back. For at least a month. I do have a drinking problem, and I need to deal with it. I don't need to manage it. I need to deal with it, to overcome it, and a lot of that means putting my life in order. When it slips out of order is when I get into problems, and in this instance, that means putting Delphine first. It also means being honest with myself. And with everyone else. It means telling the truth." Prentice paused, then looked up at Arthur. "You know what I did this afternoon?" he said at last.

Arthur stared blankly at Prentice. Did he really have to listen to some sort of testimonial at this point? What he had to do was tell Prentice about Delphine and the gardener. As soon as possible.

"I finally replied to all those messages the police have been leaving on my answering machine," Prentice said. "I drove home. I listened to all the messages again, and then I drove right to the police station, turned myself in, and then told them exactly what really happened. I told them everything. I told them I had been drunk when I went to see my kids. I told them that things got out of hand, that I yelled and screamed at my ex-wife, and that it was the alcohol that made me do it. I said I couldn't be more sorry and that I'd accept any punishment the judge felt was warranted. And I told them I was getting help for my drinking. That's the way you've got to do these things. Come clean. Tell the truth. Accept what's coming to you. I guess I knew that. But it's one of the things the doctors in Lausanne kept telling me."

Needless to say, Arthur was shocked. The insult of Delphine falsely accusing him of social crimes was now quickly receding as Arthur again considered the lies he had told the police.

"You didn't tell them I was with you when you got drunk, though," Arthur finally said.

"Well, that's what happened," Prentice replied. "I told you, I've got to be more straightforward. Duplicity is probably why I lost my family in the first place. Duplicity and drinking."

Arthur abruptly stood up and started making a mental tally of where his things were in the cottage and how quickly he could get them into his suitcases. "I need to leave," Arthur said.

"Yes," Prentice said thoughtfully.

"No, I need to leave now. I went to the police department and told them all sorts of lies. Under oath. To a prosecutor. I said I was with you and that you had nothing to drink. They said they'd send me to jail if I was lying. It's just a matter of time before they come to get me."

As Arthur got to the end of this statement, Prentice burst into laughter. "Arthur. This is the French police we're talking about. They don't care about this. Or they care about me, not you. Trust me. They're all at home watching soccer and not thinking twice about what you told them."

Arthur stared at Prentice. Or he stared at the vacant space to the left of Prentice's head. It appeared that Arthur was thinking the matter over. But he wasn't really thinking about anything. He was only trying to ease out of the panic he was now feeling. The experience was purely physical. Prentice again said, "Don't worry about it, Arthur," and only then did Arthur suddenly come back into focus.

"The deputy prosecutor was very adamant," Arthur said. "He was very clear what would happen to me if they caught me lying. Also, I'm afraid I'm on rather good terms with a police officer there. I really feel quite bad that I've lied to them all."

Once more, Prentice laughed. Arthur looked at him for a moment, trying to absorb some of his ease. But just as he tried to tell himself that perhaps Prentice was right, he felt a sudden flash of anger, anger because he had done something very distasteful to protect Prentice and now Prentice was sitting there laughing at him—just moments after kicking him out of his house, no less. Arthur suddenly felt that he would be well within his rights to throw something close to a tantrum at this point. But he only managed to say, "I'm sure they'll try to do something. They can, and they promised they would. And I lied to someone who was, in the end, very nice to me. He even invited me over to dinner."

"Well, there you go," Prentice said, smiling. "If he invited you over to dinner, he's not going to prosecute you."

As Prentice said this, Arthur wondered why he so often felt like this, like the things that were important to him, or caused him so much anxiety, were so easily dismissed by the people around him. He suddenly recalled a conversation he had had with Rebecca when his business was failing. He had finally confessed the whole thing to her one evening just before going out to dinner. He was drinking a glass of scotch, and feeling brave enough to admit to his failures. All Rebecca could do was to respond with declarations of how little his business mattered in the first place. "And what if it is time for the business to come to an end?" she said. "Is that the worst thing? We have plenty of money. And it's not like the business has ever really done much for us. In the last few years, at least. I've inherited more in that time than your business has brought in. You should be happy."

It occurred to Arthur as he thought of this, sitting there with Prentice, that there are, in fact, times when this kind of advice is appropriate, when it is given to relieve a person of his or her pain. That is, it makes sense when it's delivered to help a person realize that the world is not at an end just because of some crisis. But this particular statement of Rebecca's—like what Prentice seemed to be saying right now—was more of a willful refusal to feel empathy, to try to understand that Arthur's pain was real and that it wasn't going away with a little laughter and a roll of the eyes. As Arthur thought about all this, he wondered just how weak his ego really was. Part of him wanted to punch Prentice right in the jaw. But Arthur found that as this fantasy played out in his mind it just as quickly dissolved, because it was hardly the sort of thing Arthur did, and for good reason. Instead, he finally just said, "I'm leaving tonight. I'll go to Switzerland."

"Maybe at least stay for the weekend," Prentice replied. "Delphine can deal with it. I'll make sure of that."

"No. I need to leave tonight. I don't want to be here when the police come."

Prentice still looked confused.

"I'm not sure you're quite understanding my position," Arthur continued.

"Arthur, this is the French, for Christ's sake. They don't worry about harassing wealthy Americans."

"Well, they certainly worry about harassing you. I think given all the trouble you've been in you'd be a little more wary of just how far they might be willing to go to harass me."

Prentice didn't seem to have much of a response to this, but he also didn't acknowledge the point. All he did was sit there smiling. Finally, though, he said, "Stay to the end of the weekend. I haven't even shown you my airfield and my planes yet. I'll take you up for a ride. We'll see all of the Alps."

Arthur exhaled deeply. Maybe he *was* being ridiculous. But then Arthur thought about sitting in the questioning room at the police station and lying over and over to Inspector Laurent. He thought about the wheels turning in the mind of the deputy prosecutor, and how he was probably issuing instructions now to pick up Arthur, and Arthur at last stood and said, "I have to pack." And then he said it once more: "I have to pack. And I've got to leave. Tonight."

"You've really got to be kidding," Prentice said again. And again Arthur felt like punching him. But just as quickly he felt a kind of loneliness and regret, as though this was not at all how he had hoped things would have turned out. He pictured himself going back to New York and having to face his wife's impending second marriage, and felt very, very alone.

"I'm afraid I really want to get going," Arthur said. "Perhaps we should say goodbye now. I really think it's best if I leave tonight." And as he got to the end of this, and much to his surprise, he let forth just a bit of a gasp—not quite a sob, but an unexpected expression of his anguish—and then turned and walked off to his bedroom.

11

As Arthur drove away from St. Loup that evening, he tried to take some comfort in the fact that he would finally be escaping what was a very stressful situation. He had been totally isolated, the woman he shared the grounds with hated him and actively tried to have him sent away, and he was kept in a constant state of apprehension by the police because he was, in truth, lying to them. Switzerland didn't seem like such a bad option at this point, and Prentice had been right when he said that Arthur was far from being destitute (as troubling as Prentice's assertions were). Arthur began to think about where he'd like to stay in Geneva, and decided that he was going to treat himself to a first-class hotel for the next week and eat as extravagantly as he could. He felt he needed something of a vacation at this point.

Arthur was still a little apprehensive that perhaps there might be some type of alert out for him. Maybe his license plate number was now circulating on the police computer system and an earnest young patrolman would spot him heading for the Swiss border. This was unlikely, but still disconcerting enough to prevent Arthur from entirely enjoying the anticipation of a high-end Genevois hotel.

There was also the matter of the border. Whether or not he would even be asked to stop was a matter of pure chance. The French and Swiss border police had long since only done routine spot checks, keeping the borders mostly open, especially for people who drove Mercedeses. All the same, what if they did have Arthur's license plate? As Arthur approached the border, he tried to adopt some of Prentice's lack of concern—it was true that he could hardly be at the top of France's most-wanted list. On the other hand, how hard was it to call in a license plate number? Maybe Inspector Laurent ordered them to make a report but was going to leave it at that. But if Arthur was caught—was spotted at the border—a low-level cop would hardly wave him through if he knew he was wanted.

And Arthur was in fact stopped. The three cars ahead of him passed through without slowing down, but Arthur was ordered to halt—and on the French side.

"Passport?" the officer said after Arthur rolled down his window.

Arthur was extremely nervous, but managed to hand over his passport. The man disappeared back into his booth and all Arthur could think about was how news of his incarceration would reach Rebecca and his various difficult family members, and how everyone would roll their eyes and think that this was just exactly what they had come to expect from Arthur. But in another minute, the officer returned, handed Arthur his passport, and waved him into Swiss territory. Finally, he could look forward to checking into his hotel.

Arthur drove through the outskirts of Geneva, and then made his way inward, to the Hotel Barnave, which was located in the Old Town, just above the ancient city ramparts and overlooking the university. He had stayed there before, and he liked everything about it, including its cheerful bar and its ancient formal dining hall. They also had a vacant room for him, which was something of a relief, and before long Arthur was stepping over the threshold of a small suite on a high floor with a view of the University of Geneva's main grounds. Since he had no currency yet, he tipped the bellhop with a ten-dollar bill he had tucked away in his wallet—it seemed more appropriate than giving a Swiss inhabitant euros—and as the door shut behind him, he felt, for the first time in a while, the sensation of security and relief. He looked around, took note of his view again, then pulled a Kronenbourg out of the minibar and sat at a large oak writing desk to pour his beer into a glass.

He was beginning to relax. There was no question about that. And he was looking forward to his beer. But as he took his first sip and acknowledged his feeling of relaxation once again, he couldn't help but notice it was, unexpectedly, starting to slip away. True, the direct threats he faced were now gone. Delphine could spend the rest of her life slandering him and it wouldn't matter at all. He felt safe from the French police. Even Arthur didn't imagine extradition was a possibility, although he did wonder what might happen if he ever took a trip to Paris. But what Arthur was beginning to feel bad about—what seemed to be diminishing his feelings of relief and replacing them with a sense of sadness—was a kind of regret now for having left in such a hurry and on such bad terms with Prentice, who was, after all, supposedly one of his oldest friends. It was a fact that Arthur didn't have many friends in the world—or not many that he had a deep connection with—and he couldn't afford to lose those he had. He wondered if he shouldn't have thrown caution to the wind, as it were, and stuck around for the weekend, if for nothing other than the chance to bond a little more with Prentice.

But that was only Arthur's first thought. What came afterward, and what bothered him more, was another conclusion, a different realization, namely that maybe he wasn't really even that close to Prentice. Prentice had always played the role in Arthur's imagination of a kind of emblem of his youth, a person from his past who

had always known him and had seen him (presumably with affection) as his character was first forming. But as Arthur opened a small
folder on the writing desk, which contained the menus of local restaurants, and as he began examining one of the restaurant's various preparations of horse meat—a thing Swiss people seemed to like
quite a bit—he concluded that the truth was that he didn't know
Prentice at all anymore, in any real, meaningful sense. This over-
sized, alcohol-loving divorcé who sped around in Jaguars while blind
drunk only to scream at his wife and terrify his kids, and who had
a girlfriend like Delphine, a girlfriend who slept with the grounds-
keepers and made up outrageous lies about guests—this man was
completely unknown to Arthur. What Arthur couldn't figure out,
though, was whether this was all new, or if he had again misjudged
a person who had once been a constant feature in his life. Mostly it
seemed to Arthur that had Prentice not left for flight school when he
was eighteen, and then not moved to Alaska and Africa and eventually Gap, he would probably now be one of the many people Arthur
routinely saw in New York City but was never properly intimate
with—"friends" in an oddly alienating sense; people who populated
his world but with whom he only felt a mysterious and sad distance.
Arthur thought about Prentice, and his airfield, and his last-minute
offer to take him up to see the Alps in one of his planes, and for the
first time he realized that what he had somehow wanted out of this
trip had no chance of ever coming about. True, he was in part just
looking for a month or two out of New York. That desire was simple enough. But there had been more to it than that. It was the promise of spending time with an old companion that made such a trip
seem possible in the first place.

   As Arthur thought about all this, still astonished by how fre-
quently he saw horse on Genevois menus, he determined that he
really needed to take steps to put his social world back in order, and

that he had to pay special attention to those few people with whom he could establish a real connection. In a certain way, his family (or his sons) had once filled that role. But this was no longer really an option for him—his sons could hardly be expected to compose his entire social world. Still, he thought he had a chance to make things better for himself. And just as he thought this, he decided that there was something he had to do, something he had to address. He abruptly stood up and walked across the room to the phone. It had been in the back of his mind, what he was doing now. It had been just a vague idea—a thought that he dismissed before it was even formalized. But now it seemed vital that he do it. He picked up the receiver and asked the hotel receptionist if he could be connected to information in Gap. And when he was patched through to information, he asked the operator (in rudimentary French) to give him the main office of the Gap police. And when he heard "*Allô. Police*," he said, "Inspector Laurent, *s'il vous plaît*."

"*Il n'est pas là*," the person at reception quickly replied.

Arthur considered for a brief second asking for his home phone number. But instead he just asked for his voice mail. He didn't feel as if he owed Inspector Laurent an explanation for his lies, or that he thought he'd be capable of giving much of one. (After all, he was still working everything out himself.) But he had, after all, been invited to dinner, and by the one person who had shown him any real kindness in the last stretch of weeks. At the very least, Arthur felt he should apologize for not being able to come, and thank him for the invitation. It was silly, no doubt. But Arthur suddenly felt that this was also very important.

All the same, just after the outgoing message ended and the beep sounded, Arthur was overcome with a sense of utter shame. And for the first seconds of the message, there was dead air. But Arthur pressed on. "Hello, Inspector Laurent," he finally began. "This is

Arthur Camden. The reason I'm calling is that I won't be available to come to dinner on Wednesday, and I wanted to make sure that you and your wife didn't go to any trouble on my behalf. I'm very sorry, and I hope this hasn't inconvenienced you. Perhaps we'll have the chance to eat together in the future. You were very kind to invite me in the first place. You are a very kind man. Anyway, thank you again. Goodbye."

Arthur's heart was pounding by the time he hung up. But the immediate embarrassment, and the adrenaline that went along with it, was soon overshadowed by deeper implications of the call. As Arthur returned to the writing desk and his nearly finished Kronenbourg, he wondered if this was really all that he was left with: chance encounters with polite people whom he seemed to like mostly because they made an effort to be friendly. Arthur remembered his thoughts when he first arrived on his trip, about how he had always liked the Swiss and how he had wondered if this was because he mistook civility for affection. The problem was a difficult one, and it had gotten no easier, and Arthur wondered if Inspector Laurent wasn't yet another example of an imagined friendship based on flimsy pretenses.

But after some consideration, Arthur finally decided that this was not the case. As he finished his beer, he determined that he had liked Inspector Laurent a great deal, however short their interaction was. And that it had been reciprocated. He had been invited to dinner, after all, and Arthur concluded that if he could just focus on this sort of thing when he got back to New York, if he could just spend time with friends (and girlfriends, perhaps) with whom he shared this kind of glimmer of affection, perhaps he might be able to embark on a happier year. In this light, Arthur resolved to call Ken Fielder the day he landed to see if there were any events (or possible blind dates) that might be on the horizon. And he even thought he might try to get in touch with Rixa again—he had waited nearly a month after he was expelled from the Fly Casters to call, only to discover that she had left for Martinique for the winter. Perhaps she would be back by now and might like to go out to dinner with him again, although this time around he would be more careful about where he built his fires. But these were all just unclear ideas, just the beginnings of a plan. All the same, perhaps he had learned something in France. And perhaps he really could get things back on track, if he really worked hard and if he really put his mind to it.

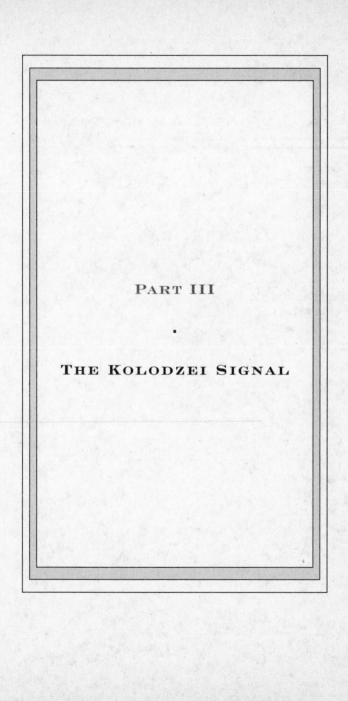

PART III

.

THE KOLODZEI SIGNAL

1

Arthur had never quite felt comfortable in a bathing suit, although every summer he found himself suffering the indignity of wearing one on far more occasions than he liked. Arthur found it puzzling that this matter caused him so much apprehension, although he was a generally self-conscious person, and his reluctance to walk nearly naked in front of other people was not too far out of character. What was odd to Arthur was that he felt all alone in his self-consciousness. It was of course true that there was an ongoing public debate, mostly in so-called women's magazines, about the topic of bathing suits, and embarrassment, and body image. But somehow this debate never actually materialized in the real world (as far as Arthur could tell, at least), otherwise why would so many people go to the beach every year? It was true that Arthur went to the beach too. But it was never his idea. He had never once suggested going to the beach to anyone, even though in happier times he and Rebecca, and his sons, David and Patrick, owned a house in East Hampton together. What Arthur liked about the Hamptons, though, was cocktail hour and white trousers, and being led from

party to party by Rebecca, who was always being invited by someone or other to come join them on their lawn or beside their pool.
It was the actual beach—all that sand and sun—that Arthur never
cared for.

But Arthur's son Patrick had decided at the last minute that the
month of August this year would be best spent on the East Coast,
and it seemed that renting a beach house was the best way to keep
his children happy and coordinate overnight visits and socializing
with friends and family. He chose Nantucket, never really liking the
hectic August bustle of the Hamptons, and after some complicated
negotiating, he rented an eight-bedroom house on three prime acres
of beachfront property so he could entertain family and old friends
all at the same time.

"It'll be like a commune," he told his father when he made his
invitation.

"I think a commune is what I need about now," Arthur replied.

It was a fact that things had still not been going very well for
Arthur. Ken Fielder had been working hard on his behalf, although
with little luck. Arthur had also resolved to call Rixa again, but he
never followed through because he heard she was in Bar Harbor for
the summer and not due back for some time. So, yet again, Arthur
found himself looking for some kind of escape, and a trip to Nantucket with his family seemed just the thing.

In addition, Patrick made it clear that Arthur was invited to come
for the entire month. "It would be really great for Sarah and Katie,
not to mention Marina and me." He added, though, that Rebecca
would probably be up for one of the weekends, so Arthur would
perhaps want to leave during that stretch—she was busy arranging
wedding details and said that a weekend was all she could swing.

"I'm afraid I've made quite a few plans for August too," Arthur
quickly said after hearing this, although it was not really true. He

had had several ideas, and had considered making travel proposals to various friends, but none had yet materialized. "I'll shift things around, though," Arthur added. "I'd of course like to come up for as long as possible."

"The place is very large," Patrick said, "so you can have plenty of space, and it's right on the beach, so we've got everything we'll need. I'll have to keep on top of my work, but I think I've arranged things so it won't be that difficult. Nothing happens in August anyway."

"What about David?" Arthur asked. "Has he figured out his schedule?"

"It looks like he can come for one of the weekends and then the third week. He doesn't have any wedding plans to make, seeing that they're not even close to coming up with a date."

"Well, David always takes his time with these things," Arthur said after a pause. "He's never been one to rush."

After hanging up, Arthur began to think about his wardrobe. Ordinarily, this would not be a troubling matter. His Hampton whites and pinstripes would be just the thing for a man of his age to wear to social events in Nantucket. The problem was that the clothes had been stored in the Hamptons, in the house that now belonged to Rebecca. For this reason, he had written them off as beyond recovery. And the truth was that this loss hadn't really been too hard to deal with. He hadn't needed things like festive bow ties for his trip to France. Arthur had, in fact, treated himself to something of a new summer wardrobe when he was headed off to Gap. But he had kept it simple—a couple of lightweight blazers, a few pairs of dark poplin pants, a pair of comfortable shoes, etc.—and now he needed something different. It would be easy enough to buy some new things, but Arthur finally decided he might be able to make a trip out to the Hamptons house. Normally he would never risk interacting with Rebecca, especially over clothes. He had pretty much surrendered the entire contents of the house to avoid any kind of painful interaction with her. But Arthur had recently discovered that Rebecca had hired a personal assistant to help her with (among other things) her wedding, and he figured that he might be capable of speaking to someone like an assistant.

The whole matter of the assistant was actually something of a psychological relief to Arthur because it meant that now he could contact Rebecca without having to talk to her directly. There would, after all, probably be future occasions for them to connect, seeing as they had sons and granddaughters in common, and that David was engaged to be married. And when Arthur first spoke to the assistant—a young woman named Hailey—he made a kind of long-winded introduction to establish that he might actually be in touch with her again soon. "The divorce only just went through this winter, you see, and there are just a few loose ends. In this particular instance, I have some clothes in the Hamptons, along with a few other things, and I was thinking there might be a good time when I could pick them up."

Remarkably, Hailey seemed entirely unmoved by what Arthur felt was a fairly pathetic introduction. "I'm sorry . . . Mr. Camden. Is that right? Mr. Camden?"

Arthur hesitated. "Yes. I'm Rebecca's ex-husband."

"Yes. I'm sorry, but I'll have to ask her if it's all right for you to go out there, and then we'll have to pick a time."

"Well, yes," Arthur replied. "That's what I'd like to arrange."

"Okay. Good. Well, then, Mr. Camden, I'll call you back as soon as I can."

Hailey, however, did not call Arthur back. Instead, and much to Arthur's shock, Rebecca called him back directly, and in a very offhanded manner told him that she had given all of his clothes to Goodwill.

"Well, my god, Arthur," she said, after Arthur expressed some surprise. "You weren't going to wear those things again. They were ancient. And they never suited you to begin with. All those ridiculous bow ties. Anyway, you're not thinking of spending time in the Hamptons, are you?"

"No. No, I'm not thinking of that," Arthur said.

"Well, Arthur, of course I'd love to see you out there. But I imagine it might be a bit awkward. You never quite seem very happy to see me."

"I don't know what you're talking about," Arthur replied, trying to be as calm as possible.

Rebecca paused, then said, "You know, I've been thinking quite a lot about this recently, but I've very much wanted to tell you again— to emphasize—that you're very important to me. You're a very important man in my life. Things ended with us going our separate ways. But I can't say I have regrets about our life together. We raised two wonderful boys, and I was always very happy with you. Well, for a while, at least."

It seemed like she might go on, but Arthur interrupted her at this point and said, "But the clothes are definitely gone."

"What?" Rebecca replied.

"My clothes. They're definitely gone?"

Rebecca paused. "Yes, Arthur. I gave them to Goodwill."

"Well, if any turn up, please have your assistant call me."

Rebecca hesitated again, almost unsure of what to say next. Finally she said, "All right, Arthur. I'll have her call you."

At that, Arthur said goodbye and hung up. He could not bear Rebecca's good-natured attempts to "put the past behind them," as she said she wanted to do. Just once he wished she'd express something closer to sorrow for what she had given up. But she had never done anything close to this. In her moments of compassion she could only manage to describe their marriage as a meaningful but now long-past episode in her ever-changing life. Arthur was relegated to a period in some sort of personal journey she was on, and that's what he couldn't bear. He thought the whole idea of marriage was to transcend the personal, solitary part of life, but, evidently, he was wrong about this. His marriage had just been a temporary pact on the way to something else—something else where he was entirely without summer clothes. All the same, this final problem was at least something he could resolve, and after hanging up the phone, he began to make a list of the things that he would need for his trip.

2

Arthur had always disliked the drive to Cape Cod and the islands, so when Patrick said that he was flying out on the jet he shared with another businessman in Steamboat and that he could pick Arthur up at Teterboro, Arthur happily agreed. He didn't really like private planes all that much either—not enough of the illusion of safety he found in commercial jets—but fear of death seemed far better than a boring drive and dealing with the ferry in Hyannis.

And it was a happy flight because Marina and the girls were on it as well, and they amused Arthur quite a bit. All the chatter interspersed with Katie and Sarah crawling over him seemed to be exactly what he needed. Of course, in the past this kind of thing wasn't always such a panacea. That is, for as deeply happy as it made him, at the end of his visits to Steamboat he always felt pressed to return to the project of putting his life back on track. But this might have just been the effect of Colorado. Life on the ranch seemed to focus on work and child-rearing, and Arthur hoped that Nantucket would be a bit different. He knew a few people who would be on the island—unlike Steamboat—and two separate members of the

Geographers Club had already invited him over for drinks, so he imagined that he would have plenty to entertain him.

There would also be his family, various members of which were listed by Patrick after they landed. "People seem excited to come," Patrick said as they rode in the back of the black SUV that took them to their house. "It's just a matter of organizing everything, and prying them away from their other plans."

"Well, I'll be excited to see everyone," Arthur said, although this wasn't exactly true. Arthur was pleased to see some of the family members Patrick named, but there were several reunions he was not looking forward to, particularly with those people who felt that he had destroyed the family business. Arthur was somewhat confident such accusations would not be made again—or at least not to his face—but after being called a "fool" and an "idiot" several times in the past, he had a hard time thinking they could all resume normal relations. Patrick, however, was mostly oblivious to these insults, which made Arthur feel better. He certainly didn't want either of his sons to know about the hard way he had been treated, especially because Arthur always vaguely wondered if he hadn't deserved it.

The thing that most unnerved Arthur, however, was that the itinerary was in such a jumble. Again, the whole plan for Nantucket was hatched at the last minute (not long after Arthur fled France), and people were still coordinating their schedules to fit in overnight and weekend trips. Patrick didn't know who was coming when, and Arthur felt that if he just knew what to expect, he might feel a little more relaxed.

The drive to the house took about fifteen minutes, and when they arrived Arthur was surprised by how large it was. Arthur had known that it had eight bedrooms, so he had had some idea. Still, it was a bit more impressive than he had imagined. The house was a long, sprawling, gray-shingled traditional with large porches on either side, a slate roof, and dozens of sixteen-over-sixteen windows. In the distance, there was a long white wooden walkway to the beach (the house came with three hundred feet of shoreline) and a newish-looking swimming pool nestled behind a perimeter of tall hedges and rosebushes. The house's trim was all painted white—it looked as if it had just been done—and although the rental company apparently called it a "Cape," the center section had three stories, the third built into the roof with large white-trimmed dormers. But it was also surprisingly welcoming for something so big, and seemed to fit well amid the surrounding dunes. Mostly, what Arthur felt about it, though, was just a little relief, because it had more than enough space for him to hide out if he needed a break from company.

They arrived at one o'clock, and Marina quickly went to the kitchen to unpack a lunch that she had prepared. "The girls are starving," she said as she darted through the front door. "Sarah's going to kill me if I don't give her something. But I've got plenty for you too, Arthur, just in case you want to kill me as well, and maybe this afternoon we can go food shopping? There's a place we can walk to that will deliver what we buy. Patrick and I are determined to last a month without having to rent a car."

"It all sounds good to me, Marina," Arthur replied.

"I saw the floor plan online, Dad," Patrick then said to Arthur, after the driver brought in the last of the luggage. "I'll show you where you'll be sleeping so you can get set up. There's what they call the 'in-laws suite,' which looks very comfortable. So long as you're not offended by the name, I think I'll give that to you."

"Not at all," Arthur said, although he did feel just slightly offended by the name.

But the suite was much more than adequate and Arthur decided that he could well spend most of the month there. It had two large rooms at the west end of the second floor, which included a large study and a bedroom just beyond that. The views were excellent, and there was a sort of enormous marble bathroom that almost made Arthur blush when he saw it.

After about an hour of unpacking, most of the day was spent on various tasks and activities, including a trip to town to buy groceries, a short trip along a footpath through the dunes, a long game of ping-pong between Arthur and Patrick, and a brief walk along the ocean to let the girls see the water. That evening they grilled steaks and drank a bottle of wine and chatted about a variety of things, including Arthur's trip to France and Patrick's plan to purchase cattle for the ranch. The end of dinner came swiftly, though, when the phone rang. David was calling, and rather than ring him back, they passed the phone around at the dinner table to say hello and ask him what his plans were.

"I'll be there next weekend," David told his father. "I can't wait. I have a job interview Friday morning, but I can be in Nantucket by midafternoon, if we can get through Boston traffic."

"What's the job interview?" Arthur asked.

"A position on the finance side of a pharmaceutical company. It's not bad. Too much travel. But decent pay. Plus I like the guys I've met so far, so it seems like it might be a good fit."

"Well, it sounds promising," Arthur said. "Let me know if there's any way I can help." After Arthur said this, though, as he passed the phone to Marina, he suddenly thought about how hollow this offer of assistance was. He might be able to recommend a good tailor for an impressive interview suit, but in terms of having any kind of pull, Arthur certainly didn't know anyone in the pharmaceutical industry. His son's career had actually been a matter that had troubled Arthur for some time, mostly because it was clear that if the family business had remained afloat, David would certainly be working there. It had seemed that he might be all right this past year—he had gotten a job working for a bond trader that Patrick knew. But the position didn't work out, for reasons that Arthur never really understood, and Arthur had once again started to worry. David had, in fact, gone through a series of jobs that ended in unclear ways. He had put in a few years at the family company when he got out of college, but it came to a point that there just wasn't very much for him to do anymore. Fortunately, he left of his own accord—Arthur would never have fired him. A friend from college wanted a partner to start a restaurant in Boston with, and David headed north. The restaurant lasted for about six months before closing, and during that time David fell in love with a woman who was working as a curator at the Massachusetts Museum of Art, and he decided that maybe he'd stay in Boston for a while. Arthur's business was clearly near the end at that point, so he didn't exactly encourage his son to return to the firm. All the same, he did say, "Well, you'll always have a job waiting for you here, David."

Arthur's various empty offers of assistance were, in fact, much on Arthur's mind after dinner and well into the later evening. It was a perplexing question: what sorts of things does a father owe his son? On one level the answer might best be nothing, since too much parental help so often had such obviously bad results. Moreover, there was no reason a person shouldn't try to make his own way in such an obviously prosperous nation. But in terms of smaller-scale help, a leg up in the world, a little nudge forward, you could say that a father should at least give his son what his own father gave him. By this logic, if Arthur matched the gifts he gave his sons with what his father gave him, he was certainly not doing very well.

It seemed especially hard at this point in David's life. He was in his early thirties and thinking about settling down. He was engaged, after all, and would probably like to have a steady job and a solid vision of his future. Arthur had had all the stability he needed when he was that age. David, however, was somehow cut loose. He had inherited money and had a trust fund. That was true. But it was the kind of money that would make a life easier, not the kind of money that could sustain one. Anyway, when he got right down to it, what bothered Arthur was not at all David's financial situation. What troubled Arthur the most was that his son might feel unhappy, and afraid, and ashamed to tell his father about these feelings. Arthur did not want his son to feel any part of what he himself had felt in the past year or so—directionless, mostly useless, and without much ability to change the course of his life.

The matter was all confusing and a bit disturbing. But just as Arthur was delving deeper and deeper into this emotional puzzle, and thinking that he might bring David to meet his friends from the Geographers Club to do a little networking, the phone rang again, distracting Arthur to other thoughts. They were now all sitting in the large living room at the east end of the house, overlooking the ocean. A wall of French doors gave out to a grass terrace and stars were beginning to appear over the horizon. The girls were in bed, Arthur had a glass of scotch, Marina was working on a needlepoint project, and Patrick was beginning a book titled *A History of Nantucket Whaling*, when he got up to answer the phone. On the other end of the line was a man named Bill Ellis, which Arthur quickly gathered when Patrick cheerfully said "Uncle Bill" into the phone. Uncle Bill was not properly an uncle. He was a cousin of Arthur's, which made him something different than an uncle to Patrick, although Arthur wasn't quite sure what. But Bill was of Arthur's generation, and a semi-regular fixture in Patrick's young life in Manhattan, and "Uncle" always seemed to be an appropriate term.

Bill was also a person whom Arthur, in particular, did not want to see. Arthur had a history with him—one which seemed extremely painful in relation to his current feelings of inadequacy toward his son. Bill had, in fact, been a sort of rival for Arthur's own father's attention and admiration, and as Patrick continued to talk on the telephone, apparently arranging plans for Bill's visit, Arthur hastily tried to distract himself by looking over the frontispiece of Patrick's whaling book. Unfortunately, he was not at all able to draw his attention away from thoughts of Bill, and how Bill and Arthur's father had gotten along so well, and, for numerous reasons, just how painful it might be to see this particular cousin again at this point in time.

3

Arthur's father died when he was eighty-nine, just three years before Arthur's divorce. He had cancer, although the disease and its pace were fairly merciful, as these things go. In fact, Arthur's father died with the kind of order and dignity that Arthur always expected, complete with deathbed farewells, declarations that it had been a wonderful life, and emphatic requests of Arthur to take care of the family. It was very sad. There was no question about that. And when he was finally dead, the sort of stunned confusion that always occurs with these things descended on the family, even though his death had been well anticipated. But there was a method to it all, and the hospice nurse quickly called the funeral home, and Arthur spoke to the lawyers the next day, and soon the death became a sort of institutional matter as well as a personal tragedy.

Arthur was the executor of his father's estate. Arthur had a sister, Helen, but she had long ago moved to San Francisco, and it was easier for his father to deal with his son when making arrangements. And since they were business partners (or since Arthur had taken over the business), he would have at least some idea of where his father's various papers and deeds and certificates were.

In truth, though, the estate was surprisingly tidy. His father's money was all with Merrill Lynch. He'd owned two homes—the apartment on Park Avenue and a house in Bridgehampton—and both sold swiftly. As for the furniture and personal effects, Arthur and his sister were able to divide things quickly and amenably, selling the remainder at Christie's in one of the numerous and surprisingly well organized estate auctions the house carries out.

Rebecca had even been somewhat helpful in all this, although not with the same compassion she had shown when Arthur's mother died ten years earlier. Arthur's father died in the midst of Arthur's marital problems, and Rebecca was already distancing herself. Just a day after the funeral she went to a spa in Switzerland for a month to deal with the stress and fatigue she claimed were "absolutely ravaging" her immune system. Still, it was she who made arrangements with Christie's, and when she returned, she continued to supervise their work.

There were only a few things that were out of order. For instance, Merrill Lynch needed death certificates for both of Arthur's paternal grandparents to establish that there would be no other claims on the inheritance. These were nowhere to be found.

"Is this really necessary?" Arthur asked his father's broker. "My father was eighty-nine. My grandparents would have to be a hundred and twenty."

"I know, I know," the broker replied. "I deal with this all the time. But it's the law. If you can't find them, there are easy ways to get copies. Especially in this day and age. For instance, if they went to a church, the church can usually draw something up."

Arthur also had to deal with making telephone calls to old friends and business associates who might not have heard the news. This was more painful than Arthur had anticipated. He had imagined that telling other eighty- and ninety-year-olds that a peer had died would not be that hard—what else could they have expected? But it was they who tended to burst into tears, or whose voices cracked as they said they couldn't believe what they were hearing. Younger people—cousins, former business associates, etc.—took it all in stride. They were the ones who managed to keep their chins up and say things like, "Well, he lived a long, good life." What bothered Arthur the most about all this was that he'd always imagined (and his assumptions were provisionally confirmed by the way his father died) that a person nearly ninety years old automatically acquired a kind of equanimity about death—it was certainly something Arthur planned to have. But now he had very specific evidence of the opposite taking place. Not one of the old people said anything like, *Well, he was nearly ninety, so you can't ask for much more than that.* The old people, in fact, seemed to be asking for quite a bit more.

Additionally, there was the matter of tracking down a few personal items. Several weeks after the funeral, Arthur went through all his father's belongings and took a certain pleasure cleaning out his closets, looking through his wallet, and examining the numerous notebooks and albums he'd left behind. There was nothing invasive about it. Arthur knew that his father must have expected this kind of thing. Arthur had been around when his father went through his grandfather's belongings after he died, so there was certainly precedent. And the truth was that his father lived a comparatively straightforward life, although there wasn't a picture or a letter or even a to-do list that didn't stir something in Arthur. It was strange how such an uncomplicated life could be so moving. Along these lines, there were a few things that Arthur wanted to keep to remind him of his father. There was a silver fountain pen, and a set of leather suitcases, and an antique shoe-shine kit that Arthur was looking forward to integrating into his own personal effects. There were also various other objects he found along the way—an ivory shoehorn and a set of enameled cuff links, for instance—that packed a sentimental force but which had been long forgotten until he uncovered them again.

There was, however, one thing that Arthur couldn't find after his father died—one thing that he wanted and knew about at the beginning of his search. The item was a wristwatch from the Soviet Union called a Kolodzei Signal, which Arthur's father had picked up in 1947 during a visit to Astrakhan, where he was setting up a deal with the Soviet Caviar Commission. The commission was looking for new distributors, and Arthur's father, who was much more imposing, much more hale and well met than Arthur, had befriended the official in charge of the deal on a visit he had made to New York. Arthur remembered his father coming home in the early morning several days in a row smelling of liquor and probably drunk, but fully in control of himself, and with his tie still neat and tight and his speech crisp and clear.

Arthur was always awake by five A.M., and each time his father met him in the kitchen over those few days he said, "Hey, there, kiddo! Waiting up for your old man? Want to make sure the Communists didn't kidnap me?"

Each time, Arthur just nodded. He never knew quite how to respond to these kinds of questions, mostly because he never understood what they meant. Or he could never quite decipher the tone of them. It seemed to demand a response along the lines of, *Out all night again, Pop? You're quite a character.* And, of course, Arthur could never manage to say anything as chummy as this, especially when he was a boy.

But Arthur did think (and thought for most of his life) that he very much wanted to be like his father when he was like this—out all night doing mysterious things, consorting with foreigners with unusual clothes and peculiar accents. Arthur was pretty sure his father was completely aboveboard in things like lawful behavior and marital faithfulness. Of course, you could never really know for sure. But the truth was that this kind of aboveboard quality of his father combined with his impressive physical stature and his ability to drink vodka by the liter was what made him the sort of larger-than-life American that foreigners wanted to do business with. He was a high-living New Yorker who was also vice-free, a man who could stay out all night drinking but who'd never get blind drunk and certainly never be caught with his pants down in a seedy (or first-class) brothel.

Arthur had, throughout much of his life, tried to mimic this. He had tried in college, in his first days in business, and right up until the business failed, and he wasn't a complete failure in the sense that he didn't achieve the opposite of this. He usually got along with foreign consulates and businessmen from far-off places. He was mostly accepted by his peers. He could generally hold his own in pleasant conversations at parties. But he wasn't ever more than a second- or third-tier member of the group. He was never the kind of charismatic, center-stage deal-maker his father had been. And, unfortunately for Arthur, the family business absolutely required that kind of personality. There was simply no room for second- and third-tier businessmen.

In any case, the Kolodzei Signal reminded Arthur very much of his father's forceful charm. It was a one-of-a-kind watch, unattainable anywhere but behind the Iron Curtain, and even there they were impossible to get. They were highly accurate military watches, manufactured with thirty-seven jewels by Swiss-trained watchmakers, and definitely impossible for Russians to obtain without high-level connections. The watch was also something that Arthur's father treasured, since it seemed to symbolize how exciting and unusual his business was, especially in the 1940s when trips to places like Astrakhan were a very rare thing. In fact, Arthur's father wore the watch right up until the illness took over his life, when it was removed after he took to his bed for the final time.

It was then, at that particular point, that the watch disappeared. Or this was when Arthur lost track of it. He had wondered what became of it, but there were so many things going on at that time, and so many people in and out of his father's apartment, that anything could have happened to it. Arthur even suspected that it was in a pocket of the suit his father was cremated in, although there was no sign of melted metal when they spread his ashes in the Atlantic Ocean. It was a mystery. And it bothered Arthur deeply. The watch was irreplaceable, and, to be frank, also worth quite a bit of money. Still, Arthur always imagined (and hoped) that it would turn up somewhere.

And indeed it did turn up, although in a place Arthur never imagined he'd see it.

Arthur first saw his father's Kolodzei Signal again nearly three years after his father's death at the first Christmas party he attended without Rebecca, their separation now official and the divorce soon to follow. Arthur was going through the humiliating task of seeing relatives and old friends he had not seen since both his business and his marriage had failed, and it was almost unbearable. He mainly came to the Christmas party to get through most of the unpleasantness in one fell swoop. He'd be reintroduced en masse as a recent failure, and wouldn't have to go through such reintroductions one by one. It was here that he spotted Bill Ellis, the person that Arthur most did not want to see, but also the person who would ultimately solve the problem of the lost watch.

Arthur and Bill had always had a strong rivalry, or at least Arthur had always felt there had been one. Bill was only three years younger than Arthur and he had once been a candidate to take over the family's business. He was the son of Arthur's father's sister, and he had grown up a member of the large and happy band of Upper East Siders who made up the Camden clan. Arthur went to grade school with him, spent summers with him, and they even spent a month together in Europe, although other cousins were there as well. And when Bill graduated from Princeton, he came to work at the family business, where Arthur had been working for the previous three years. Arthur's father was running the operation at the time, and he immediately gave Bill broad responsibilities. They did not supersede Arthur's, which had taken him all of those three years to earn, but they were definitely far beyond what Arthur was entrusted with when he had graduated from college. "Frankly, I'd be comfortable having a guy like you run the whole company," Arthur's father said to Bill when he first arrived.

But for all of Bill's abilities, and for all of Mr. Camden's confidence in him, it was Arthur who eventually took over the company, the main reason being that Arthur's father had, on principle, always been determined that his own son take the helm. True, the process of grooming Arthur entirely exasperated him. He commonly expressed complete bewilderment over various business decisions that Arthur made. But the sighs and groans were always followed with statements like, "You're going to take over one day, so this is something you really have to learn."

Bill understood what his uncle wanted, and in his younger days he bore no grudge. When he was twenty-six, he left the company to go into business with a friend—corporate real estate of assorted types—and was a huge success. All the same, Bill did still have a stake in the family company, and by age thirty-five he was elected to the board with his uncle's strong support. And when Arthur's father decided to retire, there were a series of family meetings, which overlapped with board meetings, where they discussed who would take his place. Bill had no interest in taking the helm, but he did have opinions about who should (and should not) take over, and he was tactfully but firmly against it being Arthur.

"I love Arthur," he said one day at a family luncheon. "I couldn't ask for a better cousin. He has the kinds of qualities you can only hope for in a family member. But this is business, and this is about the family's financial future, and who I like shouldn't play a part in who I support to lead Camden and Sons."

No one argued with this reasoning. This kind of clear-headed logic was what had established the family's business in the first place. But Arthur's father had a different argument—one about the nurturing and growth of younger minds, the importance of lineage, the absolute necessity of a family member holding the reins, and a small note on the absence of any other candidates. "Who else can we trust to run the family business?" he said.

"Frankly, we should just hire someone," Bill replied. "What's important to the family is the solvency and growth of the company, not whether a Camden is directing the day-to-day running of it."

Again, no one could argue with this kind of thinking. But Arthur's father had influence over the older generation, and they had long deferred to his business sense. In the end, his choice won out. Arthur was named the new president, and his father continued to carry his point with the older Camdens until he died, just two years before the company finally collapsed.

It was a story that Arthur thought about over and over, and after the company entered bankruptcy proceedings he couldn't help but wonder if Bill hadn't been right. Bill and Arthur's father always got along very well, even when they didn't see eye to eye on Arthur taking over, and while Arthur had the status of being part of the direct line, Bill was always a favorite because he seemed to represent the best of what the family was capable of producing. But most difficult was the feeling Arthur always had that Bill thought of him as an idiot—perhaps a mildly likable idiot, but definitely an idiot, tolerated under duress and spoken to because of social custom. The matter was all very hard for Arthur to think about and running into Bill was always extremely difficult, as it was at this particular Christmas party, after not having seen him since his father's funeral. Arthur thought about avoiding him. This was an absolute impossibility, but Arthur still thought about it. After catching his eye across the room, though, he felt obliged to walk over to say hello. Arthur made his way through the guests, put out his hand, Bill smiled and put out his, and Arthur said, "Hello, Bill," in a weak, quiet way that suddenly made him blush. He never made a forceful impression, but in these situations he was particularly bad.

But Arthur's concern over his weak hello, and the sort of limp handshake that followed, suddenly vanished. Arthur nodded again and began to ask how things were with Bill's family, when he looked down and saw, strapped to Bill's wrist, his father's watch. He almost didn't know what to say at first, and for a moment he concluded that it must be another Kolodzei Signal, one just like his father's. Still, despite this conclusion, he asked Bill where the watch was from. "Where did you get that watch?" he said, now, surprisingly, with a stronger voice.

Bill smiled. "Recognize it?" he said. "It was your father's. He gave it to me."

Arthur was shocked. "He gave it to you?" he finally said.

"Well, he once told me I could have it, and I got it after he died."

"You got it after he died?"

"Rebecca passed it along to me. I bumped into her somewhere and asked her if she could grab it for me." Bill paused, then added, "I hope this isn't a problem, Arthur."

Arthur hardly knew how to respond. It certainly was a problem, but what should he say? Finally he managed to reply, "I'm just surprised. It's been so long since I've seen it."

"It's a beauty," Bill said. "It would be pretty hard to buy one like it today, no matter how much you were willing to spend."

Arthur stared at the watch for a moment, and then finally nodded and said, "I suppose not." He wanted the watch back, but at this point, three years after his father had died, he wasn't sure how that would happen. It of course troubled Arthur that his father might have actually offered the watch to Bill. Equally troubling, however, was that Bill had somehow taken the watch without asking him, without at least negotiating or asking or explaining why he wanted it. It wouldn't have been hard to imagine that Arthur would have liked to have his father's watch and the reality was that it was also very valuable. And as he stepped back away from Bill (under the pretext of getting more punch), Arthur suddenly found himself consumed with a kind of rage. He just couldn't believe that Bill, of all people, had his father's watch. But what was he going to do about it? Like so many times before, Bill was in command of the situation—he had the watch on his wrist, after all—and he would most probably be able to best Arthur (either legally or physically) should Arthur try to pick some sort of fight. All Arthur could really do at that moment was to suck it up, as they say. Maybe there was a way to get the watch back, but he couldn't think of anything, and he rapidly concluded that the watch was now lost to him. Or he concluded that to get it back would cost too much in terms of stress and shame, and these were two things that Arthur was determined to avoid in the near future. All the same, this particular situation was exceptionally hard on him.

4

At any rate, that first week in Nantucket mostly passed quietly, at least in terms of Arthur's emotional state. Over the past year, Arthur had gotten much better at putting unpleasant matters out of his head, and he was able to walk on the beach, eat lunch with his granddaughters, watch baseball on television, and do numerous other things without the burden of Bill's impending visit interfering too much.

Dinner was also an event every night, and although Arthur cut his thumb while shucking oysters the second evening they were there, and then ruined a pair of pants with balsamic vinegar the following evening, he also had his share of successes, including a first-rate clam chowder, well-executed waffles one morning, and an outstanding coleslaw.

"I really think this is the best coleslaw I've ever had," Marina said. "I mean, I guess it seems weird to praise something like coleslaw. It's not exactly a soufflé. But it really is great. I'm really impressed."

"I'm a great talent with anything that involves mayonnaise," Arthur replied. "As well as celery seed."

Arthur even enjoyed himself on the beach, seeing as no one seemed to be nearby when he joined Marina and Patrick and the girls. There were no strangers that he could suspect were staring at him, amused or shocked by his aging frame and less-than-taut muscle tone. Arthur was slim, but he had never been very strong, a fact that had somehow burdened him since his early adolescence. He found it interesting, though, the sort of intimacy that the beach (or the bathing suits) made him feel. Patrick was in good shape, and so was Marina, but all the slouching and stooping and squinting that takes place on a sunny beach when you have two small children didn't exactly flatter either of them. Arthur wondered if there was something wrong about this—wrong about even considering the quality of the physical appearance of his son and daughter-in-law. But since it only came up because Arthur was surprised (and happy) about how comfortable he was with it all, it seemed a good enough thing to notice and think about.

Arthur also did things on his own around the island, trying to give Patrick and his family a bit of time alone. He went to dinner at the home of one of his friends (Ian Gray from the Geographers Club), who was hosting a kind of reunion for friends from an expedition he had taken to kill some type of elk in northern Alaska. Arthur stayed late, listening to stories about wind patterns and hiding in gullies and drinking cups of blood from the first kill (a rite that struck Arthur as fairly gruesome).

"You've got to do it Arthur," they all kept telling him. "You'll never be the same. It will absolutely change your life."

"Yes, I'm sure that's true," Arthur replied. "But I'm afraid it's probably not for me."

That particular evening was also memorable because Arthur borrowed a bike to get home and had consumed quite a bit of scotch. The bike was a lady's model with a basket and the kind of headlamp that's powered by the wheel. It suited Arthur well enough, but the lamp fell off about a mile from his own house and he spent nearly half an hour in the dark trying to find it. Eventually he gave up, assuming that no one would care if it was missing, and when he returned the bike the next day (after searching again) Ian didn't seem to notice at all. That return journey was most memorable for Arthur, however, because it was fairly shocking to see all the elk hunters in the bright light of noon, terribly hung over, sunburned, and, Arthur noticed, quite fat and unfit-looking, at least as explorers of northern Alaska go.

Arthur also played a round of golf with another of his friends, a man named Lawrence Nahill, whom he knew via family connections. The course was at a golf club in Nantucket that had recently gotten a lot of press for its newly calibrated membership fees, which dwarfed anything that anyone had ever conceived possible. Even visitors from Tokyo were astounded, as the story went. Arthur liked it well enough, although the things that made this golf club so beloved were lost on Arthur. The truth was that Arthur didn't really like golf all that much, mostly because he was never comfortable with the kind of weird enthusiasm (or monomania) that he felt many golfers possessed. Nevertheless, he was surprisingly good at it. He had a calm, straight shot that kept him on the fairway and always brought him to the green without too much trouble. He was not a very good putter. But he was often a shot or two ahead by the time this skill became relevant (with lesser opponents, at least), so he usually came out on top.

"If you don't hit at least one shot in the rough on the next nine, I'll never speak to you again," Ron said as they ate a hot dog after the ninth hole.

"I'll do my best," Arthur said. "I just seem to hit them straight. I don't know why."

Aside from golf and late-night drinking parties with hunters, Arthur did numerous other things to pass the time, and when Friday arrived, he was well tanned, much more familiar with the daily routines of Sarah and Katie, which he found fascinating, and, perhaps most important, somewhat better acquainted with his son's tolerant and endlessly interested parenting skills. It struck Arthur as amazing how much a person continued to learn about his own children, and he was quite proud to see what a natural Patrick was at fatherhood. Seeing that Friday was the day that David was due to arrive, Arthur also looked forward to seeing him in the role of a new fiancé, and wondered what he would be like on the threshold of this new stage of his life. Arthur's only concern was that this not be ruined by the fact that Bill also would be arriving the same evening.

Fortunately, David arrived first, well before he was expected, because his job interview had been rescheduled. "One of the guys was sick," David said as he stepped into the large entry hall. "Or at least that's what they told me. But it's probably true. If they didn't want to interview me, I'm sure they'd just tell me."

"I'm sure that's true," Arthur said. "But good news for us, at least. We'll get you for an extra afternoon."

David's fiancée, Alicia, was also there, and she seemed genuinely happy to be with them all. She was clearly already close to Marina—they had spent a week in Steamboat that winter skiing—so there was no awkwardness between them at all. There was just a little, however, between Arthur and her, although Arthur was sure that he was partly to blame. It was a funny emotional trick, relating to a now-future family member when all you've done is had dinner together a few times at crowded restaurants in Manhattan and Boston. Still, Arthur was happy enough to see her, and Alicia seemed the same, even if the pressures of the impending familial intimacy gave the scene some rough edges.

After David and Alicia brought their things up to their room, they all had a late-ish lunch on the east porch, which included lobster salad and some sort of expensive white wine that Patrick had discovered in California, and afterward, they did all the things a person customarily does on Nantucket. They went to the beach, they walked in the dunes (where walking was allowed), and when they made it to cocktail hour, they played several games of croquet on the lawn. Arthur was paired with Alicia on the last game, and they ended up having a great time together, even winning the match. Of course, gin and tonics eased some of the discomfort they might have felt, but Arthur was quickly convinced that their strides forward were real. Alicia took to teasing Arthur about his "girlish stroke" and kept telling him, "I can't carry you the whole way, Arthur. You've got to start making some shots." Everyone laughed, as did Arthur, although the truth was that he did make quite a few shots (as with golf, he had a slow and steady approach that paid off in the end). When they were victorious, Alicia even hugged him and said they had to be partners for the rest of the weekend. Arthur could hardly have been happier about that.

There was really only one difficult moment during the early part of that evening. It came after croquet when Arthur found himself alone on the porch with David. Everyone else was showering or changing for the evening, and Arthur was feeling a certain need to make sure everything was all right in David's life. It was strange: the Camdens were never very demonstrative, and the way to deal with problems was always to say that "everything is great" or, in moments of obvious calamity, that "things will get better soon enough." But after the last few years, Arthur wondered if this was really the best way to go about things. And so, without too much of a segue from a discussion about a beautiful willow tree on the property, Arthur broached the matter of David's general well-being in one of the few ways he knew how. "Do you need any money?" he whispered.

David was surprised for a moment. "Money?" he finally said. "Uh, no. I mean, yes, I do, we do, but only in the larger sense. We're fine. Most of Alicia's friends are museum people or academics, so it's not like we're going out to expensive restaurants every night."

Arthur paused. "Well, good. I don't mean to pry. Or insult you. I just want to make sure everything is all right with you. Boston is an expensive city and you'll be married soon enough."

"I just really need a job," David replied, sighing. "For my sanity more than anything else. I mean, I'm not going to slit my throat. But I'm really a generalist where this stuff is concerned, and I always seem to be competing with someone who has the exact right background and experience."

Arthur paused, unsure of how to proceed, but then finally spoke in an unusually frank and heartfelt way. "I wish the company was still around," he said. "I think you would have been great there. I know you'll find something you like. But I wish things could have been a bit different."

David seemed touched, and looked as though he was thinking of how to respond. But at that moment, Marina came onto the porch with a large platter of cheese and instructions for Arthur to replenish everyone's cocktails, and soon the evening was under way once more. Arthur expected the conversation might continue later, but the porch suddenly seemed so cheerful that he was soon thinking of other things. At this time, he did have one other issue on his mind, though. Bill and his family were due in an hour, in time for a late dinner, and Arthur was beginning to prepare himself for the reunion.

5

Bill arrived at eight o'clock with his sons, grandchildren, and new wife in tow. They had flown down from Maine—leaving their summerhouse in Northeast Harbor for the weekend—and arrived at the house in two of the black SUVs that ran shuttles between the Nantucket airstrip and people's homes.

There were twelve of them in all—six adults, including Bill's two sons (Justin and Blake), their wives (Erin and Christina), and Bill's new wife, Joan; and then six children, ranging in age from four to eleven, who had names that Arthur was never quite able to master. Patrick and David were nearly the same ages as Justin and Blake, so they all knew each other well. Patrick had even hosted Justin and Blake in Steamboat over the past two Presidents' Day weekends, so they were in close contact even though the family was spreading apart geographically. And (as was again very clear to Arthur) Patrick and his Uncle Bill had always had a certain affection for one another.

Despite his apprehensions, Arthur played his part in the warm greetings as well. He hugged and shook hands with everyone in the house's large entryway, and kept saying, "It's so good for all of us to be together like this." In some ways he meant it. He liked Justin and Blake a great deal, and had gotten to know them through countless sleepovers and weekend visits to the Hamptons in their youths. He had also attended many of their grade school events when they were in school with Patrick and David. He liked seeing them as adults, with wives and children of their own, and they seemed to be very happy to see him. "It's been too long," they all said, acknowledging the extraordinary ways that even family members living in close proximity can go for lengthy stretches without seeing each other.

After a few minutes, the welcome moved onto the porch, commencing another round of drinks. Marina and Alicia went back and forth from the kitchen, where they attended to the rack of lamb they were making for dinner, while David and Blake took all the kids onto the lawn just off the porch to play in the grass. Everyone else continued to carry on cheerful conversations about the expected weekend weather, the need to do more things like this, and so on. Erin and Christina, whom Arthur did not know well, chatted rapidly about how excited they were to come to Steamboat that winter. Bill kept saying things like, "My sons say it's one of the nicest places they've ever been to," and Patrick kept replying that what he really wanted was for everyone to come live with him.

"I mean it, Uncle Bill," Patrick said. "A computer and an airstrip is all you need these days."

Arthur did his best to keep up with the cheerfulness, and he kept telling himself that he was cheerful, and that any anxiety about Bill's arrival had been unfounded. He smiled, and laughed along, and nodded whenever it seemed appropriate. All the same, after the performance had continued for a while, Arthur began to lose something of his bonhomie. And just as Bill started describing a recent trip to Shanghai to look at an office building his group was thinking of buying (after describing another building in Macao they had just bought) Arthur finally looked down at Bill's wrist, which was now bare because he had rolled up his sleeve, and saw for the first time that evening his father's Kolodzei Signal. Arthur stared at the watch for a few moments, and then glanced up at Bill. He was such a tall, overpowering man—someone Rebecca used to describe as "remarkably handsome"—and his now-graying hair combined with his still-muscular body made him look something like an aging Marine colonel. He was friendly and affable, but he still looked more than capable of laying off five hundred line workers, or firing a slew of middle managers, or, frankly, of beating a man to death without losing his happy grin. And as Arthur thought about this, and how much he disliked Bill, and how Bill, in truth, was nothing less than a professional enemy, Arthur wondered how he was going to get through the weekend. Finally he stepped back, weakly excused himself, and soon found himself chopping onions for Marina, who always seemed to be able to find him a job when he needed one.

Arthur's nervousness around Bill carried on through dinner. They sat down late—at about ten-thirty. The children were either in bed or playing in the expansive basement playroom, so the dinner had a bit more of a formal air. There were eleven people in all, fitting comfortably around the large dining room table, and the stories that passed between them seemed now to be a bit more thoughtful. The good weather and personal victories were not mentioned, and instead things like education reform and medical scares (especially, for some reason, brain tumors) were the topics of choice.

David's career also came up, and David seemed comfortable talking about the difficulties of continually changing directions, but how he had avoided getting too stressed about it all.

"I've even been thinking about law school," he said. "I live in Boston, I have good grades from college, so maybe that's what I'll do."

"How did your interview today go?" Bill said. "Patrick mentioned you had one."

"The interview was rescheduled," David replied. "One of the guys was sick. I believe it because these guys aren't the type to beat around the bush. They'd tell me if they wanted someone else."

"Well, let me know how that works out," Bill said. "I know a few people in Boston." Then Bill paused, although, in retrospect, Arthur could not figure out how long, exactly, this pause lasted. In memory, it seemed like a full five minutes of silence, where no one said anything in expectation of Bill's next words. Finally, Bill leaned forward and said, "Of course, if your father hadn't destroyed the family business, maybe you wouldn't have to be dealing with this kind of thing at all."

It was a strange moment. Arthur was fairly sure that total silence took over the table, although he couldn't be positive because the shame and embarrassment he felt seemed to make a noise of its own—a sort of buzzing that drowned everything out. It was an odd kind of shame, though. He wasn't sure if he felt it for himself, or for Bill for saying such an unpleasant thing. And as an instant passed, and Arthur regained some perspective, he looked up at Bill, who, after a moment of looking as if he were going to pretend he hadn't said something extremely cruel, added, "Well, the company was run on an outdated business model. It would have taken a bit of innovation and creativity for the company to keep going." He paused and then suddenly flashed a look of exasperation, adding, "But let's face it, Arthur, it could have survived if you had a better sense of what the hell you were doing." Bill then cut a big piece of lamb off his bone, indicating that he had done an adequate job of explaining himself and was now ready to move on.

Needless to say, however, he had not done an adequate job of explaining anything. But what was next? Was Arthur expected to make a reply? Arthur watched Patrick glance over at Bill with an unmistakable look of fury. Arthur, however, didn't feel a bit of comfort in this and, instead (and for the first time in quite a while), felt like bursting into tears. His son's inclination was not to roll his eyes, as though this drunken uncle couldn't be taken seriously. Rather, it was more like a kind of burning rage at his uncle for pointing out something that was very harsh but also absolutely true. Arthur never really knew what his sons understood about the way the business fell apart, the ways in which he was blamed him for it. The older family members didn't discuss much with the younger generation. But now Arthur was sure that his sons knew that at least one family member—a successful one that they all liked—held a certain kind of malice toward him.

Arthur now knew it better as well. In the past, Bill's animosity had always been couched in friendly assertions about how likable Arthur was and what a good sort of guy he had always been. Bill had never quite explained his feelings with such bitterness before, and certainly never in front of the younger people in the family. Maybe it was the alcohol. Maybe that was why he let his guard down. But it also seemed that he had somehow become tired of humoring Arthur. This seemed to be a trend these days. It seemed to be Rebecca's justification for her own behavior—that she had had it with pretending, that she had reached the age where she could be blunt about what she saw around her, and that she was sick of humoring Arthur when he was making her so unhappy.

Arthur finally let out a nervous laugh, in preparation for making a kind of general statement about the nature of talent and luck and responsibility. But just as he was trying to formulate his thoughts, Marina stood up and began to ask people if they needed more wine, or more mint sauce, or anything else that might be missing from the table. Just after this, David asked Alicia to tell everyone about the new wing they were considering at the Massachusetts Museum of Art. "You wouldn't believe the politics," David said. "All these people chiming in on how it should be built. It's amazing anything ever gets done. Tell them about it, Alicia."

Alicia paused, but not long enough to let anyone interrupt her, and soon the table was listening to a story about a patron who would only complete his promised donation if they hired an expert on medieval theatrical costumes.

Arthur listened attentively too. He was relieved that the focus was off him. He didn't think he could handle any sort of argument, especially in front of his sons. But the relief was mixed with shame and, now, with quite a bit of anger. It seemed that yet again he was going to have to suffer some kind of ridicule without a response. The sad fact of this all was, though, that Arthur still wasn't sure if Bill's assessment was that wrong. Maybe if he had been a better businessman, or if he had been able to see some new way to make the company work, he wouldn't have destroyed what at one time was, after all, a very valuable asset, and a thing that perhaps David, at this point in his life, might like to take over.

6

Arthur went directly to bed after the table was cleared, and, surprisingly, managed to fall asleep. But the next morning the things Bill had said were very much on his mind, and he went out for a walk on his own to think about what had happened. The walk was somewhat frustrating, though, in that it didn't lead Arthur to any conclusions. He simply rehearsed what he now realized would be a never-ending story about him and the family's company.

On his way back to the house, Arthur decided he might like to go for a swim in the pool. From a distance, the hedgerows and rosebushes seemed very appealing, and Arthur felt like he needed to do something refreshing. He was wearing shorts, so he could go straight in, and as he came alongside the hedge he found himself relaxing a little. It was a welcome feeling. The walk hadn't done much for him, but he loved pools. He disliked swimming in the ocean, but he did love pools because they seemed a bit more private, and he found himself very much looking forward to a morning swim. But just as he got his shirt off and took a few steps beyond the hedge near the water, he looked to his left, and there, beneath him, was his cousin Bill, reclining on a white wicker chaise longue.

"Hello, Arthur," Bill said, holding up his hand to shield his eyes from the sun. "It means you're getting old, when you like to swim in the morning. I don't know why, but it's always something old people do."

Arthur wasn't sure if he had any evidence for or against this, so he said, "I suppose that's right."

Arthur thought about turning and going back to the house. He certainly didn't want to have any kind of one-on-one conversation with Bill. But his shirt was off, and it didn't seem as if there was any dignified way of avoiding getting into the pool. And then, in a flood of feelings that took Arthur very much by surprise, he had the sudden urge to tell Bill exactly how much he resented his comments from the previous night. It was very unlike Arthur. Again, his tendency was always to hide from this kind of confrontation, especially when he felt that he might really be at fault. Even when Rebecca's criticisms were their harshest, for instance, he tended to promise change and improvement rather than defend himself.

But now seemed like a time to strike back, as it were. At the very least he should say something about being insulted in front of his sons. *Be angry with me,* he imagined saying in that split second, *but leave my family out of it.*

Arthur even thought he might be able to make some sort of sophisticated remark about how in the modern, globalized economy small import-export firms really couldn't make it anymore, although he also imagined that Bill could just as easily reply with some phrase along the lines of *innovation is the cornerstone of stability* and that a better man could have found a way. But just as Arthur was rapidly weighing up these various scenarios, Bill glanced up and saw two of his older grandsons walking toward the beach with a surfboard.

"Where'd you guys get that?" Bill yelled, suddenly leaning forward.

"In the garage," the older one replied. "Patrick said we could take it out. Dad said he's coming down in a few minutes to watch us."

"Well, wait for me," Bill yelled, standing up. "I want to come too." And before Arthur could think of an appropriate way to bring up dinner the evening before, Bill had his towel wrapped around his waist, and his shirt on, and was running toward the wooden walkway.

Arthur stood still for a moment. A kind of fatalism and depression began to take hold of him, but he also still felt anger, anger at any number of things, from Bill to Rebecca to his bad luck with the family business. It was a confusing kind of resentment, and one that Arthur didn't feel was very flattering. He had never liked people making blanket complaints about how the world was against them, although for a brief second, Arthur felt that it was. He was sure Bill was, at least. Bill was definitely against him.

But just as he thought of all this, and thought for a moment that he might still be able to swing some kind of showdown, he looked down and saw, lying between a glass of water and a thick stone candleholder, his father's Kolodzei Signal glimmering in the sunlight. Yet again, Arthur felt mocked by it. But only for a moment. In the next instant, Arthur was thinking something very, very different. After taking a look around to see if anyone was watching, Arthur bent down, touched the candleholder, moved the glass of water, and then, in a single motion, took the watch and put it in his pocket. He looked around again. No one seemed to be watching. A moment later, he was walking quickly up to the house with his heart beating at a very uncomfortable pace.

7

It was a puzzle what Arthur would do next. But as he arrived in his room, he was mostly thinking about how fast his blood was circulating, and how frightening all this was. He sat down on his bed and began to inspect the watch, the whole time thinking about where he might hide it.

Arthur stood up and looked out the window. His view of the beach was at an angle, and partially obstructed by dunes. But he could see the pool well enough, and saw that Bill wasn't down there yet searching for his property. Arthur almost laughed at the thought of it. He almost laughed, and then, for an instant, he thought he'd better put the watch back immediately. He'd never be able to pull this off. Bill would surely suspect him of the theft. But then Arthur felt an odd sensation of excitement, and he felt happy that he had regained the watch, and in the end, Arthur put the watch in one of his dresser drawers, just beneath a small pile of shirts, and then went back downstairs. He'd think about it. Arthur just needed time to think. As he walked to the kitchen, and then out the side door, and then around the front lawn, he began to calculate the possible outcomes of his actions. He could still put the watch back. Or he could put it somewhere else and the missing watch might look like the result of Bill's absentmindedness. But mostly, Arthur wondered how he might be able to get the watch back to Manhattan without anyone finding out. Arthur thought about this possibility as he walked up the driveway, and into the small lane, and then around a long looping meadow, and then back again. But when he arrived back at the kitchen, probably thirty minutes later, he still didn't know what he'd do.

Alicia was now in the kitchen, though, peeling potatoes for dinner that evening, and before he could set off on his own to keep thinking about what was next, she quickly engaged him in conversation. "I hope you're not going to be upset if we get married in Ann Arbor," she said as he was darting by. "It's home," she continued as Arthur suddenly halted, "but I know what easterners think of the provinces. We've been thinking about Boston too. But I know everyone will love Ann Arbor, and it's a lot easier to organize a wedding there than in Boston or New York."

"Yes, well, that's probably true," Arthur said nervously. He wanted to look out the dining room window to see if Bill had returned to the pool, but Alicia seemed eager to talk about wedding plans.

"My dad occasionally teaches classes in the law department at the university," she said, "so he can get use of most of their buildings. I went to undergrad there. It's a beautiful campus. Lots of great spots for parties. So maybe we'll do it right on campus. I'm sure you'll love it."

"I hear the campus is lovely," Arthur said rapidly.

"Your sons would have died there," Alicia said, dropping a potato in a large pot of water. "It's way too big. I don't get the sense that they were the most devoted students when they were younger, and you can get away with skipping a lot of classes at big schools like

Michigan. I'd say the best students at Michigan are as good as the best students anywhere. But there's room for a lot more slackers if you've got lecture halls with five hundred kids in them."

"I think you're right about that," Arthur said. "I think you're right." Arthur was now craning his neck around the doorway to see if he could spot anything. But the house seemed to be very calm. He now desperately wanted to go upstairs to check on the watch. Maybe there was a better hiding place. After all, his shirt drawer was hardly secure, although he also couldn't come up with a reason why anyone would look there.

"I know it seems like we're delaying this wedding, because we don't have a date yet," Alicia continued. "But it's really me. I need my career to move forward another notch first. Maybe Boston isn't the best place for us, and if I got offered something in New York, or even San Francisco, I'd probably take it. It's hard to move up too fast in curatorial work in Boston, believe it or not. Too many people with advanced degrees."

"Yes, ha ha," Arthur said. He was now ready to bolt away, no matter what Alicia expected out of the conversation. But just as he was going to say that he really needed to "head to the gents'," he looked out the kitchen window and saw Bill's two grandsons walking back to the garage with the surfboard. He really had to leave now. "You know what, Alicia," he said, but stopped short when he heard the porch door swing open and Bill yell, "My watch is missing. Did someone take my watch?"

Arthur looked at Alicia, but both remained silent. Arthur wanted to run up to his room immediately to find a better hiding place. But he did his best to restrain himself and hide his panic, and in the next instant, Bill was in the kitchen asking again if they had seen his watch. "Did you grab my watch when you were down by the pool, Arthur?" he said. "It was right where I was sitting."

The question seemed innocent enough. That is, Bill didn't seem to be implying anything. But when Arthur said, "No, I didn't see it," Bill flashed a glare at him as if to say he knew everything and it was exactly the sort of thing he had always expected from Arthur. But the look quickly disappeared, probably because it was such an outlandish suspicion. Still, Arthur couldn't help but feel that the blood was rushing to his face, and that the tremors he felt in his hands were already giving him away.

"You're sure?" Bill said again.

"Of course I'm sure," Arthur replied.

Bill looked like he was going to ask again, but then said, "Well, maybe one of the kids grabbed it. They're always asking to play with it."

For the rest of the afternoon, all the family members at one time or another looked for the watch. A team of young people looked through the hedges and under the seat cushions on all the couches. Bill directed the operations, asking the kids at several points if they were sure they didn't pick it up. "I won't be mad," he said. "I know that sometimes people do things and then realize they shouldn't have and don't know how to make it right. I promise I won't be mad at any of you."

Arthur felt extremely guilty that the children were under suspicion. Still, he could hardly confess at this point, although he did promise himself that were any of the children actually directly accused of taking the watch, he would come forward. He also had to keep track of the kids for other reasons. One of Bill's granddaughters (an eight-year-old who Arthur thought was named Lisa) tried to enter his room in her enthusiasm for a completely thorough search. Fortunately Arthur was right behind her, and was able to explain gently that there was "no possible way" that the watch was in his quarters.

Arthur too pitched in on the search, diligently looking in several places around the house. He also suggested that maybe Bill lost it when he was in the ocean.

"I didn't wear the damn thing in the ocean," Bill yelled.

"But maybe you forgot," Arthur said.

"I didn't forget, goddamn it."

The whole time, Arthur was still mulling over what he had done, and was again thinking that he could still back out of what he had started. If he needed to, he could put the watch in his pocket, walk down to the hedges by the pool, and pretend to find it. He could say, *I guess we missed this spot when we looked here earlier.* But as the afternoon wore on and the search became more sporadic, Arthur became more and more determined to go forward with what he had started and keep the watch for himself. Part of this came from simply deciding that the watch was his property in the first place and that he was fully justified in what he had done. But another part of this resolution stemmed from Bill growing more and more testy with him, and asking him in blunter and more pointed ways if he was sure he hadn't "picked up the watch inadvertently."

"You were right there!" he kept yelling.

Arthur found these kinds of comments to be a bit offensive, and Patrick once again started glaring at his uncle. Arthur thought the whole thing was very strange—how you could feel deeply abused by what felt very much like a false accusation, even when the accusation was absolutely correct.

By the time evening arrived and the adults were having cocktails on the east porch, the search was mostly over, and although Bill said he'd look again the next day and asked everyone to keep their eyes open, the matter was now dying. They had looked. The watch was nowhere to be found. It seemed time to move on to other things. Interestingly, though, the anxiety of being caught, and the difficulties of pretending to be innocent, gave way in Arthur to a feeling that was something close to guilt. Even if he disliked Bill, was this really the way that he ought to be behaving?

Arthur felt this guilt for some time. But as he sipped his drink (they were all having Bloody Marys), he suddenly began to recall a specific telephone call to Rebecca following that Christmas party where he had first seen the watch on Bill. He had wanted to make sure that Bill's story about her "passing it along" to him was accurate.

"Yes, I gave it to him," Rebecca had said matter-of-factly after Arthur asked.

"But I looked all over for that watch," Arthur said. "Why didn't you say something?"

"I had no idea you were looking for it," Rebecca replied.

"But I asked everyone."

"Well, I don't remember. Maybe I wasn't paying attention. Anyway, you were very upset those days, so who knows, maybe I did tell you. Anyway, he said your father wanted him to have it, and that sounds like it would be true. He was certainly your father's favorite relative. Not many uncles and nephews get along like that, or are so similar." Then, after a pause, "You know, I think that your father always felt bad that Bill didn't stay with the company."

As Arthur thought about this, as Bill sat beside him and told Alicia about yet another property deal he was working on, the guilt subsided somewhat. Or one thing at least began to become clear. He wanted the watch, and he intended to keep it, however foolish it all was. Now he just had to get it back to Manhattan. As he came to the end of his Bloody Mary, he decided that he'd leave early the next morning on the ferry. He'd make his way to Boston and jump on a train. He wanted to leave as soon as possible so he could put an end to what had become a very stressful situation.

8

Arthur went to his room early that evening, right after dinner, to study ferry and train schedules he'd found in the kitchen. He decided he'd leave the island at nine on a boat bound for Hyannis, take the shuttle to Boston, and be back in Manhattan via train by late afternoon. After folding the schedules back up, he went to the dresser and carefully took out the watch, thinking he'd like to look at it a bit more.

The watch really was extraordinary when examined up close. It had a stark Soviet look to it, although Arthur couldn't quite put his finger on what made it this way. It had a cold black face and muscular hour and minute hands that gave it something of an authoritarian appearance. And its boxy numbers and the thick stainless steel bracelet looked like something that both political zealots and corrupt bureaucrats would respond to. The object fascinated Arthur, and as he sat on his bed, fingering the bracelet and playing with the setting crowns, he remembered his father telling him about it. His father would take the watch off and let him play with it, instructing him how to wind it and how to set the alarm. The alarm interested Arthur the most as a boy, seeing that at that time alarms on watches were not very common. And it had an unusual mechanism, the hammer actually striking the back of the jewel case, making a thick clanging sound, rather than the sound of a bell. Arthur's father also loved to talk about the importance in Russia of an accurate time-piece with a good alarm because, "If you're late for an important meeting in Communist Russia, they chop off your hands."

Arthur knew that his father was joking about this, but he also knew that his father thought of the Soviet Union as a very dangerous place, where life was cheap and injustice common. Of course, everyone thought that back then, but Arthur's father had actually been there, had done business there, so his opinions seemed particularly compelling, especially where the chopping off of hands was concerned.

Just as Arthur was thinking about all this, he heard a knock at his door. The knock came from the outer door, though, beyond the en suite study, so he had time to put the watch back in his shirt drawer. Finally he yelled, "Yes, come in." Soon after, Patrick walked through the door.

"Hi, Dad," he said. "Just checking to make sure everything's all right with you."

"Everything's great," Arthur said. "I think I might go home for a bit. Tomorrow morning. At nine. There's a small party I want to go to on Monday night. I'll leave for about a week. Your mother will be up next weekend, so I won't be here anyway. Maybe I'll come up next Monday."

Patrick looked a little surprised. "You're sure everything is all right?" he said. "I'd love it if you stayed. At least till Mom showed up."

"Well, I think it's been a terrific week. I just kind of want to get back to the city for a few days. But I'll be back soon enough."

"Okay. So long as you come back." Patrick paused, scratched his arm for a moment, and then finally said, "You know, what I really wanted to say is that it's not true. What Bill said. I know how these businesses work. My fund has looked into buying smaller import and export operations, maybe for nostalgic reasons for me more than anything else, and I don't think they work anymore. You didn't do anything wrong with the company. People don't need that kind of middleman anymore. There was nothing you could have done."

Arthur could only stand there and look back at his son with a feeling of extreme embarrassment. What he felt at that moment was complete shame over the fact that his son felt any need at all to comfort him. Did he really seem so down on his luck?

Eventually Arthur said, "Well, who knows how these things happen? But I'm fine. I really am. I know it wasn't all my fault. But the important thing for you to know is that I'm really not bitter about the way things turned out. I'm not wallowing. I have plenty to do, and I'm looking forward. I really am. I'm a very fortunate man in many, many ways. That's really how I look at things."

Arthur felt a little better as he said all this. His role seemed to be back in proper alignment, he being the one who ought to be doing the comforting. And with a little bit of relief, Arthur began to restate his declarations that all was well when Patrick interrupted him. "I just can't believe Uncle Bill spoke to you like that. I don't know if I can forgive him. Especially since you've had such a rough couple of years here." Before Arthur could tell his son once more that everything was going very well in his life, his son added, "You know, Dad, I know I've said this before, but if you ever spot some kind of business opportunity, I hope you'll let me know. The fund is very broad at this point. Property. A restaurant chain. Stakes in sports teams. We've got money in a lot of different things. I'd love to work with you if you spot something good."

Again, Arthur could only stare back with a look of total shame, wondering what his son must think of him. "Really, Patrick, I'm fine," Arthur said at last, forcing a small laugh. "I have some friends who have some business ideas, so I don't need any help. One friend wants to open a restaurant and I think I might go in on it. But other than that, the fact is that I'm not so sure I have much interest in business these days. As for Bill, I don't think there's even anything to forgive. He just had too much wine, I think. I've said lots of things at dinner tables that I wish I hadn't. I've talked to him about the business plenty of times, and he understands that I didn't cause the collapse. Things are fine between me and him. There are no grudges, and there's certainly nothing for you to worry about. It takes a lot to hurt my feelings, or to provoke me to want to retaliate."

Just as Arthur finished speaking, however, thinking that maybe this talk really might have done something to placate his son's concerns, a horrible clanging noise startled him from behind. He wasn't sure what it was at first, but when he turned and looked at the dresser—the second highest drawer, where he had put his shirts—he realized that he must have accidentally set the alarm on the watch when he was handling it, and that it was now (very loudly) going off.

"What's that?" Patrick said, looking surprised.

"Nothing," Arthur replied. Arthur took a shallow breath and hoped it would stop. But it did not. In fact, it seemed to grow louder. And as Arthur looked back and forth from the dresser to Patrick, he realized that he was going to have to open the door and turn off the alarm. He could hardly stand there pretending it was nothing.

"Maybe it's my travel alarm," Arthur finally said, his voice noticeably anxious. Then he turned to the drawer to open it. His plan was to open it just a bit, reach his hand in, and snap the alarm without Patrick seeing anything. But the drawer slid out a little too quickly, and came out a bit too far, and Arthur pulled aside his shirt with just a bit of awkwardness. And just as he finally wrapped his fingers around the Signal to turn it off, Patrick turned his head and said, at a somewhat alarming volume, "Is that Uncle Bill's watch?"

"No," Arthur quickly said. But when he looked back at his son, he realized that he knew exactly what it was, and that lying when both of them knew very clearly the truth was too shameful a thing to bear. "Well. Yes. Yes, it is Uncle Bill's watch. I'm afraid I took it from him this afternoon."

Patrick looked stunned. In fact, he looked so stunned that Arthur had the instinct to slap him, almost to start him breathing again. But then Patrick began to laugh a bit. "You took it?" He said. "You just stole it from him?"

Arthur couldn't gauge what Patrick thought about it all, but he seemed more amused than anything else.

"I stole it back," Arthur said. "You see, it was my father's, as you know, and it was very important to me, and Bill had no right to take it, or to get it from your mother behind my back. I know it seems unreasonable, but I've been very upset about it—for some time—and after what he said to me last night, I guess I was feeling very upset, especially with all that's happened to me recently."

Only as Arthur finished this small speech did he realize that he had made a terrible mistake. If his son had started off thinking this was kind of funny, maybe a sort of unexpected prank, he now had a look that Arthur could read as nothing but sadness, now realizing that the theft of the watch wasn't a kind of comic stunt, but, instead, fairly firm evidence that his father really was profoundly wounded by what Bill had said, that he was hurting in his life in general, and that it was leading him to a sort of desperate behavior. Arthur wanted to get Patrick back to the first way of thinking—the amused Patrick—but his heart was now beating wildly, and, unexplainably (and much to Arthur's later shame), all he could say was, "You're not going to tell him, are you?"

Patrick paused, looking as though the question was completely astonishing. At last he said, "No. Never. I would never tell him. I would never tell Uncle Bill anything about this."

All Arthur could do was avert his eyes, and while looking down, and hoping to bring an end to his embarrassment, he said, "Perhaps we can talk about this later. I'm very tired at the moment, and this is probably a more complicated discussion than I'm capable of having right now."

Patrick hesitated, then said, "Okay. We can talk later."

Arthur looked up, trying not to appear teary, and said, "You know, Patrick, I really am okay. I might not seem that way sometimes. I'd agree that the past few years have been hard on me. And I don't always act in my own best interest. But it would break my heart if you were worried about me. There's nothing to worry about. I'm fine. I just need to get things a bit more in order, that's all." Arthur wanted to say more, but he felt like if he did then he would surely start crying. What wasn't clear was whether they would be tears from embarrassment or a kind of love for his son, whom he desperately wanted to shield from feeling any despair or anxiety on his behalf. "I'm fine," Arthur quickly said again, stepping away from the dresser. "I really am. But I think I should get to bed. I don't want to miss my ferry tomorrow morning."

Patrick looked at his father with a kind of desperation. Again, it was that strange look of pity that made Arthur feel so terrible. "I'm really fine," Arthur said again. "We'll talk about it later, if you like."

Finally Patrick forced a smile and said, "All right. We'll talk later. But Dad, if there's anything I can do for you, you know I'm here."

"Yes," Arthur said, his eyes now certainly filling with tears. "But I'm fine for now, and I'm very tired." Arthur now turned his back to Patrick. "So maybe we'll just say that I'll see you in the morning, if that's all right."

It took a second for Patrick to respond, but eventually he said, "All right," and in another instant, Arthur heard his son walking out through the study, and then shutting the door behind him.

9

That evening, word passed around that Arthur was leaving the next day, and the following morning everyone was up to say goodbye. It wasn't so unexpected that Arthur was taking the early ferry that morning—his plans had always been tentative and the family knew he'd be back. But they still had a large farewell breakfast and everyone happily ate pancakes and sausages together. Bill and his family would be leaving that evening anyway, so the house was going to quiet down one way or another. All the same, everyone said that they'd miss Arthur's company.

After breakfast, Arthur went up to his room to pack. Everything was basically in his suitcase, but he wanted one last chance to think about the matter of the watch. It was not too late to head down to the hedge by the pool and pretend to find it. It would be suspicious, especially to Bill, but what could he really accuse him of? In the end, though, Arthur rolled up the watch in a shirt and tucked it in his bag. After looking around to see if he had forgotten anything, he picked up the bag and headed downstairs. His ferry was due to leave in forty-five minutes, and one of the black SUVs would arrive soon to pick him up.

In the center hall there was another farewell for Arthur. Actually, people were already in beach clothes and headed out, so it was more of an accidental convergence than anything else. Arthur was glad to be in his city clothes again, and hoped he wasn't taking back too much sand to Manhattan. He looked out the window and noticed that the car was there, and, trying to make the exit as simple and quick as possible, said, "Well, we've already said our goodbyes, so, so long, and I'll see all of you soon."

Everyone said their own versions of the same thing, and Arthur turned to open the door. But just as he did so, just as Bill gave him one of his big inscrutable smiles, and just as the driver of the SUV stepped out to open the door of the waiting car, there was (once more, and much to Arthur's absolute shock) another loud clanging, now coming from deep within his bag. Arthur's mind instantly fixed on two facts: the first was that he was now surely caught; the second was that it was almost impossible to imagine just how stupid he must be to let this happen to him twice. Arthur quickly beat the side of his bag with his hand, hoping it might rattle the watch and force it to stop. But the clanging continued. Arthur stepped out the front door, thinking he could get to the car before anyone made sense of the noise, but as he did, Bill said in a voice that was anything but inscrutable, "Arthur, do you have my watch?"

Arthur continued slapping the side of his bag. "No. Your watch? No, I don't have your watch. That must be my travel alarm making that noise."

"You have my watch," Bill immediately replied.

"No I don't, and I'm not sure I appreciate what you're saying."

"Let me look in the bag."

Bill was now out on the front porch with Arthur, and the rest of the family crowded by the door, watching in astonishment. Arthur was still slapping the side of his suitcase, although it was a kind of futile physical tic more than any real action plan. He felt like an idiot, like he must look like a complete idiot, but he slapped anyway, blindly hoping for something to happen. And then, suddenly (and miraculously, in Arthur's opinion), the clanging stopped.

"There, it's off," Arthur said. "I've got to get that fixed. It's old. It belonged to my mother."

"Just let me look in your bag, Arthur."

Arthur was motionless, wondering what to do next. Everyone was staring at him, and Bill looked like he was about to attack. But the car was waiting, just down the stairs and across a short stone pathway. It would look bad if he kept moving. He'd look like a fool. But it was better than Bill finding the watch. "I'm sorry, Bill, but I'm afraid I'm late," Arthur said, "and I very much resent you demanding to search my bag. You may have your opinions about how I ruined the family company, and I may very well have to hear them, but I won't let you treat me like I'm some kind of criminal."

Bill still looked like he was going to pounce, so Arthur added, "Now, I've got to go," and then, just a little more rapidly than normal, Arthur walked down the stairs and across the pathway to the car. He wasn't sure if Bill was going to grab him by the back of the neck and throw him to the ground. But when Arthur turned to look, Bill was still standing on the porch, now looking at Arthur with what amounted to hatred and disgust. Still, a look of disgust was something of a relief, given the alternatives. And as Arthur stepped into the car, waving to the rest of the family in a slightly ridiculous gesture, he realized that he was safely on his way.

The drive to the ferry passed almost without any real thoughts. There was just a cascade of images in Arthur's brain as he tried to make sense of the scene he had just left and to piece together what everyone else must have thought. Did they think Arthur was a thief or that Bill was an aggressive blowhard? Searching the bags of cousins was hardly acceptable behavior, but if they identified the alarm the way Bill did, it would seem reasonable. Arthur wondered how many of them had heard the alarm before, or would remember it.

These thoughts continued on the ferry, although Arthur was beginning to process things a bit more clearly. He went to the concession counter and bought a carton of orange juice, and then sat in the forward compartment, where the view was best. Now the images were clearer. Or the images had transformed into concepts and questions, and Arthur was weighing the consequences of everything. What if Bill reported the lost watch to his insurance company? This was one of Arthur's first concerns. The watch was valuable. If Arthur didn't come forward, was he committing insurance fraud? It was worth at least ten thousand dollars. Possibly much, much more. Would they interview him? Would he have to lie? Arthur could hardly fail to recall his experiences at the police headquarters in Gap and just how difficult he found such situations. Along these lines, Arthur began to wonder if it was possible that Bill might even call the police. He could, and Arthur's apartment could be searched, and then what would happen? This thought was hard on Arthur. He felt like the scenario was unlikely. But as with most worries, it was the consequences, rather than the probability of the incident, that was so fixating. But then, why was it improbable? Bill wanted the watch back, it had sentimental import, and was worth a lot of money, and Bill knew with some certainty that Arthur had it.

As Arthur thought about the police unexpectedly showing up one day, and being caught red-handed, and the story circulating through the family—and to Rebecca, and maybe even to some kind of tabloid gossip column about deranged Upper East Siders—he found himself taking the watch out of his bag, and then walking to the side of the boat. He didn't think he'd throw it over. But he might. He wasn't entirely sure. And as he finally reached the side, and leaned over, it did give him some comfort at that moment, that he could put this behind him once and for all.

It was strange. Arthur had certainly embarrassed himself more than once in recent years. But the embarrassing incidents always had a fortuitous nature to them—something just a little beyond his control. He'd never really stood a chance with his company. It was not his fault that the chimney at Maidenhead wasn't clean (although it was clearly wrong to bring an outsider there), and when he lied to the French police, he was doing it for a friend, as questionable a friend as Prentice turned out to be. But this incident was somehow different. He was clearly the cause of this particular problem. Or he had acted with much more agency, at least. He had taken the watch. He had looked on as the rest of the family searched for it, without saying anything. And he had lied about it, even when the alarm was going off in his bag in front of Bill. But what Arthur couldn't quite figure out was whether or not, in the last day, he had behaved with the pettiness of a child or whether this was the kind of thing he should have been doing with his life all along. Would Bill have agonized over all this? If the roles were reversed, Bill would have told Arthur to take the watch off the first time he saw it at the Christmas party. He would have asserted himself immediately, and without second-guessing himself. Why shouldn't Arthur? Rebecca had no right to "pass it along." Bill had no right to have it without Arthur's permission, no matter what the final legal determination might be. So why shouldn't he take it back? It was his. That was clear. It belonged to him.

In the end, Arthur put the watch back in his pocket. He didn't know quite what would happen, but he decided he'd rather ride out the consequences than throw the watch into the ocean. He thought about Patrick and the night before, and how ashamed he had felt when his son saw the watch. Arthur decided that perhaps he did need to be a bit stronger, take back the things that belonged to him and not be such a weakling all the time. If the cops came, he'd tell them the truth. The watch was his and Bill had no right to have it in the first place. Maybe he'd go to the police himself. Maybe that was the kind of aggression he ought to be presenting.

But as Arthur turned and headed back to his seat, he had another idea. Perhaps it would be more funny, more original, to simply take the watch out the next time his sons were in town and show it to them while laughing and telling the story of how he stole it right out from under Bill's nose in Nantucket. It was an amusing story, after all, if you really thought about it. And maybe his own sons would inherit the watch and tell their children and grandchildren about their crafty grandfather and the blustery Uncle Bill and how Arthur had turned the tables on him in a moment of great cunning. As Arthur sat down and took a sip of the remaining orange juice, he decided that this was definitely how he'd proceed, and should he run into trouble, he'd deal with it when it arose and hope that things turned out for the best. Adopting that sort outlook, after all, was what it seemed he needed to do with his life, and this seemed as good a place as any to begin.

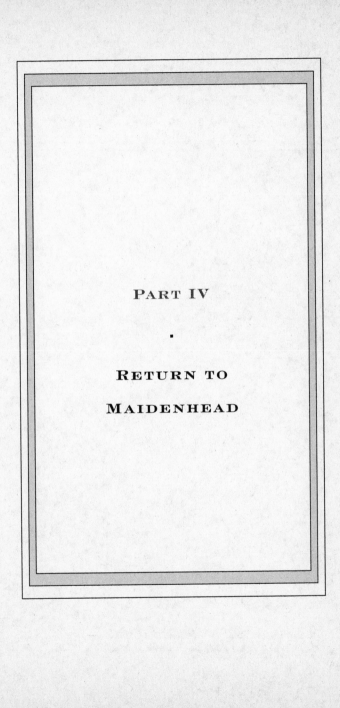

PART IV

·

RETURN TO

MAIDENHEAD

1

Arthur was, of course, no longer privy to the decisions of the Hanover Street Fly Casters, and although he was still on fair terms with some of its members, the subject of the club rarely came up when he bumped into them at various social occasions. All the same, by the last day of August (now not long after returning from Nantucket) Arthur had gotten wind from several sources that plans to rebuild the lodge had stalled somewhat. He heard numerous explanations, most of which hinged on fairly lofty things like locating the best architects, perplexing ecological concerns—the Fly Casters were, after all, great conservationists—and the necessity of finding exactly the right materials to build with. "We can hardly use just anything," Arthur overheard Charlie Feltham say at a reception at the Geographers Club. "As a matter of fact," he continued more quietly, "and I shouldn't say this because there are other interested parties, we're thinking of using wood from a soon-to-be-sold replica of the *Cutty Sark* that's been touring the North Atlantic. Now, that would be something. Can you imagine? Teak aged in arctic waters!"

But Arthur also heard other explanations of the delays and finally gathered that the real problem was, in fact, money. Specifically, there was something of a gap between what members wanted and what they could afford. Maidenhead had been grossly underinsured—the fault of a now-deceased surgeon "who had no business dealing with that kind of thing in the first place." The subsequent problem (and also the more troubling one) was that most of the members were having difficulty themselves coming up with the kind of capital to replace what they lacked from insurance, especially since everyone had such high expectations for the new lodge.

Of course, by anyone's estimation these were all wealthy men, and each of them hardworking and successful—not one was simply living off family money. But none were the captains of industry that their great-grandfathers had been, and after several generations (and with numerous second and third cousins to share in the inheritances) no one quite had the resources their forebears once did. They were all millionaires, to be sure. But a man whose net worth is, say, eight million dollars can rarely chip in four or five hundred thousand when the money can never be recovered, will provide no financial return, and will be spent on what, in essence, is a house he wouldn't use more than several weekends each year. Needless to say, in the minds of the Fly Casters, Maidenhead Grange was more than just a weekend house. It was a singular event in the history of America. Still, most of their assets were tied up in their homes, and they had children to educate, and summerhouses to keep up, and wives who had other (better) ideas for the money.

Basically, what the Fly Casters lacked was the sort of member who was worth hundreds of millions of dollars, who could sink four or five million dollars into a Newport-sized fishing lodge (complete with brand-name architecture and arctic-aged teak paneling) without noticing the hit. Much to the annoyance of the membership, not one of them had amassed that kind of capital.

It was, however, true that Patrick Camden had that sort of money, and news of the Fly Casters' troubles spread faster than anyone might have thought. And it was, with some surprise that Arthur found himself discussing the matter with his son on the telephone one evening at the very beginning of September, just as Patrick and his family were reacclimating to Colorado. After discussing the children, and affairs in Steamboat, and David's employment prospects, Patrick said, with just a bit of a laugh, "I hear the Hanover Street gang can't raise the money to rebuild Maidenhead." There was something of an awkward pause after Patrick said this. After all, it was easy enough to put the blame for all this trouble squarely on Arthur. But Patrick quickly followed the pause by saying, "I guess I've been thinking about it all, Dad. I've always felt bad about losing our membership there. Or yours, which would have become mine. My family built that place too, and that chimney should have been swept. Any fire in the fireplace would have burned the place down. It wasn't your fault. It was stupid bad luck. Anyway, it's a ridiculous rule, in my opinion— no outsiders. My god, a weekday night in winter and you're not allowed to show someone around? No one was there. There was no chance of interfering with anyone. The way it all played out really pisses me off."

Arthur was a little surprised at Patrick's increasingly heated words, and he quickly did what he could to calm him down. "It's all right, Patrick," he said. "I appreciate your concern, and what you're saying, but I knew the rules. Another member was kicked out for the same reason in the 1950s. Anyway, perhaps I should have checked things out a bit more—made sure that it was safe to use the fireplace. And I wasn't exactly forthcoming about everything I should have been."

"I think you deserved a pass," Patrick abruptly replied, "and the truth is that this isn't just me coming to your defense. It's also selfish. I wish you had gotten a pass for my sake. I'd like to go there myself one day. I guess I've been thinking about it a lot."

There was another pause. Arthur then heard a bit of a sigh on the end of the line, and assumed Patrick had something else to say. But the pause continued, and Arthur quickly decided now might be a good time to change the subject, since this one was always difficult for him. However, just as he was about to ask Patrick what he thought the ski season would be like that year, Patrick continued. "I really have been thinking about this a lot," he said again, "and I have a bit of a proposal. It's a proposal for me as well as you, so I hope you'll take it the right way. I'm thinking that I might propose that I help rebuild Maidenhead—or entirely rebuild it, as the case will probably be. I've got the money, and this is pretty important to me. I'd make the proposal depend on you being reinstated, and you could keep your membership as long as you liked. When you were ready to give it up, or even if you kept it till you died, it would pass to me."

Arthur paused for a second, barely able to work through the implications of all this. Finally, he said, "I'm afraid my days with the Fly Casters are over. I can't imagine that all that would be a good idea. Even if you put up the money, they won't let me back in. They can't. It would be against the rules. But maybe you could propose yourself as a member, on the basis of your family's previous membership and what you'd be willing to contribute."

"That's not the way I'd want to do it," Patrick replied. "It would have to go to you first. And my bet is that they might rethink the rules some. I don't think they'll have much of a choice, if they want to build anything like what they're talking about, that is. They don't have too many options."

Arthur started to contradict Patrick again, but halted just as quickly and in an instant tried to calculate what all this meant. It would mean undoing the damage he had caused. It would mean restoring the Camdens to what had been a very important club to Arthur and his father and grandfather. It would mean that Patrick would inherit the membership, which seemed to be important to him. Furthermore, it might somehow restore to Arthur the sort of deeper friendships he felt he was missing. He'd love to be able to go up to the club again to fish and hang around with people like Ken Fielder and Charlie Feltham. All the same, Arthur told Patrick once more that the whole idea was impossible. "They won't reinstate my membership," he said. "I know they won't. There's no point in even considering it."

"But if they did? How would you feel?"

"I don't know. Maybe more important, I don't know if I like you spending all that money. I know you can easily afford it, Patrick, so I'm confident it won't be coming out of Sarah and Katie's pocket. But still, I just don't know if it's such a good idea."

"But if I told you that it was important to me? That it was something I really want. For myself. You'd think about it?"

Arthur hesitated. "Well, I'd think about it," he said at last. "But I can't say that I think it's such a good idea, or that it will work."

"Well, let me work on how to pitch it to the members, and you think it over. We can talk about it later."

"Well, all right," Arthur said. "I'll think it over."

2

And Arthur did think it over. For the rest of that evening, and for the following day, he turned the proposal over and over in his mind. But it was such a baffling idea that he could hardly evaluate it in any kind of sophisticated way. The financial implications alone were too much for Arthur to quite understand, although over the past several years he had gotten used to the idea that his son brought in the kind of money that was far beyond anything he had ever imagined making.

The fact was, however, that Arthur had other pressing matters. After all, it was just after Labor Day and Arthur had promised himself that that fall he would arrange dinners, attend plays and musical events, and be present at every social function he was invited to. He would not go back to wallowing in self-pity. He was not going to flee the country to hide out in foreign lands. Most of all, he was not going to avoid places where he might run into Rebecca. He had to learn to face her and get on with things, otherwise there was no way he would ever rise out of the malaise that had been gripping him.

With this logic in mind, Arthur agreed to attend a charity ball for the Central Park Preservation Council, which the organization was holding on the Friday evening following Labor Day weekend at Tavern on the Green. Arthur had bought seats just after returning from Nantucket, and even arranged a sort of date. He was going with a woman named Rosalie Wilson, whom he had known since he was fifteen. There was no romantic aspect to their relationship, however, as Arthur understood. She had made this clear one night several months earlier when she said, seemingly unprompted by anything, "Isn't it wonderful that there's no sexual tension between us? It's often so hard to be friends with a man. But you're like one of my girlfriends, Arthur. You're kind of like a woman to me. And I couldn't be happier about that." Arthur said that he was very glad about this too, although needless to say he would have preferred it if Rosalie expressed her feelings a bit differently. He did also feel some disappointment. He wasn't sure why. He hadn't really felt any attraction himself, but it seemed to sting a bit that there wasn't at least a little sexual tension—or, worse, that there was sexual tension of the unpleasant kind, and that Rosalie had decided to put an end to it. But they were friends, and they liked spending time together, and when he suggested the Central Park event to Rosalie, she happily agreed.

On the evening of the benefit, however, now a few days after Patrick had first broached the topic of rebuilding Maidenhead, Arthur began to feel very tense. It was strange: he was always so full of enthusiasm and extroversion on the nights he sat home alone in his apartment, but now that he was going out (on a beautiful, breezy September night) he fantasized about staying in his apartment to eat Chinese food and watch the Yankees. This was in part because of his general social timidity, but he was also specifically apprehensive about this event because it was one that Rebecca was likely to attend. He had even gone to this same benefit with her in years past and they always had a wonderful time. They had lots of friends who attended, they loved the park at that time of year, and the truth was that they both had a sort of embarrassing weakness for Tavern on the Green. All the same, Arthur bought the tickets because he specifically wanted to confront his demons, as it were, and one of the first events of the fall season seemed to be the perfect place to start.

And when Rosalie and Arthur arrived at Tavern on the Green, Arthur found that despite his apprehensions, he felt just a bit of excitement as well. "I'm so happy we're doing this," Rosalie said. "You'll be a good wingman for me this fall, if you'll pardon my son's expression."

"Exactly what I was thinking about you," Arthur replied. As he said this, he had a quite pleasing image of a full social calendar with a steady date who didn't make him feel the sort of romantic pressure that other dates might. Of course, this was only temporary. In his new vision of his double-fisted bacchanalian social persona, Arthur could only conclude that he would be going on romantic dates very soon. But it was at least a pleasant fact that he had a standby with whom he could attend events like this.

And when Arthur finally saw Rebecca—before dinner began but after he had safely made it to the bar and ordered a whiskey— he found he was able to handle his feelings of loss with just a little equanimity. She was dressed in a black embroidered gown, and had her hair beautifully highlighted and done up in a kind of elegant ponytail, and he could hardly fail to notice how attractive she was. The truth was that he did feel a sort of pain in his stomach when he thought that he was going to have to spend the evening in the same place as her. But it was at least promising that he didn't run out of the room. Instead, he strode across the entryway, came up behind her, and said, "Hello, Rebecca."

Rebecca turned abruptly and then replied (a bit nervously), "Hello, Arthur." Arthur couldn't help but notice her apprehension, so he quickly added, "I just came over to say hi."

Rebecca still appeared flustered, but then she looked away and exhaled and said, "I'm sorry. I'm just a bit on edge. I'm glad you came over to see me. It's very good to see you." She leaned forward to kiss Arthur on the cheek, then said, "Can we catch up in a bit? I've got to run just now."

"Of course," Arthur said. This wasn't going very well, but Arthur was more confused than anything else. Still, she hadn't insulted him and he hadn't burst into tears, so to a certain extent the evening was already an astonishing success.

Arthur never entirely relaxed for the rest of the evening, but as dinner passed and the dancing went on, he could not help but feel that the fall social season might be somewhat tolerable. Toward the end of the night, however, Arthur did run into some trouble. He left the dance floor—where he had been fox-trotting with a second cousin he hadn't seen for several years—and was crossing the entry hall to find the men's room when he saw Rebecca and Stephen standing off to one side, talking in a very heated way.

"Why are you being like this?" he heard Rebecca repeat several times, now sounding near tears. Arthur could not quite hear Stephen's response—it was deep and hushed and spoken with his mouth toward the wall. But it seemed from the gruff intonations that he was losing his patience. Needless to say, Arthur wanted to hear more, but he was now at the hallway leading to the bathrooms, and couldn't stop without looking like he was eavesdropping. Given who he was trying to listen to, he couldn't afford for that to happen.

Arthur visited the lavatory as quickly as he could before walking swiftly back to the main entrance, and when he arrived he hoped he might hear more. But as he glanced around, he only managed to see

Rebecca as she walked out the door, her wrap now tightly around her shoulders and Stephen walking quickly after her. He still wasn't able to tell what exactly the dynamic was between the two, and he couldn't help but want to know more. He even took a somewhat awkward step toward the doors, hoping for more information. Just as he did, Rebecca turned toward Stephen and yelled, now apparently near tears, "How can you be like this? How can you do this to me?"

Stephen halted and then glanced back toward the door, as did Rebecca, nervous that someone might be watching. And, in fact, there was someone watching. It was Arthur, who was very startled and very embarrassed that he had been spotted. In an instant, he considered smiling and waving, but he thought better of this, and instead averted his eyes and turned back to the dance floor. It wasn't his fault he'd walked by, he told himself, almost muttering this aloud as he entered the dimly lit room, although he was sure they would conclude that he was somehow spying. The whole thing was very awkward, but it was true that Arthur's feelings of embarrassment were overshadowed at this point by quite a bit of curiosity.

There was also, at first, a kind of exhilaration. As Arthur got home later that night, he felt just a bit of satisfaction that Rebecca's life was somehow troubled—that life after Arthur was not all one big celebration. He had no idea why Rebecca was yelling, but (he was ashamed to admit to himself) seeing her in a bit of distress did soothe him some.

All the same, as he stood in front of his dresser mirror, placing his studs and cuff links in the small silver box where he kept such things, his mind started turning in another direction, and he suddenly began to feel an odd kind of loneliness, or, more particularly, an overwhelming lack of intimacy because there was absolutely no one in his life who might do something like yell at him at Tavern on the Green. That is, his life affected no one to the point that they would even have much of a reason to lose their temper with him, for whatever reason. Even if someone like, say, his cousin Bill yelled at him, it was out of some ancient dislike or an indictment of his character, not because Arthur's behavior had some kind of immediate impact and needed to be changed. It was true that Rebecca had yelled at Arthur an inordinate amount—although never near tears—and he was very glad that was gone from his life. Nevertheless, it might be nice if something he could do in the world might affect a companion so deeply. Or even not so deeply. It would even be a relief if he had someone to reprimand him for a minor faux pas, or one too many helpings of roast beef, or even discarded toenail clippings in the bedroom. If Arthur did nothing but sit naked in his living room all day drinking vodka and eating potato chips (perhaps while scattering his toenail clippings across the floor), absolutely no one in the world would object.

It was very disconcerting. Despite it all, though, Arthur still tried to be optimistic. He had a busy fall ahead of him, and it was this that Arthur tried to think about as he fell asleep that night. This loneliness and lack of intimacy surely couldn't last for long if he really made an effort to change things, to make things different for himself.

3

The next social event for Arthur was (to his great excitement) a party at Ken Fielder's apartment. Arthur had not seen Ken for over a month, and he was looking forward to catching up. But the party was going to be reasonably large, about sixty people, and Ken said on the phone with a certain amount of forcefulness, "My god, Arthur, you're not going to waste your time 'catching up' with me. You're going to be talking to women. If you want to catch up with me, let's have breakfast sometime. My wife met lots of single women this summer, and she's on a mission to nab one for you. 'God help you,' is what I say, but she's a determined woman and there really are a lot of newly available women our age running around looking for a new pal."

"Well, if your wife can face disasters like the ones last year, I suppose I can be brave too," Arthur said.

"My wife loves you, Arthur. If things don't work out between you and a woman, it's the woman she blames. You can't ask for a better ally than Lauren."

The truth was that Arthur actually felt this. It really was all very exciting. Arthur was skeptical about the whole thing, and more resigned to failure than hopeful for success. But he really liked Ken and Lauren a great deal, and he liked being included in their plans, and after he got off the phone with Ken that night, he felt quite fortunate. Ken and Lauren had real affection for him—good-humored affection that seemed cheerfully to acknowledge Arthur's shortcomings and even take pleasure in them.

At any rate, on the night of the party, Arthur arrived at nine-thirty. He had forced himself to go to a movie earlier in the evening because he was afraid of showing up too early, a habit he tended to suffer from. When he finally stepped through the door, the party was well under way. A hired coat-check person took his jacket, a caterer handed him a glass of champagne, and soon Lauren was leading him around the main reception rooms introducing him to people.

Arthur already knew a few of the guests who were there. There were even one or two women he had taken on dates. They were all gracious and seemed not unexcited to see him, although it was clear that they still didn't view him as any kind of sexual suitor. There were also a few other people he knew from other places, some of whom he hadn't seen since Rebecca left him.

Of particular interest to Arthur was a couple with the last name of Martin. They had been friends of Arthur and Rebecca's for years, although they seemed to be more Rebecca's friends, especially now, since the divorce had gone through. Of course, that made sense, given that Arthur had, in essence, gone into social hiding, afraid to bump into Rebecca at one place or another, whereas Rebecca had embraced the social world as though she had been locked in solitary confinement for thirty years. But the Martins were friendly, kind people. Arthur couldn't deny that. He was happy to see them, and they seemed pleased to see him. "Arthur!" they both called out when he made his way to their side of the room, and soon he was catching them up on what he had been doing for the past year.

It was a fact that Chrissy Martin also liked to drink quite a bit, and later on, after Arthur had been at the party for about an hour, she approached him again and trapped him against the piano to tell him all sorts of information that, frankly, he would rather not have heard. Rebecca was a slut, apparently. "Or not a slut," Chrissy corrected herself quickly, "because that sounds bad. But she hasn't wasted any time catching up on things, if you know what I mean. But my god, who wouldn't? There's a lot left to do. We're not too young, you know. Especially these days. We're younger than our parents ever were at this point." Then she added, "And who knows how things will work out with Stephen? I mean, it's hardly a match made in heaven. They're not two peas in a pod. But these things always take some negotiation, and god knows Rebecca is a difficult woman. But look at me telling you this. I mean, you know better than anyone. She can be very demanding. But maybe she's simply the type to know what she wants. If she can't get it, she's certainly proved herself to be strong enough to move on. That's what's important in life. Knowing how to move on."

As Chrissy said "move on" for a second time, Arthur couldn't help but think he spotted a bit of regret in her eyes for saying all this, as though she knew she was taking things a little too far. But then she added (very unexpectedly), "But I hear she slept with absolutely everyone, and during your separation, no less. Most people have the sense to wait till the final paperwork is done. But from day one it was like she was on Spring Break."

Arthur determined that it was certainly time to excuse himself now and find the bathroom—perhaps to stand in the dark and weep. But just then, Gresham Martin, Chrissy's husband, arrived and said, smiling at Arthur, "All right, Chrissy. Time to go. Enough bothering poor Arthur."

She turned, tightened her lips, and squinted at her husband. But after a moment, she finally smiled and said, "Oh, all right. I'm so terribly, terribly bored right now, so what do I care?"

Arthur was just trying to evaluate the implications of Chrissy's statement about being "terribly bored" when he turned to his left and saw a woman staring straight at him and beaming. He recognized her immediately. Or he immediately understood that he knew her, but since the meeting was so unexpected it took another split second to piece everything together. Before he could open his mouth to say hello, however, she said, "Arthur! It's me, Rixa. I helped you get kicked out of your club. Surely you haven't forgotten me."

"No, no," Arthur quickly said, stepping forward, smiling, and kissing her cheek. "I haven't forgotten. How could I forget the woman who brought about my disgrace?"

"I'm so sorry," Rixa said, laughing and still smiling broadly.

"Well, people were quite impressed with me, even if I did get kicked out. I've always been known as a rebel, though, so most people expected it."

Rixa continued to smile and look at Arthur, sizing him up somehow. Arthur was about to ask her how she had been all this time—he knew she had been in Maine and Martinique but didn't know much more than that. But before he could speak, Rixa leaned toward him and said, "I have to leave now. I'm afraid I'm with someone horrible. But I'm back in town for a few weeks, so maybe you'd like to ask me to dinner? I'm free Saturday night."

Arthur tried to remember if he had anything to do that Saturday night, but after an instant he realized that if he did have something, he surely ought to cancel it. "Of course. Saturday night. Let's go to dinner."

"Okay, then." Just as she said this, a large square-jawed man whom Arthur had never seen before approached.

"We should get going," he said to Rixa. "They'll be expecting us."

"Yes, all right," she said. Then she smiled at Arthur and said, "Well, it was good to see you."

"Yes, good to see you too," Arthur replied, just a bit confused. But when she and the square-jawed man turned to leave, she glanced back at Arthur and mouthed the words "Call me," and then turned away again, leaving Arthur alone with his sudden and unexpected feelings of happiness and good fortune.

4

Arthur had written down Rixa's number in his telephone book around a year ago, and when he called the next day she answered after the first ring. He tried to act relaxed. After a quick hello, he launched into a story about getting locked out of his apartment that morning. "I had to find the doorman in my bathrobe," he said, "although it wasn't the first time. Still, it was pretty embarrassing."

He had told the story because he thought there was something happy and charming about it, but as he came to the end, he decided that he should have stuck to subjects closer to the weather. The story was not quite as flattering as he had first thought. All the same, Rixa laughed, and soon they were making plans for dinner. It was Friday afternoon at this point, and since it was a relatively warm September, they decided they should try to eat outside. Arthur suggested a place called Le Safran, which had a back garden, and after agreeing to meet at eight the following evening, they said goodbye and hung up.

For the rest of the day and night, Arthur thought about the date, and even allowed himself to be happy about it, despite his hard conviction that being happy about a date was a certain way to jinx it. The next day he even went to Barneys to buy a new tie. He wanted to look fashionable, after all, although not too fashionable. He was feeling as though his wardrobe was a bit out of date, however, and this was exactly what he said to a salesperson named Samantha, who picked out three ties for him, and convinced him to buy a new sports coat as well. It all cost him more than he wanted to spend—Arthur had always felt it was important not to be too concerned with the latest clothing. But he was in such a good mood, and the day held such promise, and before long he was in the cab back home trying to figure out which of the ties to wear.

When the evening finally arrived, Arthur decided on a light blue tie with a repeating pattern of a small white flower. "It's appealing and disarming," Samantha had told him, although as he tied it around his neck, the disarming quality seemed mostly unnecessary since he was simply not a very threatening man.

After putting on his new sports coat, and giving his shoes a quick polish, Arthur was finally ready, now a full hour before he was due to leave. They had reservations at eight, and at seven Arthur poured himself a scotch diluted with plenty of water and turned on the television to pass a very slow forty-five minutes before he could justify heading to the restaurant.

But the time passed, and soon Arthur was stepping through the front door of Le Safran at exactly 7:59. He quickly looked about for Rixa, who was not there yet, then went to the bar and ordered another drink. Rixa arrived five minutes later, and before long the two were sitting at a quiet table in Le Safran's unusually peaceful back garden.

And everything went as Arthur hoped it would. In fact, the date was so pleasant that Arthur hardly recognized it as a date. He had prepared several funny stories and developed a number of talking points to fill any lulls in the conversation. But as they looked over the menus, they started talking about their children, and the pleasures of being a grandparent, and as the dinner came and they ate, he found that his talking points (regarding New York City politics, global warming, travel in East Asia, etc.) were not necessary at all. Global warming did come up, but only in reference to the low price of lobster in Maine, and Arthur didn't get to deliver his prepared remarks on the subject, specifically that the world's leaders better wake up before it was too late. Before Arthur knew it, he found himself looking over the dessert menu and considering whether he could manage to eat anything else, although he was having such fun that it seemed he could consume an entire chocolate cake.

"I think I'll have to have the raspberry tart," Rixa said to the waiter with some authority. "Maybe we can share it, Arthur? Let's have a cognac too, since it's a special occasion."

Arthur readily agreed, although he wasn't quite sure what she meant by "a special occasion." But the comment passed, and the waiter ran off to the kitchen, and soon they were discussing how much Rixa loved New York, now that she was gone for ten months out of the year. "It's my favorite place in the world," she said, "and it's my home. But I'm not sure how happy it makes me. I don't know if that makes sense. But I always feel so exhausted after a few weeks. Too much to think about."

Arthur said that he understood her perfectly, then asked if she preferred Maine or Martinique, the two other places where she had homes. "Well, I like them both," she said. "I know it all sounds very fancy, and I suppose it is by most standards. But in Maine I have a little apartment above an antiques store in Bar Harbor, and in Martinique I live in what most people would call a shack, although I love them both. I mean, I'm very fortunate as world standards go, and I don't mean to downplay my good luck. But I'm definitely not living on oceanfront property in East Hampton. My husband liked that kind of thing. He was a good guy. Not affected, really. But he liked expensive things. When he died, though, I kind of lost my taste for them. Or I lost my taste for a lot of the things we used to share together, and when I struck out on my own, I definitely wasn't drawn to the things he would have wanted."

As Rixa said this, Arthur determined that this was the most she had ever said about her dead husband, and he wondered what the proper etiquette was when it came to questioning her further on the subject. Rixa was remarkably low-key, so it didn't seem like any kind of question would bother her, and if it did, she'd certainly say so. But just as Arthur was mulling all this over, another thought came to mind, which was, very specifically, that Rixa was easily the most attractive woman he'd been out with since Rebecca left him. She looked exactly like a very happy and athletic model he saw on a jar of vitamins he'd purchased just a few days earlier, almost to the point that he asked if it was her. It was just all very puzzling because Arthur couldn't figure out what exactly she saw in him. A bitter, far less attractive woman than Rixa—one that Arthur would have probably married, had she shown any interest—would have called it a night hours ago. She probably would have left him at the bar. But Rixa seemed to like him, for some reason. Or they got along well. Arthur didn't think he was imagining that. And just as Arthur was wondering if he hadn't somehow been underestimating his own attractiveness all these years, Rixa said, "I don't know why I like you so well. It's just hitting me now, I guess, because, oddly, this is only our second date, if you include the one where you burned down your club. I hate to say this because of the obvious bizarre implications, but you remind me a little of my father and my brothers. Only on a superficial level, maybe, because I actually don't know you all that well, when you think about it. But my father was a very gentle man. He was a very gentle, kind man. Almost to the point of being unable to defend himself. Same with my brothers. I think it's an admirable quality, though. A total lack of aggression. I mean, maybe I'm all wrong about you. Maybe you're a seething furnace of anger. But it doesn't seem like that. Not to me, anyway." She paused, then quickly added, "But I mean I'm attracted to you. Don't get me wrong. I'm not giving you a 'you're like a brother' speech. I used that the other night. With the good-looking guy I was with at the Fielders' party. I wasn't attracted to him, for some reason. But let's face it, Arthur, if you two got into a fight—over my affections, for instance—you wouldn't do so well, would you? I'm pretty sure he'd win."

Arthur wanted to contradict her, feeling some sort of obligation to explain that fighting skills were sometimes very hard to assess and that you never really knew what a smaller man was capable of. But he thought better of it, mostly because if he was the example to prove this lesson, he'd hardly be making a compelling case. "I suppose you're right about that," he finally said. "But I wonder if I've ever really thought of myself as gentle." He paused, then added, in a moment of semi-serious introspection, "Needy, maybe. Insecure. Desperate to be liked. That kind of thing. But not gentle." Arthur looked up and then suddenly became very nervous. "I'm just kidding, of course," he said. "That was just a joke. None of that is really true."

Rixa cocked her head, then said, "I really think you are desperate to be liked, Arthur. I actually think that's really true. But don't worry, because I'm not bothered by it. Maybe I even like it. But I do think you're desperate to be liked. I think that's a fact."

Arthur wasn't sure what to say and sat silently for a moment, thinking of something to add. But in the next instant, the cognacs came and they were soon chatting about their respective travels in

Europe, and the difficulty of making pie crust, and numerous other small things that struck Arthur as very insignificant but also very pleasurable, given what was passing between them.

As dinner came to an end, and they left the restaurant, and then stepped out onto Seventy-seventh Street, Arthur was thinking that he could hardly have had a better time. But this was always the tricky part. It wasn't that he had any expectations or desires that needed to be satisfied, but rather that he was at a complete loss when it came to protocol and expected behavior. Doing the proper thing was really all he wanted. He had kissed her before, though—the night he burned down Maidenhead. It might seem odd if he didn't kiss her again. Perhaps he should take her back to his apartment. Or maybe they should check into a room at the Mark. Maybe that was what he was supposed to suggest. It was just all such a complete mystery. But, fortunately for Arthur, and as he may well have expected, Rixa spoke first. "Listen, Arthur, my sister's in town visiting, otherwise I'd invite you home. I'd suggest we go to your place, but I think you might have a heart attack, and maybe that wouldn't be a good idea anyway, since I really do like you. So I have a proposal, if you don't think I'm being too forward. I'm going up to Maine next weekend. For a couple of weeks. I'm shutting down the place before I head south. I was wondering if you'd want to come up to visit me. Maybe in three weeks? I have quite a lot to do between now and then, otherwise it would be sooner. And I've got a spare bedroom, so you could have all the privacy you'd need, if you wanted it. The crowds have died down and I think this is the time when Mount Desert Island is most beautiful. You could leave on a Thursday, since you don't appear to have a job these days, and you could head back on the following Tuesday, if you'd like."

Arthur lowered his head, trying to remember if he had any previous commitments. But once again, just as it had been when Rixa had suggested that he ask her to dinner, he quickly determined that any previous plans should be immediately changed, and that there was no reason in the world not to go. "I'd love to," Arthur said. "I haven't been to Bar Harbor in years. That sounds wonderful."

As he said this, Rixa stepped toward the street and held up her hand. A taxi was passing, and it came to a swift halt beside them. Rixa turned, then kissed Arthur on the cheek. "Great," she said, smiling. "I'll call you." Then, as Arthur watched, she opened the cab door and got in.

5

Three weeks was a long time to wait, but Arthur thought he could manage, and the next week brought its own distractions, beginning with Patrick calling to announce that he was flying to New York to meet with the Fly Casters about his proposal to rebuild Maidenhead.

"It's just the opening salvo," Patrick told his father on the phone. "But they seemed pretty interested and agreed to meet, so I'm already ahead of the game."

"I'm astonished," Arthur replied. "Did you tell them that return of my membership was part of the package?"

"Not yet. I want them to see what they're getting first. Make it harder for them to say no."

"Patrick, I'd really hate to think that this is all being done for my sake. I'm fine, you know. I'm very happy right now. I don't need you to do this for me."

"I know, Dad. But it's for me too. Or for the family."

Arthur considered this for a moment. It still didn't quite add up, and he couldn't help but feel like this was another offer on Patrick's part to bail him out of something. But he was in no position to refuse. Patrick did also have his own stake in the matter. Anyway, Arthur couldn't deny that he vaguely wanted this thing that Patrick was proposing, although he felt very ashamed of this desire.

Patrick arrived two days later, and met his father at their apartment in time for dinner Wednesday night. Patrick's room had long since been converted into a guest bedroom—a transition Rebecca had begun to make when Patrick was still in prep school—but Patrick was happy to have the room all the same, and said as much when he arrived. "It's funny how much this feels like home, given all the times Mom redecorated."

"I know," Arthur said. "Although I wonder if I'm getting tired of the place sometimes."

"Maybe you are," Patrick said. "You could always move. Maybe you'd like someplace new."

"Maybe," Arthur said, although the idea of moving anywhere seemed completely out of the question.

They went to dinner at a small Italian restaurant off Lexington that they had been going to for years, and then went to sleep right afterward. Patrick's first meeting was early in the morning—a game of squash at the University Club followed by breakfast—and he wanted to be well rested. "It's important that I win, I think," he told his father. "And it's been a while. There aren't many squash courts in Colorado."

The meeting was with a man named John Mason, a Fly Caster whom Arthur never really felt he got along with. They were never particularly close, at any rate, Mason being a kind of toughened and silent man. But Mason was smart, and he was a good administrator, and he had taken the helm of the rebuilding plans soon after Maidenhead burned down. He was the man Patrick had to impress, and it was Mason who knew in the clearest terms what the Hanover Street men wanted to see built on the land.

Patrick was out of the house before Arthur awoke, and didn't return until lunchtime, looking flushed but amused. "Well, I heard about the plans," Patrick told Arthur as he met him in the kitchen. "Basically it's what we thought, what we've been hearing about. Lots of hardwood paneling, extravagant moldings, elaborate parquet, that kind of thing. But they want the facade to look like the old Maidenhead. Or as close as possible and as makes sense. Mason kept stressing that fact. They're 'rebuilding,' not 'starting over.'"

"Well, I guess that's best," Arthur said, now feeling slightly wistful. "You can't do better than the old Maidenhead Grange. It was a beautiful building."

"Yes, it was," Patrick said. "But listen, they've set up another meeting for me this afternoon. I think you should come. None of the Hanover Street people will be there. It's with some kind of fish scientist, which should be interesting. I think Mason wants me to meet him to get me excited about all this. Any interest?"

Arthur hesitated, but then thought he might like to spend the afternoon with his son and finally agreed. "All right," Arthur said. "I don't have any other plans."

Patrick smiled, then said he had to get changed, and quickly disappeared down the back hall toward his room.

The meeting that afternoon was with a man named Christoph Petersen, a tall white-haired ichthyologist who worked mostly on the Delaware River and its tributaries. He was a professor of biology at Columbia, and had an additional post at the Museum of Natural History, where he managed local freshwater collections. Christoph had a surprisingly aggressive affability, and as they sat in his office at the museum, Arthur couldn't help but be just a little intimidated by him. He spoke with a very pointed, staccato intonation, and Arthur pictured him being something of a tyrant with his students, and with his children, if he had any.

The nature of the meeting was about plans for a sort of fishery, or fish-science lab, to be set up on the Maidenhead grounds. The idea was a pet project of Mason's and he wanted Patrick to solicit Christoph's help and expertise. But Arthur quickly understood that Christoph was, at best, lukewarm about the idea. Or what he wanted was unreasonable and what the Fly Casters would offer would be insufficient. After all, a real lab along the river would mean that strangers would be coming and going, which would be entirely unacceptable for the Hanover Street men. Christoph did make a small proposal, though, which seemed like it might work. If the Fly Casters liked, Christoph suggested, they could build a small water-monitoring station—just a little hut, away from the bank—and then fund a graduate student to drive up once every two or three weeks to take readings. "It won't provide much data," Christoph said. "But students like that type of thing, and it will put a little money in their pockets. You can build it just at the edge of your land, so no one will ever know that someone's been there."

Patrick, who had by now warmed up to Christoph, smiled and said that the Fly Casters would probably go for something like that and then mentioned that he wasn't quite in on the deal yet, though, so it wouldn't be his decision in the end. He then mentioned returning to Colorado and leaving things to other people, and Patrick and Christoph quickly began talking about the West and how Christoph had spent every summer near Steamboat Springs as a boy because his father was a paleontologist at the University of Copenhagen and did a lot of his research there. The two talked about fishing on the Yampa River, and how happy the Rocky Mountains made them, and soon Christoph was explaining just how extraordinary he found

East Coast conservation culture sometimes. "The blue bloods can get to be a bit too much," he said, losing sight of who he was talking to. Arthur also now noticed that his accent became just a bit sharper and shriller. The aggression of the accent, however, compared not at all to the content of what Christoph said next. He smiled, shook his head, then said, "But the stories are all very funny. Mason can't stop talking about the idiot who burned the lodge down in the first place. I think there's been too much inbreeding in these people. Mason is a case. But by all accounts, the guy who put them into this position is the worst of them all."

Arthur could do nothing but turn his head and exhale. He tried to stay calm, but he was positive he was now bright red. Christoph noticed this, then said, "I'm sorry. I've insulted a friend of yours. It was just a story I heard. I'm sure there are other circumstances. John Mason, to be honest, doesn't seem that reliable to begin with."

"No, no," Arthur said. "You haven't insulted anyone. I've just thought of somewhere I'm meant to be right now. Patrick, perhaps we should go. Or I should go. You could stay, and I could meet you later."

"No, I'll come with you, Dad," Patrick immediately replied. "I've got to take care of a few things as well."

It wasn't until they sat down at a small café across town, on Seventy-fifth and Madison, that they discussed what had happened. Patrick had said he was sorry in the cab, and Arthur told Patrick that he wasn't as upset as he appeared. But they didn't begin really to talk about the implications of what Christoph said until they had glasses of whiskey and a small bowl of cashews in front of them.

"I think I needed this," Arthur said as he took a sip of his drink. "I feel like the blood is still rushing to my head."

"I'm really sorry about that, Dad. But John Mason is an idiot. I mean, I spent the morning with him and there's not one thing I liked about him. He's petty, self-involved, and completely boring. What that guy says about you should count for nothing."

"I know," Arthur said. "It's just so hard to know who my friends are. After the fire, everyone patted me on the back and said it could have happened to anyone, but you never really know what they're thinking. I've got to say, Patrick, that it makes me feel as though this whole idea of rebuilding Maidenhead and getting us back into the club isn't such a good idea. Or I don't know what it's all for. I mean, what do I need this for?"

Patrick looked at Arthur with a very pained expression, then finally said, "Look, Dad, I know what you mean. I do. But I think it's because of the way all this has played out that you should go ahead. I mean, fuck John Mason. Forgive me, but that guy can go fuck himself. The important thing is that you don't let people like that dictate what you do. More important, the club is more than just him. What about people like Ken Fielder? It's their club too. And it should be yours as well. Your great-grandfather helped build it. You can't let guys like John Mason intimidate you."

Arthur paused, then said, "My sense is that you haven't exactly told Mason that my reinstatement is part of the package. Does he think it's just going to be you?"

"We haven't talked about it directly. But I'm pretty sure he understands that it will be part of the deal. And Dad, he'll go for it. He'll have to. These guys throw their weight around like they can have anything they want. But they can't. They can't have one-quarter of the things they're planning with the rebuilding. They can't afford it. But we can. What else are they going to do?"

"I don't think you should underestimate these people," Arthur said. "They can be stubborn, especially where things like tradition are at stake. They're not going to like some young fellow waving money in their faces."

"Maybe. But I have a legacy. By their standards, I'm still one of them. Or I'm closer to one of them than anyone else they could find to come in and fund them. I was once a future member, after all."

Arthur considered this for a moment, but he still couldn't help but feel that it was all a doubtful proposition. What he really wanted most at that point was to go home, get into bed, and stay there until he went to Bar Harbor. "I just don't know," he said at last. "I just don't know. I just wonder what it would all be for."

Patrick took a long sip of his whiskey, then said, "Look, Dad, I don't mean this to be a criticism, but I'm going to say it because I'm worried about you. You need to learn to fight a little harder. Give people around you 'a little stick,' as my hockey coach used to say. Make them flinch a bit more. I mean, I don't like that kind of aggression any more than you do, and I guess that's part of the reason I don't live in New York anymore. That being said, you've got to assert yourself. Not because you have to overcome a character flaw—you could hardly be a better person, in my opinion—but because you're never going to figure out how to make yourself happy. You can't let people walk all over you. I hate to say this, but family members did it with the business, I've seen peers of yours do it, and I saw Mom do it. Mom did it all the time. I saw it for my whole life. I mean, I don't know what to say. I feel like I'm being pretty harsh here. I really couldn't ask for a better father. I mean it. But, Dad, you need to force yourself on the world a little bit more. I think it should begin with Mason. Fuck that guy for talking like that behind your back. It's because he tells stories like that that you need to reclaim your stake. You loved Maidenhead. You always felt comfortable there. And even if people do talk behind your back, you have real friends there. Ken Fielder has been great to you over the past year. You've told me so yourself. Why shouldn't the club be about you and him rather than about John Mason? Let Mason leave if he doesn't like it."

Arthur didn't quite know what to make of all this, but he couldn't help but begin to feel that his son might be right, that his son had described the kind of thing he had already been thinking about himself. Giving people "a little stick" wasn't exactly the sort of thing that he was good at. But perhaps he would enjoy being the one to show up with the cash to save the day (via his son, of course). Maybe that was the best way to deal with the fact that John Mason thought of him as such an idiot. All the same, it was hard for Arthur to quite believe he would be capable of assuming this identity, of making anyone "flinch," as his son said.

6

Patrick was due back in Colorado in about a week, and for the next several days he took business meetings and met with a few more of the Fly Casters to discuss plans and hopes for the rebuilding of Maidenhead. Arthur and he didn't come to any decision about whether or not they would actually proceed, but they did talk more about it, and Arthur began to feel less dread over the whole thing. Patrick had also begun the process of suggesting at his meetings with the Fly Casters that Arthur's reinstatement in the club would be a condition of him putting up the money. While the Fly Casters certainly showed no wild enthusiasm for this condition, Patrick reported to Arthur that people also hadn't put up too much of a fuss about it. "Obviously they said they'd need to consider it, that they'd need to have a vote," Patrick told his father. "But they're pretty excited about their plans for the rebuilding and I don't know where else they're going to get the money, so I'd say they won't have to think too hard."

"I'm still doubtful," Arthur replied. "This can be a prickly bunch."

The one other matter of importance that arose during Patrick's trip had to do with Rebecca, whom Patrick visited on his final night in the city. She claimed she was "inundated with wedding obligations," but was able to have dinner with her son on Tuesday evening, and they met at a restaurant called Clovis, which had just opened a few weeks earlier. Patrick left for dinner early—he and his mother were meeting for a drink beforehand—and he didn't get home until quite late. Arthur wouldn't have waited up for him, but Patrick was leaving at five the next morning, so he made a pot of tea and watched a made-for-television movie, and was still awake when Patrick finally came home.

"Well, how is she?" Arthur said when Patrick came into the den and took a seat opposite his father.

Patrick just smiled, as if to say there was too much to describe. But then he glanced at his father, seeming to remember who he was with, and said, "She's fine. The same." It was a neutral response, and Arthur concluded that his son might not be an appropriate person for him to probe for information about his ex-wife. Arthur was going ask him about the food instead—Clovis had become extremely popular—when Patrick unexpectedly looked over at his father and said, "What do you think Mom's after? I mean, why is she getting remarried?"

The question startled Arthur. The truth was that he had never really talked at all about the divorce with Patrick—nothing beyond the absolute minimum, at least—and he hardly knew how to begin answering such a question. But before he could say anything, Patrick continued with another equally jarring statement. "I just don't see what Stephen has to offer her," he said. "It seems like he's making her very unhappy."

Arthur recalled seeing his ex-wife yelling at Stephen at Tavern on the Green and thought that he might have something to say on this matter. But in the end, he determined it was best to be as impartial as possible on the subject of Rebecca when talking to his son. "Your mother is a willful woman," he finally said. "She knows what she wants. You shouldn't worry about her."

"I guess I don't, really. I've never really worried about her, to be honest. I just don't understand what motivates her. But I guess these are hard things to ever know about your mother."

"Yes, I suppose they are," Arthur said. He wondered how far this conversation was going to go, but Patrick stood up, ran his hands through his hair, then said, "Well, I think I need to go to bed. I've got a long day ahead of me. I have to hit the ground running in Colorado. Conference calls all afternoon."

"Well, go to bed. Make sure I'm up when you leave. I want to say goodbye."

"It'll be early. The cab is coming at five."

"That's fine. I can always go back to bed."

The subject of Rebecca's happiness was interesting to Arthur, though, and for the next few days he thought about it quite a bit. It was a puzzling question—perhaps Rebecca really was a person who sought out difficulty. She had always acted as though Arthur was a source of frustration and disappointment. Again, he wondered if maybe, now that she had left him, she realized she simply needed a level of discomfort in her life to function properly. That weekend, however, Arthur came to a very different set of conclusions.

He was at a benefit for the New York Public Library—an event he had always attended with Rebecca—when he spotted her standing off to the side, next to a glass display case that held some kind of medieval manuscript. She was bent over the case and looking very intently at the large book, which was opened to a series of religious illustrations. Arthur approached her from behind, although with a bit of hesitation, thinking that perhaps he shouldn't disturb her. But after considering the matter for a moment, he decided it was important for him to get this particular reunion over with. He'd say hello, tell her it was wonderful to see her, and then be free for the rest of the evening. This time around he also had another means for keeping up his courage. As he stepped behind her, he focused very intently on thoughts about Rixa and his trip to Bar Harbor—now only a week away—and told himself that happiness was right around the corner. But as he finally reached Rebecca, his attempts to maintain an emotional sturdiness faded. He said, "Hello, Rebecca," expecting a cheerful kiss and a few customary remarks about how well he looked, but when she glanced up from the display case and then stood up and faced him, Arthur saw that she was in tears. And when he took a step closer, the tears began to come even harder.

"Oh, Arthur," she said, trying to force a smile. "I don't want you to see me like this. But I'm afraid I'm not having a very good night with Stephen."

"What's wrong?"

"Oh, nothing. Nothing. I shouldn't be crying like this. I should leave."

"But what's the matter?" Arthur asked again. He had never seen her like this, especially in public, and he was quite astonished to find that he actually felt a bit of sympathy for her.

Rebecca, however, just shook her head, indicating that she didn't want to talk about it. Arthur didn't move, though. He wasn't sure how he was supposed to behave. Should he ask her again? Should he insist that talking about it would help her? There was also the unmistakable fact that he was starting to feel just a bit of happiness, that maybe Rebecca was now appreciating what a good-natured (or submissive) husband he had been to her. She had certainly had her frustrations with him, but he had never reduced her to tears. Rebecca kept shaking her head, though, indicating that she couldn't talk about it, and after a moment Arthur decided he had to leave her alone. As he stepped backward, however, mumbling a few words about being sorry that she was upset, she suddenly blurted out, "Oh, Arthur, he's cheating on me. I'm sure of it. I can barely keep myself together. I confronted him. But he denied it. Of course he denied it. But I know it's going on. I've heard from so many sources. How can I marry this man? But it's absolutely out of my hands. I can't bear to be without him. Now he's doing this to me. After all I've been through for him."

Arthur was so stunned he couldn't manage to say a word. These were not tears of anger and frustration over an intractable boyfriend. Rather, they were tears brought about by love, or infatuation, and a kind of desperation and dependency. It occurred to Arthur that in all the time he and Rebecca had been married, and even in the time before they were married, when they were only getting to know each other, Rebecca had never once cried for him like this—had never once felt this kind of despair or pain. He had been devastated by Rebecca's celebratory behavior over the past year, by the fact that she was so happy to be done with him, but now that she was standing there crying he realized this was a million times worse. It was a million times worse because she was not crying like this for him. She was crying like this for someone else.

All this passed through Arthur's mind in only a few seconds, but clearly the thoughts registered on his face because Rebecca quickly tried to wipe away her tears. "I'm sorry to talk to you like this, Arthur," she said. "I should keep my mouth shut. But after all, it was never like this for us. It was never this kind of love for us. It was easy for us to part ways. There wasn't so much at stake. Not like this."

It was here that Arthur realized that his only option was to turn and walk away, otherwise he was going to have his own public meltdown, and he was positive it would not make him feel better to "let things out," as the saying went. This was certainly a time for maintaining a stoic front. He said, "I'm sure things will look up, Rebecca. You're a wonderful woman. I can't imagine Stephen is cheating on you. But I'm afraid someone is waiting for me on the dance floor, so I really have to go."

Rebecca smiled at Arthur and nodded, as if to say that she understood why he was leaving and that she had to bear her pain in solitude. But it was such a pathetic kind of smile—so frightened and so pained—that Arthur suddenly (and very shockingly) found himself again feeling an uncontrollable affection and desire for this woman. He hadn't expected this at all, and his only recourse was to quickly nod and walk off. But the desire did not recede, and as he circled around the dance floor, and then started walking toward the exit, it only seemed to increase, as did Arthur's confusion. For the past year, people had told Arthur that he was much better off without Rebecca. Even her friends had said it, knowing full well that Rebecca had not treated him well at all over the last many years. Arthur always agreed as best he could, finding the logic and the rationale impossible to argue against. But the truth was that he never quite felt it, he never quite believed he was better off, despite whatever good evidence there was for the argument, and now that he had seen her in the throes of love-induced agony for a man who was not him, all he could feel was that he wanted her back more than ever, that he was burning (more painfully than he ever had) with a kind of wild jealousy and hatred for Stephen, and that if Rebecca would only say now that she wanted him back, he'd be euphoric and accept her with uncontrollable gratitude. The whole idea was shameful. Arthur knew that. It was the most outrageous and unexplainable feeling he had ever had. As he finally arrived at the library's expansive marble entryway and saw the street ahead of him, he did what he could to make the feeling go away. But it didn't. It was so clear, his feelings were so completely bare to him, that he couldn't even resort to the kind of denial and self-inflicted confusion that he had recently depended on so much. All he wanted, at least at that moment, was Rebecca back. All he wanted was for Stephen to disappear. Mostly, though, he was absolutely shocked that these were his feelings. They seemed so outlandish and so reprehensible. Still, as he stepped out on Forty-second Street and turned toward Bryant Park, they showed no sign of diminishing.

But there was at least Maine. Arthur at least had that. And after that night at the public library, this was what he tried to focus on. It had all been confirmed with Rixa in a short but cheerful conversation on the telephone, and the trip was now a week away. Arthur did his best to think about what was ahead and forget any longings he still had for Rebecca. And when Thursday finally arrived, he could hardly have been more relieved, and found that he had been able to shake these unwanted emotions somewhat.

Arthur decided to drive to Bar Harbor, rather than fly to Bangor and rent a car, because he felt that a long drive might help to clear his head. He bought an audiobook about George Washington, two corned-beef sandwiches from a deli on Lexington—a thing his doctor had forbidden him—and on Thursday morning, about ten o'clock, he headed north toward New England.

And the drive did actually turn out to be just a little therapeutic. The weather was perfect, and although the highways were hardly scenic, he lost himself slightly in his audiobook and managed to eat his sandwiches with a frugality that allowed them to last for the entire trip, finishing the second one only as he arrived at the bridge to Mount Desert Island. It took about an hour to get from the bridge to Rixa's house. Traffic was still light, but the roads were winding and Arthur had never been a particularly fast driver. He made it to the town by about six, and found a parking space in a lot Rixa had told him about—behind the antiques store that was below her apartment—and soon he was walking up a set of outdoor stairs to Rixa's door.

The building seemed ancient, although it was in good condition. It was white, freshly painted, and had an ornate wooden trim along the roof and along the windows. As far as Arthur could tell, the entire second floor was Rixa's. He also noticed that there were dormers off the attic in the back, and he assumed that this third floor was probably hers as well. The fact was that it was all very appealing to him, although he didn't quite know why, and by the time he was pressing the doorbell he was smiling and trying to calm himself down, because, after all, he hardly had a good record with this sort of thing.

It didn't take long for Rixa to arrive, and when she opened the door Arthur couldn't help but think she was indeed a beautiful woman—one not likely to like him, if you added things up. Again, he thought about the model on his bottle of vitamins, and wondered what exactly she saw in him. Her initial greeting didn't help his anxiety any. "Arthur!" she said when she saw him. "This is quite a surprise. Was I supposed to be expecting you?"

Arthur suddenly tried to figure out if he had made some gross mistake and was about to insist that he had been invited. But Rixa quickly said, "My god, Arthur, you're going to have to develop more of a sense of humor. Or you're going to have to toughen up. I'm not very nice, and I'm very sarcastic, and if you can't handle that, you might as well turn around right now." This time, though, Rixa's meaning was unmistakable—it was all said with warmth and excitement, and Rixa was grinning happily. She put her hand up, grabbed hold of the back of Arthur's neck, and kissed him warmly on the cheek. "I'm thrilled to see you," she continued. "I really am. I've very much been looking forward to it."

"Well, I have too," Arthur said, beginning to relax.

"Good. Good. Really. I'm so glad to see you. But come in. You have bags, I assume. Maybe they're in your car? We'll get them later."

Rixa grabbed hold of Arthur's hand and led him into a reception hall decorated with what looked like very old so-called naive paintings of (Arthur assumed) local Maine gentry.

"It used to be a captain's house," she said as Arthur looked around. "A captain of some kind of merchant ship. These are actually the quarters where he kept his three sisters. He lived downstairs. A bachelor, as I understand it. Are you hungry? I have some excellent cheese. I thought we'd go out for dinner. I'm not a bad cook, but there's a restaurant I particularly like, and since I won't be back for a while I thought we should go there. Anyway, my cooking is much better in Martinique than in Maine. I don't know why, but I'm much better with limes and peppers than I am with potatoes and lobsters. But let's have a drink first. It's six o'clock. Cocktail hour by any reasonable standards, and you're on vacation, so you can drink whenever you like."

"All right," Arthur replied, trying to keep track of everything Rixa was saying. "I'll have one of whatever you're having."

"I'm going to have a gin and tonic. You're sure that sounds good to you?"

"It sounds perfect."

They had their drinks on a large second-floor deck that looked out on the ocean. The house sat on a sort of promontory on a road through town, and even though it was fall the harbor was still bustling with activity. Sailboats were taking advantage of the autumn winds, motorboats jetted back and forth, and people walked on the small streets that wound down to the water. And Arthur found his drink to be very refreshing. "I needed this," Arthur said. "Nothing like a day of driving to get you ready for a cocktail."

After spending an hour or so on the deck, finishing a second gin and tonic and eating the cheese Rixa promised, they left for the restaurant. The walk was about half a mile and it was very pleasant in the now-dimming light. Rixa kept her hand through Arthur's arm the whole way, and Arthur was beginning to feel like this was all about as good as he could have possibly hoped for.

The restaurant was called Ourson and had an American country store quality while managing to serve food at Manhattan prices. But it smelled wonderful, and Arthur looked over the menu eagerly.

"I'm quite hungry now," Rixa said. "I've had a long day. I sailed with friends out to a nearby island for lunch, and the wind was very trying."

Finally the waitress came to take their orders. Rixa suggested a bottle of wine that she said she had grown fond of that summer, and Arthur assented, never really knowing enough about wine to offer his own opinions. Then Rixa ordered a salad and the bouilla-baisse, and Arthur ordered steamers and the duck. This order, how-ever, did not meet with Rixa's approval. "Good lord, don't order the duck," she said. "It comes from New Jersey. That's a fact. I'm not just saying that to be funny. I know the chef. He'll have a lobster. Unless he's allergic. Are you allergic?"

"I don't think so," Arthur replied.

"Then that's what he'll have. The lobster. Arthur, you're going to embarrass me. Please remember that I have to live here."

"I like duck."

"Well, everyone likes duck. But that's not the point, is it?

Arthur nodded. Rixa's bullying really had the unlikely quality of being deeply affectionate, and Arthur was happy that it was becoming more pronounced now that he had been there for a bit. The teasing was very relaxing, even if he was somehow the object of her nudging, and this nudging only increased, although Arthur could hardly have been happier. "Why do I like you so much, Arthur?" Rixa said after their entrées had arrived, now launching into something of a speech. "You're a bit of a fop, after all. I mean the way you're dressed. You're wearing a tie, of all things. A little much, don't you think? A little stiff. A little deferential. Maybe I like pliable men. Does that alarm you? I'm afraid I like to have my way. But I like you. I do. And now that I think about it, maybe I don't really need to be in charge so much. Maybe I just like nice people who don't think much of forcing themselves on me. That's not the same thing as me being in charge."

"It's not," Arthur said, unsure if he was even supposed to be speaking at this point.

"But I'll tell you this: I'll never go on another date with any sort of brute again—like that man you met at the party—unless I'm tricked into it. You can't avoid being tricked into things. That's the truth. Maybe I like you because you're so guileless. How does that make you feel? Do you like being guileless? Maybe you have more guile than I'm giving you credit for. You never really know. Am I being manipulated? Are you manipulating me? What if your guilelessness is all a ploy? I've seen it before. My Great-Aunt Jane was duped by a man pretending to be guileless. Do you have a lot of mistresses somewhere? I bet you do. I bet this is all an act so people don't find out about your mistresses. Perhaps you have a secret life in Monte Carlo. I've seen it before, and more than once. Have you ever been to Monte Carlo, Arthur? I bet that's where you carry on your secret life."

Arthur sat listening to all this feeling somewhat stunned. He had been trying to crack through his first lobster claw with at least a tiny bit of grace, but it was very difficult to do while also keeping up with Rixa's conversation. After all, she was asking several questions of him, although he had no idea how to answer them—or when to, since she wasn't providing much opportunity for him to speak. He did like, though, that he was being accused of keeping mistresses in Monte Carlo, even if Rixa was clearly taking some descriptive license and that there was, of course, no chance that she suspected he had mistresses there, or anywhere else, for that matter. All the same, he finally managed to play along. "Zermatt," he said. "That's where I like to keep them. I'm a very popular man in Switzerland. But not Monte Carlo. Too pleasant for me down there. Too many happy people. Everyone trying to be friendly to me. I'm afraid this might disappoint you, but I tend to have a great affinity for Swiss people."

"Well, the Swiss love Martinique," Rixa said. "They go in droves, although mostly the French-speaking Swiss. The Calvinists. Well, that makes things easy. I was thinking I'd ask you to come down to visit me, and now you can hardly refuse. It's your people who run things down there, and very efficiently, I might add. It's a sort of Swiss Disney World."

Arthur was surprised by the invitation and didn't quite know how to respond. But he couldn't help but nod and say, "I'd love that," because visiting Rixa in Martinique sounded like an excellent idea to him, and it also could only mean that this visit was now going as well as he thought it was.

They stayed at the restaurant late, ordering dessert and coffee and more drinks, and by the time they left they were the last people in the restaurant. Arthur could hardly have felt better, and as they stepped out into the cool night, Rixa quickly put her arm into his and stepped very close to him. The air was colder than earlier.

Arthur felt it, and Rixa seemed to be shivering just a bit. Arthur began to feel that this was the moment when, perhaps, he should kiss her. That's what he was there for. But Arthur's heart was now racing and he didn't exactly know what to do next. Before he could arrive at a plan, however (and there were several plans now turning over in his mind), Rixa turned toward him, leaned forward, and kissed him. And from there Arthur was perfectly happy to let her take the lead.

They kissed for some time, standing in the cold on a buckling sidewalk, and Arthur could barely catch his breath as they kissed, although after a while Rixa pulled away and gave him just a bit of a reprise.

"Let's get home," she whispered.

"All right," Arthur replied. "I was just going to suggest that."

They were silent on the walk, but they huddled together as they made their way through town. Arthur was feeling just a bit of panic, but it was happy panic. Completely pleasurable, really. He was venturing onto new terrain, and unless he managed to burn down Rixa's house, he would soon be on very intimate terms with her. That, after all, was the rub. Sex. It had not happened since Rebecca, and even then, over the last decade they were married, Arthur was sure that what passed for sex was only barely that, and hardly the kind of thing a person expects from a relationship. As they walked, Arthur began to feel quite a bit colder, although he was trying his best to act as though he were perfectly comfortable and entirely relaxed about his present situation. He even thought about offering his jacket to Rixa—she only had a light wrap around her—but he thought that if he gave up his jacket his teeth would surely start chattering and he'd look like such a fool that Rixa might make him sleep in the car.

But he made it back. And soon he and Rixa were climbing the stairs together, and before long they were in her bedroom, and Arthur found that it was all much more of a straightforward thing than he expected. He was much more comfortable about everything than he would have anticipated. Soon he was happily in Rixa's bed wondering why he had ever been so nervous, especially with Rixa, who was a remarkably warm and kindhearted woman, especially in this setting.

And the next morning, Arthur found that he was still entirely relaxed and happy. He was naked, and so was Rixa, and he could hardly fail to remark on the new social dynamic that had unfolded. He got out of bed as soon as he awoke, made a pot of coffee, and by the time Rixa came out of the bedroom and walked to the kitchen table, where Arthur was happily reading the newspaper (now in his pajamas), there was not a trace of awkwardness. "Did you sleep well?" she said, leaning forward and running her hand through his hair.

"I did," he said. "I slept about as well as I ever have."

"Mmmm," she said. "Good. Me too."

She stood there for another minute with her hand on his head. Then she turned and said, "I'm going to make you something to eat now," and she set about preparing Arthur's breakfast, which included a so-called salmon frittata, several sausage links (evidently made by a Tuscan-trained sausage maker living in Augusta), and grilled tomatoes, a thing Rixa ate almost every morning in Maine. It was maybe the best breakfast that Arthur ever had, and he soon came to the conclusion that making this trip north was the best thing he had done for himself since Rebecca left him, perhaps the best thing he had ever done in his life.

For the rest of the day, and the day that followed, this kind of gentle, effortless happiness continued, and Arthur hardly knew what was happening to him. He couldn't quite get used to how easy everything was, and how quickly time passed, and by the time he was packing up his car to return home, he wondered where the time had gone.

They hadn't talked in any detail about what would happen next—about the visit to Martinique Rixa had mentioned at that first dinner—and Arthur was determined not to ask any questions that might make things difficult for them. But on his final morning, Rixa said, "I'm in Martinique as of next week. So how about you come down soon? You could stay for a week, and if we have a good time, you could stay for another. Or you could go home and then come back again. I really like you, Arthur. I've had a wonderful time. I'm very comfortable with you, which is something I have a hard time finding with other people."

Needless to say, Arthur agreed, and before he even drove past Bar Harbor's town line, he was thinking about what Martinique might be like for him, and that he certainly wanted to visit Rixa as soon as was practical. It was hard for him to get his mind around it all, though. The happiness was puzzling, to be sure, but it was the lack of struggle that was most confusing. He had to work so little for all this, and he finally concluded that he was simply very lucky to have met Rixa, because the truth was that she seemed to like him a great deal, and for no apparent reason. And affection for no apparent reason (Arthur concluded as he left Mount Desert Island) was the only true affection there was.

8

Plans for Martinique were still a little ways off, though, and by the time Arthur got back to New York, he was thinking he shouldn't get too far ahead of himself. As wonderful as the weekend had been, he decided it would probably be best if he didn't start making plans to buy property in Martinique or tell his sons that they would soon have a new stepmother. He called Rixa when he got back to tell her he was safe at home and to restate what a wonderful time he had had. But then they hung up with the promise of talking in about a week, after Rixa had flown south, and Arthur realized that he still had to go back about his life, one way or another, and try to keep his head about all this. Again, for as well as things had gone, it was still just one long weekend and there was still much that had to be considered. The fact of the matter was that he was still just a little upset about what had been going on with Rebecca. Maine had helped him put some of that behind him, but from the moment he stepped back into his apartment, he couldn't help but think about seeing her crying that night over Stephen and how crushed he was by her capacity for feeling such pain over another man. As brilliant a stroke of luck as the whole thing with Rixa was, he was still not past feeling very deep sadness over what he had lost with his marriage—or sadness over the fact that his marriage had never been much to begin with.

Still, there was nothing he could do about Rebecca. That was clear. Moreover, he really did have things to look forward to, and he could find happiness in them if he just made an effort and kept focused. He talked to Patrick when he got home, and his son said that he had now talked to almost every member of the Hanover Street Fly Casters and that they understood what the terms of his financial involvement would entail. Arthur was still uncertain about the plan, but it was in play and he thought he'd let it unfold on its own and thereby avoid having to make any decisions. He also talked to David, who sounded very upbeat because he had gone to a series of interviews with a computer animation company in Boston that was looking for someone with business experience.

Arthur also embarked on more minor pursuits. After finishing his excellent audiobook on George Washington on the drive back from Maine, he decided that he knew far too little about the Revolutionary War and that it was time to address this gap in his education. He went to a bookstore and bought several popular biographies on key figures from that time period, and even purchased a so-called *Encyclopedia of the Revolutionary War* so that he could look up any references he wasn't familiar with. He was a bit embarrassed by all this. It seemed a little too cliché—he had always found it astonishing that all the adult men he was friends with seemed only to read books about war and powerful men. But he couldn't deny that he had been riveted by his book on George Washington, and that he was quite amazed by what he learned (particularly that so much of the Revolutionary War happened in New Jersey, of all places), and so he gave in to his current inclinations and decided that for the next stretch of time, at least, he would read about "the heroic fathers of the American experience," as one book phrased it.

It was just such a book that Arthur was reading one evening, nearly a week after his trip to Maine, when something fairly astonishing happened. He had talked to Rixa that night, and they had agreed that he'd fly to Martinique in just ten days for a visit, and he was quite happily learning about the centrality of New England waterways for eighteenth-century military tactics when his doorbell rang. It was eleven thirty at night—later than Arthur normally stayed up—and he couldn't imagine who it was. The doorman hadn't called, so his first thought was that it was one of his neighbors, but when he looked through the peephole, he was shocked to see Rebecca on the other side of the door, looking very staid and serious.

And when he opened the door, her expression didn't change at all. She hesitated for a moment, then said in a very somber tone, "Arthur, I was hoping we could have a talk." But just as she came to the end of this sentence, just as she said "talk" with a forced and deep tone, she burst into wild tears and begged Arthur to let her in because she absolutely had to speak with him. Her life had become an "absolute shambles ever since I made the terrible mistake of leaving you" and she needed to "undo" all that she had done.

Needless to say, Arthur let her in because a person can hardly say no to such a desperate request, and because (it was true) it suddenly, despite all common sense, made Arthur feel elated to hear Rebecca so clearly state this kind of thing. And as she pushed past Arthur, now with a kind of dramatic stagger, still weeping and now holding her hands to her head, he turned and tried to get hold of what exactly he was feeling. He had just come to the firm conclusion (again) that he had spent far too much of his life with people who didn't properly appreciate him. He had even thought that if things didn't work out between him and Rixa, at least he learned what it meant to be with someone who liked him, who was happy to be around him, despite his numerous and entirely obvious flaws. But as he saw Rebecca stagger forward down the hallway and into the living room, where just a few seconds before he had been reading about Lake Champlain and the cannons of Fort Ticonderoga, he couldn't help but wonder if this terrible period in his life was finally on the verge of being over, and that Rebecca was finally coming back to him, that she was about to make him whole again and repair the almost incalculable damage she had done.

He caught himself. He told himself that what was now going through his mind was outrageous. He didn't want her back. And he was sure she didn't want him back. Not really. She just needed attention. That was why she was here. He told himself this over and over as he followed Rebecca into the living room and saw her, again in a state of high drama, collapse on his couch. For all his understanding of the situation at hand, though, he still couldn't help but conclude that it was very likely that he'd take her back right there, that night, and never say a bad thing about her as long as he lived, if that, in fact, was what she was there for.

"Oh, Arthur," she said, lying back on the couch and running her hands through her hair. "You can't imagine what it's been like. You can't imagine. To be treated like this. You don't know what it's like. You simply don't know. Oh, I'm so happy to be here with you again. Oh, Arthur, can you ever forgive me?"

He didn't know what to say. But the feelings of elation continued. Arthur knew they were irrational. But they continued.

"Can you ever forgive me?" Rebecca said again. "Please tell me you can forgive me."

Arthur paused. He looked down at her in a state of total arrest. But finally, without being sure that he really meant it, he said that he could. "I forgive you, Rebecca. I forgive everything. I forgive you."

But just as he got to this last phrase, just as he got to this last assurance of forgiveness, the spell broke just a bit. The elation diminished just a little. Just a little, though. He was still overcome with joy. He could hardly imagine anything better ever happening to him in his entire life. But there was a chink, a dent, a small tear in his feelings, and he couldn't help but notice it.

"Oh, Arthur," Rebecca quickly said, continuing in her state of distress. "I can't tell you what it means to hear that." Arthur was still standing, and Rebecca now rose from her seat and put her arms around him. She smelled like gin, and she was clearly unsteady on her feet, and Arthur was now even more distrustful of this situation. He knew this was somehow unreal. But when Rebecca reached her hand around Arthur's back and placed it beneath his shirt and on his skin, he almost started crying. He couldn't deny his happiness. And when she began to undress him, and then pulled him toward their former bedroom, his exhilaration only increased. He felt like a drug addict, deeply aware of the self-destruction that was taking place but still thrilled to have the drug that was killing him. And soon they were in bed, and undressed, and embarking on a kind of carnal love that had not really existed between them for most of their marriage.

And when Arthur finally regained his composure, when the frenzy was over and Rebecca was lying next to him, drifting into a deep and drunken sleep, the happiness continued, although Arthur now wondered just what he had gotten himself into. He stayed awake for some time afterward, letting his mind turn over everything that was going on, and he found he didn't grow tired for what seemed like hours. Finally, though, the confusion transformed into dream, and Arthur was soon curled next to Rebecca, drifting off to sleep himself.

When he awoke, he had the sensation of not knowing where he was. He looked to his right and began to distinguish his dresser and his writing desk, and then it all came back to him, and he turned to see if it was all still real. And it was real, in the sense that there was clear evidence that someone had been in the bed with him. But Rebecca herself was gone. He got up and walked through the house. "Rebecca?" he called out several times, but there was no answer. It was seven thirty in the morning and she was gone.

It didn't seem that unreasonable, though. It had been quite a night. There was a lot to think about. Surely Rebecca felt as confused as he did. But Arthur also felt a kind of sickness. It came on slowly, but as best as Arthur could tell, the sickness came from a sense of loneliness—or, rather, a deep fear of loneliness—and he had the strange and simultaneous thoughts that, first, he needed to erase this woman from his life once and for all and, second, that he needed to do absolutely whatever he could to get her back.

9

He didn't call Rebecca that day, or the next after that, and by the third day after she had come over, he had heard not a word from her. His mind was gripped with a kind of psychosis—a sort of free-flowing fantasy that spanned everything from marrying Rixa and living out his life on a sailboat to remarrying Rebecca and having long talks with his sons about the importance of respecting the sacred vows of marriage. He barely ate—or he ate little that was healthy—and when Patrick called to say that apparently the Hanover Street men were about to take a vote on whether or not Arthur should be readmitted into the club, he said he didn't really care what the outcome was, and that he'd simply respect what everyone else decided.

"We can still back out if you want," Patrick said. "But I don't think we should. They'll say yes. I'm certain of it. They'll be employing a blackball rule, so all they need is one no. But a no will pretty much put an end to rebuilding Maidenhead Grange, so I'd be shocked if anyone pulls something like that."

"Well, whatever you think is best," Arthur said with little enthusiasm. "I leave it up to you."

By the fourth day after Rebecca had slept over, however, Arthur began to regain his perspective. Or, rather, he started feeling more concrete kinds of pain, and began to conclude that he was out of his mind to have even considered letting Rebecca reenter his life. He couldn't deny the deep kind of unexplainable pleasure it would give him—the elation from the other night was absolutely undeniable. But in the end she was poisonous, and being with her would make him miserable. Finally, Arthur concluded that he needed to put it to rest. He needed to talk to Rebecca about it. After a day of deliberating, mostly by way of uneasy walks through Central Park, he decided to call her. He walked home, went up to his apartment, and without considering the matter again, called her up. He was feeling composed, but he was half afraid that he might immediately start screaming, or beg her to come back to him. But neither happened, since Rebecca's assistant answered, catching Arthur just a little offguard. "This is Hailey," she said when she answered.

"Ah, is Rebecca in?" Arthur replied.

"Who is this, please?"

"This is Arthur Camden."

"Can I tell her what this is regarding, Mr. Camden?"

"Tell her I need to speak to her."

"You can't tell me what it's regarding?"

Arthur paused. "I don't think so," he said at last.

"Okay," Hailey replied. "One moment, Mr. Camden."

Hailey put Arthur on hold, and, he assumed, went to get Rebecca. But it took some time for her to arrive, and when Rebecca did finally pick up the phone, she seemed to be in the middle of some sort of task. "Let me see the other one, Hailey," she said. "No. The other one. Am I not being clear? The other one!" Then she sighed and said, "Arthur?"

"Yes. Hi, Rebecca. I'm just calling to say hello. I haven't heard from you. So I thought I'd call."

"This is a terrible time for me right now, Arthur," Rebecca replied. "I'm sure you want to talk about the other night, and I do too, but I'm hoping it can wait because I'm absolutely swamped this afternoon and probably for the next few days too. Can I call you back? Soon? By the end of the week?"

Arthur didn't know what to say. This was clearly not what he wanted to happen, or what he expected. Finally Arthur replied, "That would be fine. Just call me when you have a minute," and then said goodbye and hung up.

It was strange how unsettling it all was, given that the correct course of action for Arthur was so completely obvious. He understood that this woman cared not at all for him. Not at all. She had used him the other night and felt not one bit of interest in making sure that he had not suffered from the event or misunderstood what had happened. And, if by some miracle, they did get back together, she would continue to mistreat him and deny him any kind of happiness or security. She would treat him like a fool and probably leave him again when it struck her fancy. So what was there even to think about? He simply had to wash his hands of it all. It was time to move forward and leave this terrible year behind him. But as clear as all that was, Arthur still felt exactly as he did the day his wife told him she was leaving, and by the time he sat down on the small sofa by the phone, he found that he was in tears. He couldn't help it. The thing he most wanted was Rebecca to say she was coming back to him. Arthur knew he was behaving like a four-year-old. But the tears were real, and they were coming hard.

Finally, though, Arthur ran his hands across his face, sat up straight, and picked up the phone again. He was going to call back, and he was going to tell her how if she couldn't take ten minutes out of her day to talk about what was clearly a very important thing that had happened between them, then she was the most reprehensible person he had ever met. But after starting to dial, he halted. He thought the idea over again, and before long, he put the receiver back on its cradle. He wasn't going to call. What was the point? He stood up and looked around for his jacket. It looked like he would be spending more time walking through the park. Still, that seemed better than staying at home and weeping on his couch.

10

The next days were not much better, although it was true that they were just a little better than Arthur expected. That is, for as upset as he was, that wasn't the only way he felt. He found that interspersed in the gloom of Rebecca's hardness, he also actually had real feelings of optimism about Rixa and the year ahead. In addition, Ken called Arthur the day after he talked to Rebecca to invite him to lunch, so he at least had some opportunity for conversation and fun.

Ken and Arthur met at a new place called Trout that had a sort of Old World sportsman motif and was in the unlikely location of the West Village—unlikely for all the mahogany and antique fishing equipment, at least. Arthur found that he felt quite happy when he got there and saw Ken, and they cheerfully took their seats at a small table by the window. They each ordered large open-faced sandwiches and pints of warm dark beer and took time to admire their British-countryside motif that made up their surroundings.

"Who knew that fly-fishing would make such a good decorative theme?" Ken finally said. "For a downtown restaurant, that is. But I like it here. I'm sold."

"I like it too," Arthur said, and as he drank his beer, and his sandwich came, he thought that this was what he ought to be eating every day.

Ken appeared pleased too, although something seemed to be on his mind, and after taking a long slow sip of his beer, he finally looked at Arthur with a serious expression and said, "Let me ask you something, Arthur. Are you sure being back with the Fly Casters and your son rebuilding Maidenhead is really what you want? I mean, Maidenhead Grange means a great deal to me. I love being one of the Hanover Street Fly Casters for all sorts of sentimental reasons. I know you do too—or did. So I might be dismissing what might be a very real desire of yours. But I see a lot of faults with the club too. I see a lot of bad things about the place. The exclusivity. The ridiculous bylaws. The old-boy thing. And I'm not sure what it all adds up to in the end. Sometimes I think I'm just a victim of a nostalgic idiocy and that if I were really a strong person I'd walk away from it without thinking twice."

Arthur didn't quite know how to respond, although it was true that Ken was saying a thing that had already vaguely been on his mind. And despite the kind of deep loyalty he felt toward the Fly Casters, he also couldn't help but wonder if this group of men felt the same toward him. Or, worse, that loyalty was exactly what they felt toward him, but that it was loyalty without affection—they accepted him simply because he was "one of them" and for no other reason.

"It seems important to my son," Arthur finally said. "It's important to me too. I suppose I can't deny that. But I'm not sure I'd be pursuing it without him. I mean, I guess I wouldn't really have that option because I don't have anything like his money at my disposal. But it's important to him." Arthur was about to continue, but the waitress came by and asked if there was anything else that the two men needed.

"I think we're fine," Ken quickly said, and Arthur nodded in agreement.

Ken looked back at Arthur, but said nothing.

"I understand what you're saying," Arthur continued at last. "Oddly, I've been thinking very deeply about exactly these issues, and I understand what you're saying. I'm all for doing things out of tradition and out of common interest and all that. And there's something mostly straightforward and simple about a bunch of men, silly as they may be, building a house on a river where they can escape from the city to fish. That being said, and aside from the larger philosophical issues (like, why should anyone have anything nice, let alone a luxurious fishing camp, when there are so many bad things going on in the world?), the simple fact is that I wonder what this social world really means to me. I suppose it's what you were just saying. Why do I want to be a part of it in the first place? I don't even know if I fit in." At this point, Arthur thought that he might say something about Rebecca—about what had happened and how similar the situation was. But he couldn't bring himself to start because it just seemed too embarrassing. Any idiot in the world would see right away that Rebecca was not the kind of person Arthur should spend his time worrying about, and the fact that he had slept with her, and then been so tortured afterward, seemed impossible to explain, even to someone as understanding as Ken. Arthur looked down at his sandwich—it was herring and sour cream on a kind of German seeded bread. It suddenly seemed much less appealing. What was he supposed to say?

"I think I'm a very fatalistic man," he finally continued, looking up at Ken again. "I can't decide whether it's simply a character trait or a very deep flaw. The larger events in my life all seemed to have just happened to me—I'm not sure I was actually behind any of them—and in this case I'm really of two minds. On the one hand,

I don't see why I need the Fly Casters at all. I can always find a place to fish, and I'm not sure how close I even am to any of the members, although I see them every so often. I'm also very nervous about my son spending so much money, even though I think he has far more money than he'll ever know what to do with. What he gives away to charities each year is staggering. But aside from that, and on the other hand, I can't help but feel as though a drink by the fire at Maidenhead after a day of fishing and before a big dinner of roast beef and potatoes is about as good a thing as I can imagine. Nights like that are some of my best memories. And with those two opposite positions in the balance, I guess my inclination is to do what I always do: turn my head and let the decision be made for me."

The moment was an unusually introspective one. Or, verbalizing the introspection was unusual. And Ken seemed at a loss as to how to reply. Arthur finally shook his head and said, "But what am I even talking about? I spend too much time thinking about myself. Anyway, what I should really be worried about is all of you voting on me being readmitted. Blackball rules and all that." Arthur smiled as he said this, and the truth was that that particular question didn't worry him very much. If he was blackballed, if he had some kind of secret enemy, it wouldn't surprise him, and the fact was that it would make his life easier. As he had just said, he'd have much less to commit to if someone else made the decision for him.

Ken, however, looked as if he had more to say on the subject of the vote. It looked, in fact, like something was troubling him quite a bit. But he finally nodded and smiled and took a sip of his beer and said, "Well, Arthur, I'll let you know how the vote goes. It's in two days, you know. We've reserved the back room at Sprague's. We're having a big meeting about the future of the club, and how to rebuild, and you're definitely on the agenda. But if anyone blackballs you, Arthur, you and I will head to where he lives and vandalize his apartment while he's out at the theater. So don't worry. You'll have at least one person watching out for you."

"Well, I really appreciate that, Ken," Arthur said. "I like the idea of vandalizing someone's apartment to teach them a lesson. I've never done such a thing before, but what do I have to lose? It's time I started trying new things. Perhaps behaving like a thug is exactly what I need." Arthur glanced down at his sandwich again, and decided it was looking a little better. He took a large sip of his beer, spread out some of the sour cream with his knife, and, still with just a bit of a worried mind, resumed eating again.

11

Patrick called too—that night—to say that the lunch at Sprague's was happening that Friday. He said it was to be a three-hour affair, and Patrick said that that was when they'd be making their decisions about the rebuilding of Maidenhead and Arthur's fate as a member.

"I wanted to go and make another pitch," Patrick said on the telephone the night before. "But they didn't think that would be a good idea—secrecy, closed doors, all that. But we're going to win this, Dad. This is when the fight is fun, and worth it, and I'm really happy we're moving forward with it all."

"Well, then I suppose I am too," Arthur replied. It gave Arthur a great deal of pleasure to hear Patrick so enthusiastic, and he managed to fall asleep that night without too much trouble. The next morning, however, Arthur felt quite a bit different. He had started to think about what an insult it would be to be blackballed—that the Fly Casters would be so determined to keep him out that they'd prefer not to rebuild Maidenhead at all rather than admit him. Patrick was probably right that this was unlikely. But it was a possibility. It might not make any financial and practical sense, but Arthur well knew that none of the men in the club would be happy about the idea of bending rules to raise cash. The scheme was fairly humiliating, as good as the reasons might be to go ahead with it.

And by eleven Friday morning, Arthur was starting to worry even more. The lunch meeting would not conclude until around three, and it seemed that he would be spending yet another day walking aimlessly through the park. It amazed Arthur that he was able to so masterfully juggle various points of trouble in his life. He was now so focused on being blackballed that thoughts of Rebecca had receded, and he marveled over how his last experiences of walking through the park would be so substantially different from today's walk, at least in terms of the content of his mind. But just as he was putting on his jacket, the phone rang. He answered it, and after a moment of silence he heard, "Arthur? This is Rebecca. I'm sorry it's taken me this long to get to you, but here I am, calling you back."

This was not something that Arthur particularly wanted to face at the moment. His inclinations that morning were actually just to let Rebecca keep blowing him off, and let her slip quietly out of his life. Whether he could do this or not was a different question. He hadn't been able to before. But he did feel a bit differently this time. He seemed a bit too aware of how terrible being back with Rebecca would be. But the question was what exactly he was strong enough to say, and the fact of the matter was that his record on this front would indicate that he would not be very strong at all.

"Well, I'm glad you called, Rebecca," Arthur said at last, but before he could continue—saying he knew not what—she quickly began speaking again, pointing out that if a person really thinks about it, "we don't need to have this talk at all."

"It's totally normal for two people who have shared so much together to slip back into old routines," she continued, "and I don't think there's much we need to say about it. I have so many other things on my mind right now, with my wedding around the corner. I guess I had a bit of a breakdown. But I wanted to thank you, Arthur, for being there for me, for really taking care of me that night. I don't know what I would have done without you. It really made me see things clearly, and I think I can really look forward to my new life with Stephen now."

Arthur had no idea how to respond. Or he had several ideas, but wasn't sure which one to proceed on. But at last he just commented on the thing that shocked him the most. "You're still going to marry him!" he yelled.

Rebecca laughed. "I'm a passionate woman. I tend to overreact. Marriage is about finding a balance and we're still finding ours. But things are running very smoothly right now. It would be a terrible mistake not to marry him, given how happy we are—I mean, when you really look at things carefully."

Arthur groaned, although he had the sense to do it away from the receiver. "I'm not sure what to say," he at last said, in a bit of a breathy whisper.

"Well, that's the point," Rebecca replied. "We don't need to say anything. We're close enough, we have enough of a history, that things like this can pass on without too much worry."

Needless to say, Arthur didn't feel that they were looking at this in the same way at all. He was hardly ready to start protesting, though, and before he could say more than, "Well, I guess that might be how these things work," Rebecca interrupted him and said, "Hailey's just come in with something I need to deal with right away. But I'm glad we talked about this, Arthur. I'm glad we have an understanding." Arthur wanted to reply to this somehow, but found himself, in the next instant, simply saying goodbye and hanging up the phone, once again staring into space and wondering what had just happened. He was still wearing his jacket, so he was ready to embark on his walk, although he wondered what exactly he should think about in the park now—the impending vote of the Fly Casters or mistreatment at the hands of his ex-wife.

Arthur was gone for about two hours but returned—now about one thirty—with nothing resolved other than he had decided to buy a sandwich and a bag of potato chips, despite having absolutely no appetite. There was another call coming, and he was feeling very nervous about the news it would convey.

And at three fifteen, his phone did ring, and it was in fact news from the Fly Casters. Thankfully it was Ken, although this did make Arthur feel just a moment of alarm because, after all, he would be the natural choice to pass along bad news.

But it wasn't bad news. "Well, Arthur," Ken said, "I'm calling to tell you that we took a vote and you're in again if you want."

Arthur hardly knew what to say, but finally managed, "Well, that is good news!"

It was surprising: he had tried to tell himself he didn't care all that much, but the truth of the matter was that he was far more excited than he thought he would be. Or perhaps it was relief. Being accepted might not have been such a prize, but being rejected would have led to a sort of emotional catastrophe. And the fact was that it somehow made him feel just a little better about what had gone on with Rebecca that morning. There was little chance that anything would start up between him and Rebecca again. She would never be a reliable partner. But the Hanover Street Fly Casters were a different matter. Here was something that he could really embrace. "This is really very good news," Arthur said again.

"It is good news, Arthur," Ken said in response. "It is good news. I'll be glad to have you back." Ken then paused, and repeated himself: "I'll be glad to have you back." But this time around there was a little bit of hesitation in his voice. Arthur was about to ask if there was anything wrong when Ken said, "Look, Arthur, I'm glad about this. I really am. I can't wait to get on to the stream again with you. I'm definitely looking forward to having drinks by the fire. I also think it's wonderful that your family will have a stake in all this again. But I feel I ought to tell you something."

Ken suddenly fell silent. Arthur thought he was about to resume again, but the silence lasted for longer than he expected.

"Yes?" Arthur finally said.

"Well, I'm not sure how to say this, but I guess most generally I'd say that if I were you I wouldn't say yes to this. I wouldn't come back. I mean, it's a hard thing to discuss, but because I like you so much, and because we've become such better friends in the past year, I think I should tell you that you've got quite a few enemies in the club. Or maybe enemies isn't quite the right word, but I'd say there are quite a few people who speak very badly about you. In my opinion, they're a bunch of jackasses, and, frankly, in the last few meetings I've wondered myself why I'm involved with them. I mean, I'm as old school as any of them, and my great-grandfather built Maidenhead just like theirs did, so I don't know how critical I can be. But the thing about these clubs is that they're all well and good when they're strange artifacts that are hanging around and which don't bother anyone and which kind of have a life of their own. Funny old men who like to talk about insects and what might be good to eat for lunch. There's nothing better than that. But to make such an enormous effort for a thing like this. I just don't know. And, well, I guess this is really what I have to say: So many of these men dislike you. And it's not just John Mason. They all make fun of you, Arthur. Charlie Feltham. Casper Moore. All of them. And in the most reprehensible and hostile ways. And today, at the meeting. Normally I'd never tell you this because I'd never want to hurt your feelings, but I also care about you, Arthur, and I don't want you to make a mistake here. I just don't think you need to waste your time with it all. If your son wants to have a place to go fishing with you, then build your own place. Lord knows I'll come up anytime you like to fish. I love sponging off other people's goodwill, especially when there's good water. We could start our own club. But I think the Hanover Street men have taken this as far as it should go, and I'm not sure you should reenlist."

Arthur wanted to say something, but he was so astonished (and so crushed, frankly) that he didn't know how to respond. But he felt as though it was his turn, as though Ken had been forced to say far more than he had wanted, and that he needed to say something reassuring. But Ken started talking again: "And you know what, Arthur? I knew my great-grandfather very well. He died when I was eleven and he was about the nicest man I've ever met. He never had an unkind word to say about anyone. And to him, Maidenhead was just a happy clubhouse and a place to go fishing more than anything else. It wasn't about these people getting together and ganging up on someone who isn't there—ridiculing him behind his back—or taking someone's money when they clearly want nothing to do with him." Ken paused and sighed. And then he sighed again while Arthur continued to listen. Finally Ken said, "Look, Arthur, I don't know if I've done the right thing here. I don't want to influence you too much on this in the end. I know that you loved Maidenhead, and the club, and your family's legacy. And I know that despite what I've told you this past year, you still feel some responsibility for the fire and all that. So if you want to go ahead and join up again, that's fine with me. I'll be happy as a clam and I'll look forward to palling around with you on the stream again. But I really feel like you need to know the truth about what you're getting into. It's up to you, though, and I won't think a bad thing about you if you decide to go ahead with this anyway."

Ken paused. But this time he didn't start up again. Now it really was Arthur's turn, but by this point he was so touched by Ken's kindness that it was really all he could think about.

"Well, I can hardly thank you enough, Ken," Arthur said at last. "I know this must have been hard to say and I'll always appreciate it. I guess I have a hard decision ahead of me, given all that's at stake. But maybe there's no decision to be made at all—maybe it should all be perfectly clear to me. It's just so hard knowing what to do."

"I know it is, Arthur," Ken replied. "And I mean what I said. Whatever you decide, I'll be very happy with. I mean it." Ken paused, then laughed a bit, saying, "Anyway, this isn't even my main concern with you because my wife has been driving me completely crazy for the past few days asking me to find out when you're free next. Apparently half of her friends are getting divorced all of a sudden and she wants you to get to know them. All of them. This is going to be a very good year for you, Arthur. I can tell right now. I know you're interested in someone right now. But believe me, this isn't like the ragtag bunch we set you up with last year."

Arthur laughed a little as well, a bit relieved that the subject was shifting to other things. But he told Ken that perhaps for the moment they should keep these women at bay. "I'm still thinking about Rixa these days, I suppose," he said. "But let's not tell Lauren to give up her work yet. Rixa may dump me soon enough, and then I'll be your responsibility again."

The conversation ended after this, and Ken didn't revisit the matter of Maidenhead because, after all, he had said what he needed to. The two men said goodbye with a certain gravity, and Arthur knew very well that he had quite a choice to make at that moment. Although having a choice in all this now seemed to be a very dubious advantage.

12

Arthur knew that Patrick would be calling soon, and that the rest of the Fly Casters would assume that their approval and endorsement would naturally lead to Arthur's joyful acceptance of the offer of renewed membership. But just minutes after hanging up with Ken, Arthur found himself in the surprising situation of suddenly wanting nothing to do with the Fly Casters. And it really was surprising, even if by outside standards a man would have to be out of his mind to link up with people who evidently disliked him so much, and made fun of him so often, and were only willing to accept him because of his son's money. But it was a fact that Arthur had a kind of deep and irrational affection for Maidenhead. It really had meant so much to him—and to his more robust male forebears. And, of course, he was the one who had burned Maidenhead down, whatever the arguments were in his defense.

There was also the matter of Arthur trying to be tougher, to be tough enough to fight it out. Maybe this was what his son was talking about when he said that he had to learn to stand up for himself more, to give those around him "a little stick" to protect the things that were important to him. Why should the Hanover Street Fly Casters be the club of the John Masons? Why shouldn't it be the club of the Ken Fielders and the Arthur Camdens? Surely this was the time to press on, to take what was his, as it were.

And there was also just a bit of shame. After all, this was a chance to reclaim what belonged to Arthur's family and its future generations— what Arthur had, in fact, lost. Along these lines, Arthur wondered what his father might say about all this. The question was a difficult one, but Arthur was sure that, for whatever instincts his father had in guiding him (via stern warnings about lobster Newberg and careful lessons about useful camping equipment), and given how hard his father had tried to encourage him to make friends and tolerate difficulties, he himself certainly never would have put up with ugly gossip and mean-spirited meetings at Sprague's, and probably would have broken quite a few noses at this stage of the game. That was a fact. Arthur had heard stories to this effect. Breaking noses was hardly in the cards for Arthur, of course, but the truth of the matter was that he did have quite a bit of leverage at this moment, and if his father was in the same position, he'd definitely use it. Or, more important (and more to the point), he'd do exactly what he wanted and not sit around worrying about what was expected of him. But did this mean Arthur should take back what was his, or just walk away?

In the end, though (and perhaps this really was finally a sign of some sort of transcendence on Arthur's part), he didn't have to labor over this question very long. It all just seemed so unnecessary, and soon Arthur was on the phone making a call that was far, far easier than he imagined it would be. He thought again about John Mason and various other Fly Casters making fun of him, and by the time Patrick answered the phone, Arthur hesitated not one bit and said, "I don't want to do it."

"Dad?" Patrick said.

"Yes. It's me, your father, and I don't want to do it."

"What?"

"I don't want my membership back. I want nothing to do with the Hanover Street Fly Casters."

"Did they say yes?"

"Yes. They said yes. They said I could be a member again. But I don't want to do it. I'm not upset. It's not a problem. And if you want me to pass along my membership to you, I'll happily do that too. I think they'd be very happy with that arrangement—taking you instead of me. They could easily justify it, since you're part of one of the original families. But it's not for me, Patrick. I can't quite explain how I came to that conclusion. But I have, and I don't think there's much you can say to change my mind."

Arthur paused, giving Patrick a chance to say something, but Patrick seemed to be at a loss for words. At last he said, "Are you sure about this, Dad?"

"I know I'm not very good at big decisions," Arthur replied. "But I can tell you now that I definitely don't want to be back with them. It's a bit too complicated to explain, but you'll just have to trust me that I'm making the right decision."

Again, Patrick paused. But then he said, "All right. You sound like your mind's made up. Maybe we just had to see this through to come to a decision. I'll call John Mason today."

"But you really are free to stay in if you like and if you can work out some kind of agreement with them. I'm sure they'd be happy to make you a member."

"No, no. If you don't want to do it, neither do I. I want us to decide this together, and I'm really happy you're letting me know this. I want us to be thinking about this in the same way. Anyway, we can always build our own fishing camp. We don't need the Fly Casters' permission for that."

"That's true," Arthur said. "That's very true. I was already thinking about that."

And then Arthur abruptly (and because he didn't want or need to talk about this matter anymore) said that he had to go. He said he was going to be traveling soon, and that he needed to make some arrangements and do some shopping. "I have a friend in Martinique I'm going to see," he said. "A woman. Named Rixa. And there's a few things I need to prepare."

"Really?" Patrick said. "I had no idea. That's great. Martinique sounds great, Dad."

"Yes," Arthur said. "I'm surprisingly happy about it. I'm surprisingly happy about a lot of things right now."

After hanging up, and without much introspection at all, Arthur began making a list of errands he needed to do and things he needed to buy. And it was totally pleasurable making this list. It occurred to him for just a moment that this kind of forward thinking, this happy list-making, might be some kind of defense mechanism, a method of deferring pain that he would surely feel sooner or later. It had been a big day. He had lost a lot. But he couldn't deny that at least for the moment he did feel happy. It was a kind of excitement that was very rare for him. It was not just about a coming event, but about how things were going in general, in the broad scope of things. It really was a very unusual experience and one that he certainly wouldn't have expected, given what had just transpired.

Arthur did get one more difficult and unexpected telephone call that day, however, although it too had something of a therapeutic value. The phone rang and when Arthur answered he found that he had a very angry man on the other end of the line. "Arthur!" the voice said. "This is John Mason. Is what I heard from your son true? Do you have any idea what you've put us through?"

It occurred to Arthur at this point to start yelling. Perhaps now was the time to give John Mason "a little stick," as his son had said. But as this idea turned over in his mind, he found that he had no real desire to act on it. Instead, he simply told Mason about how happy he had been as one of the Fly Casters and how it had meant the world to his family, but that it was time for him to do something else now with his life. "And after all," he said, "it's really my son you want. I suggest you make your pitch to him. He's really the heir to all of this, when you think about it."

"But now he doesn't want to be in either!" Mason yelled.

"Well, that's up to him," Arthur replied. "He's very independent, and I'm afraid I don't have much sway with him once his mind is made up."

Mason exhaled in disgust, but before he could start yelling again, Arthur told him that he absolutely had to go. "I'm going to Martinique," he said. He then told Mason that he wished the Hanover Street gang all the best, and that he was sure he'd see them around the city and that he'd look forward to catching up with them and finding out how things are going.

"Don't count on it!" Mason snapped.

"Well, I hope to, at least," Arthur replied. And with that, he said goodbye and hung up the phone.

13

It could hardly escape Arthur's notice, once he was back at JFK and about to embark on another trip abroad, that this time around he was in fact going to a sunny exotic place that was nothing but a beach. He wondered whether he should stick to city-bound women if things didn't work out with Rixa, thereby ensuring that he would never be expected to do things like lie in the sand all day and endure all the endless sun that he would surely find in Martinique. But the fact was that he could not have been more pleased about all that was ahead of him. He had bought two new bathing suits at Barneys—from Samantha, the woman who had helped him with his recent neckwear purchases—and both of the bathing suits, Arthur felt, were surprisingly flattering. He also bought an outrageously overpriced "beach robe," as it was named, that seemed to be exactly the sort of thing he'd need for afternoon cocktails after a long swim in the ocean. And as he made his way through airport security, he couldn't wait to see Rixa's so-called beach shack and, he hoped, keep taking things further with her. Where it would all lead was hard to say. But things were certainly going well at the moment, and

would probably get better. Whether they would stay together forever was a hard thing to predict. Rixa was an independent woman,
and there was no telling what she might want in the future. But that,
after all, was one of the things that made her so appealing. Perhaps
it was also the thing that made her like Arthur so much. He was
a decent kind of man. Incompetent, perhaps. An imbecile when it
came to women. This was true. But he didn't take pleasure in bullying others. He liked to spend time with his sons more than anything
else. And he could hardly help but notice that the person who had
been the greatest friend to him in the past year—Ken Fielder—was
himself one of the kinder and more compassionate men he had ever
known. That was certainly an endorsement of some sort. Probably
the only kind of endorsement that mattered.

As Arthur found his way to his gate, he also couldn't help but
note the sort of calm and distanced perspective he now had about
everything that had recently happened. He could see he had been
hurt and had been rejected, but the thing was, at this particular
moment, he couldn't actually feel it. He didn't feel bad at all. There
were so many things to sort through. So many questions about what
had taken place. But for some unexplainable reason—and it really
was unexplainable; perhaps the most unexplainable change in the
last many years of his life—he really didn't care. He felt a sort of
momentum, a forward propulsion, and he could only think of drinking rum (or tequila, or gin, or whatever it was they drank in Martinique) on the beach with Rixa and getting tan and showing off his
expensive beach robe and feeling very comfortable and relaxed. He
even found that he was looking forward to Rixa's teasing—Arthur
knew full well that she would quickly ride him for his pale com-
plexion and fear of large waves. But maybe this was at the root of it
all—Rixa's strange affection for him despite his ridiculous behavior. He thought about his sons and then about Ken and how they

seemed to appreciate him despite whatever it was that made others think he was a buffoon. And then he thought of Rixa, and how she seemed to feel this way as well. Arthur could hardly help but conclude that maybe things weren't at all in such a state of disaster with him. Maybe, for all the terrible things that had happened, he might be better off. He was (to be honest) uncertain about whether or not he could, in fact, deal with the endless sand Rixa would surely make him face. Part of him also understood that he would probably look completely ridiculous in his beach robe, as magnificent as it obviously was. But he was still excited about it all. That was a fact. And for the time being, as fleeting as it might be, he was going to enjoy this feeling. He was going to make a determined effort to enjoy it, despite how things might finally end up.